The Hiding House

Malcolm Richards

Malcolm Richards crafts stories to keep you guessing from the edge of your seat. He is the author of several crime thrillers and mystery novels, including the PI Blake Hollow series, the award-nominated Devil's Cove trilogy, and the Emily Swanson series. Many of his books are set in Cornwall, where he was born and raised.

Before becoming a full-time writer, he worked for several years in the special education sector, teaching and supporting children with complex needs. After living in London for two decades, he has now settled in the Somerset countryside.

Visit the author's website:

www.malcolmrichardsauthor.com

Available in large print from Malcolm Richards:

PI Blake Hollow
Circle of Bones
Down in the Blood
The Dark Below

The Devil's Cove Trilogy
The Cove
Desperation Point
The Devil's Gate

The Emily Swanson Series
Wish Me Dead (Prequel)
Next to Disappear
Mind for Murder
Trail of Poison
Watch You Sleep
Kill for Love

Standalone Books
The Hiding House

In memory of my grandmother, Laureen Trembath.

Chapter 1

The day that Nana May died was hot and syrupy and clung to the skin in tiny beads. The sun sat at its highest peak in a cobalt sky, searing the earth until it cracked open, scorching the grass until it singed brown. There was no breeze to bring cool relief, no rain cloud to break at any time soon. As each minute of the day dripped by, the world slowed down, hissing and spitting like an old car engine.

Nana's many cats crawled from one shady place to another as midday shadows shifted across the dusty front yard. A young ginger tom named Red found solace beneath the rusty shell of a pick-up truck. Other felines pawed their way under hedgerows and the lush woodland canopies that surrounded Nana May's whitewashed house. Even the birds, usually so full of song, moved on their branches, spreading their feathers to expel the warmth. Crickets in the foliage chirped lethargically. Fat honeybees swayed drunkenly through the air. For miles around the land lay flat on its back, melting away on the last Sunday of July.

It could have been the coldest of winters before Nana May looked up to notice. Upon returning from the village church, she'd spent the last hour and twenty-four minutes of her life preparing the culinary delights that now baked and sizzled in the kitchen.

There were butter almond cookies, sweet bread, and sponge cake. Sugary smells permeated the air, mingling with the delicate scent of tea leaves that were steeping in an old brown teapot.

Nana May finished pumping pink icing onto the cooling cookies, paused to wipe perspiration from her brow, and was on the move once more, shifting her large frame toward the kitchen table.

A battalion of gingerbread men smiled up at her. Nana May smiled back as she pictured the wide, hungry eyes of her grandchildren. They had seen more than their fair share of horrors, but if they could finish off a mountain of her butterscotch fudge (which contained more butter than sense) and still come back for more, she knew they were over the worst of it.

This was her gift to them. Every Sunday, a different tasty mountain to fill their stomachs. Every Sunday, a little further away from the past.

Nana scooped up one of the biscuit men and frowned.

'Your smile's not big enough for my little ones,' she sighed. The gingerbread man looked pensive, melancholy even; his eyebrows pulled down over sad blue eyes. 'Oh well, plenty more where you came from.'

Pinching his leg between finger and thumb, Nana May tore it from his body.

'Sorry about that,' she chuckled, as she popped the gingerbread limb into her mouth.

It was hot against her tongue, so she sucked in a deep, cooling breath. Caught up in the sudden rush of air, the leg flipped over, hit the back of her throat, and lodged itself in her gullet.

Nana May's face flushed red.

Her free hand reached for her neck. She stared at the gingerbread man with wide eyes, then watched it slip from her fingers and break into pieces on the flagstone floor.

Panic scrambled up Nana May's throat.

Her heart fluttered, beating faster and faster, then not at all, then in mad, erratic measures. Nana spun a full circle, her long skirt billowing like sheets on a washing line, her arms flapping at her sides. Scarlet rivulets filled her eyes as blood vessels started to burst.

The coal oven that she refused to replace with a modern stove emitted enough heat to keep out the coldest of winter nights, and now it blasted her with molten waves.

She stumbled, striking her hip on the corner of the table. The back door swung into view and she lunged towards it, a cacophony of gurgles and squawks punctuating every step. Trembling fingers curled themselves around the door handle and with one final and tremendous effort, Nana May wrenched the door open and staggered outside.

The first thing she saw was her rocking chair.

A summer evening had not passed without her sitting in this spot, rocking back and forth, listening to the evening chorus of birds and insects. She told stories to her grandchildren from this chair—stories that filled them with laughter, sometimes with fear. This was the chair that had rocked her to sleep each night at the bedside of her cancer-stricken husband, the chair she'd wept in when he'd died. It was as much a part of her as her own bones.

Nana May slumped back into the chair's well-worn grooves. Her head rolled back and she saw the sky falling towards her. The sun was coming down with it, setting fire to the world. Where the woodland met the garden, she saw a darkness lurking in the trees, and it terrified her.

Above the din of her hammering heartbeat, she heard an irrevocable quiet. Then there was only beauty. Then there was only light.

Nana May found she could breathe again.

Chapter 2

Sebastian Montgomery sucked in a breath as he watched Elise freeze on the bottom step, her fingertips turning white as they gripped the rail.

'What did you call me?' she said, without turning around.

Sebastian tried to speak, but a dry croak and a squeak sprung out. Slowly, his sister turned, her tangled mass of blonde locks writhing like a nest of vipers.

'S-sorry!' Sebastian stammered.

But Elise was already advancing, emerald eyes ablaze, hands curled into angry balls.

The broken blue toy car Sebastian was holding clattered to the floor. He took a step back, dark hair falling over even darker eyes.

'Do you even know what that word means?' his sister raged.

Sebastian shook his head from side to side. 'No! I'm sorry, Elise—I don't!'

It was true. He'd heard the word for the first time a week ago, on the last day of the school year. He and his gaggle of nine-year-old friends had been sitting around a picnic table, eating their lunchtime sandwiches in the sunshine, when Billy Tooms had looked up and declared: 'Miss Barker's a whore!'

The other boys had exploded with shocked laughter, but Sebastian had knitted his brow into a confused frown. He thought Miss Barker was a wonderful teacher, but the word Billy had used to describe her sounded harsh and unpleasant.

When Elise had wandered into the hall and accidentally stomped on his favourite toy car, the word had shot from Sebastian's mouth like a firecracker.

Now, he stared at his sister as she welled with fury. Elise's clumsiness was getting worse. Nan May had said it was because she was going to be a teenager soon, and that all teenagers were clumsy (and bad tempered, although there would be none of that under her roof). Even so, it didn't mean Elise could break his toys and get away with it. That wasn't fair!

'When will you ever learn to keep your big mouth shut?' she cried, her voice breaking.

A tear slipped from her eye and Sebastian watched it sail down the contours of her cheek. Before he could reply, Elise turned and hurried away in the direction of the kitchen.

Confusion overwhelmed him. Usually, their fights ended with Elise pinning him to the ground and pinching his ears until he wept. Sebastian was small for his age, his clothes always hanging off his slight frame. Elise was tall and healthy, and strong like their grandmother. It was unnerving to see her so quickly crushed, her fight snuffed out like a candle flame.

Guilt flooded Sebastian's veins, and although he was still unsure why that word had had such a devastating effect, he vowed never to utter it again.

A thought struck him. What if Elise told Nana May?

Sebastian's love for his grandmother equalled his love for Elise, and he loved them more than everything else. The looks of shame and disappointment his grandmother might bestow upon him would be enough to break his heart into a thousand pieces.

Standing in the hall, he felt tiny splinters already beginning to spread.

* * *

The kitchen was a furnace. Heat from the stove turned the air into treacle. Wisps of steam puffed up from the cookies cooling on the table and the tea steeped too long in the pot. Elise had been standing here for just a few moments, but beads of perspiration were already clinging to her skin and hair.

She wrinkled her nose at the unpleasant odour hiding behind the sugary smells. Smoke was spilling from the edges of the oven door. Grabbing a towel, Elise removed a blackened loaf of bread and dumped it onto a cooling tray. She stood for a moment, wiping her stinging eyes.

Stupid Sebastian, she thought. Always picking things up from his stupid friends and not knowing what to do with them!

The kitchen closed in on her as something else stirred her emotions. For as long as she could remember, she had never known her grandmother to burn a single thing.

'Timing is like breathing,' Nana once said, while showing the children how to bake the perfect apple pie. 'Get it wrong and you're going to run into some trouble.'

Elise looked towards the back door that led to the garden. It stood wide open like a hungry mouth.

'Nana May? Are you out there?'

As she waited for Nana's soothing voice to reply, her gaze flitted about the kitchen, fixing upon the shattered gingerbread man lying on the floor, then darting back to the loaf of burned bread. Ignoring the unease creeping into her thoughts, she edged towards the open door.

So, Nana May had finally gone and burned something—did it really mean something bad had happened to her?

Elise stepped outside.

The first thing to hit her was the scent of the roses that sprang from well-tended beds.

The second was the staggering heat, which made the temperature of the kitchen seem tepid.

As Elise allowed her body a moment to adjust to the discomfort, she turned her head. Nana May was sitting in her rocking chair, eyes closed, hands folded on her lap, chin resting on her chest.

For the briefest of moments, she looked like an old woman taking a much-needed afternoon nap. Elise sighed with relief. Then she noticed little things that filled her dread.

Strands of hair, usually drawn back into a flawless bun, had sprung loose. The skin on Nana's face, usually so radiant despite the ravages of age, was now so pallid and waxy that not even sunlight could penetrate it.

Then there was the matter of her chest. It did not rise and fall like someone in the throes of sleep. It did not rise and fall at all.

Nana May had been petrified like the people of Narnia. She was an ice sculpture sitting out to melt on a summer afternoon.

An odd, strangled whimpering disturbed the air. Almost a minute went by before Elise realised it was coming from her own mouth. She snapped her teeth together and the sound ricocheted back down her throat, slamming into her stomach.

The world turned full circle. She saw the ground rush past overhead. Then it swung right back and struck her on the temple.

Oblivious to the pounding in her head and the trickle of blood darkening her hair, Elise pulled herself up from the garden path. Her grandmother's left shoe had slipped from her foot and was now hanging precariously from her toes. How they had always laughed at Nana May, whose feet never reached the floor when sitting, whose shoes always slipped off as she rocked back and forth, enchanting them with wondrous bedtime stories.

Elise willed it to fall, but the shoe remained.

'Nana!' She was dead, of course. Elise had known it almost instantly. 'Nana May!'

How she longed to rush over and bury herself in the folds of her grandmother's clothes! How she yearned to feel the beat of her heart against her aching head! Elise extended a trembling hand towards Nana May, wishing her touch to be one that healed.

'What are you doing?'

The voice was startling, shattering the silence that had enveloped her in a protective shroud.

'You're bleeding,' Sebastian observed.

Any trace of guilt had clearly vanished the second he'd stumbled across the feast in the kitchen. Now, he stood in the doorway, cramming warm cookies into his mouth. Chocolate sauce decorated his cheeks and fingers; smears that his grandmother would have wiped away with spit on her handkerchief after scolding his impatience.

Elise burst into a fit of hysterical giggles.

'Quiet!' Sebastian chided. 'Nana's sleeping.'

Elise stopped laughing.

'Go inside,' she muttered.

Sebastian stepped from the harbour of the doorway and onto the path. He stood over Elise, pointing a finger at her bloody temple.

'Maybe we should wake Nana up. You need a plaster on that.'

'I can put a plaster on it myself. Go inside.'

'Yes, but Nana should take a look at it in case it gets infected.'

'I'll clean it with the antiseptic from the medicine cabinet. Now go inside.'

Sebastian ignored her. 'How'd you do it, anyway?'

'I fell. Please, Sebastian.'

But Sebastian was already stepping over her and tapping Nana May on the shoulder.

'Nana?' Sebastian smiled at Elise as he waited. 'Nana, it's time to wake up.'

He shook her, sending the chair rocking back and forth. The shoe came away from their grandmother's toes and flipped over onto the grass. Nana's hand slipped from her lap. Her head rolled around on her neck.

Sebastian took a step back, his face the colour of sour milk.

'She won't wake up.'

Elise stared at the gravel path, at the trees, anywhere but his stricken features.

'I know,' she whispered. 'Please, just go inside.'

Sebastian didn't move. 'Why Elise? Why should I go inside? What's wrong with her?'

'Nothing's wrong. Why don't you go and get the antiseptic for my head?'

'No!' Fat salty tears coursed down his cheeks. He threw the cookies he was holding onto the ground and grabbed Nana's shoulders with both hands.

'Nana!' Sebastian shouted in the woman's face. 'Nana May!'

'For God's sake, she's dead!'

Sebastian stared at his sister.

'It's true,' she whispered, as she curled into a ball on the garden path, not caring that the gravel was scratching her skin.

Sebastian let out a low, painful moan. His knees buckled and he fell onto the lawn. He sat there for a moment, his mouth twitching, the veins in his forehead popping. Then his eyes rolled back in their sockets.

Elise watched helplessly as he tumbled into darkness.

Chapter 3

He was dreaming of floating in sunlight, of flipping and diving through the rays, ducking down to skim the surface of an ocean so blue it hurt his eyes to look at it. Then he was hurtling upward, further and further, until the world was a pinpoint, until it disappeared below him and was replaced by time and space.

There was a voice somewhere at the back of all this; its words dancing past him like fireflies. He couldn't hear what the voice was trying to tell him, but its tone was soothing and familiar.

Elise was here too, somewhere in the distance, drifting towards a constellation of vibrant purples and vivid reds. She was lost, motionless, allowing herself to be pulled along by an unseen force. As she drew closer, the constellation suddenly dissolved, revealing a colossal, churning ball of fire. Sebastian tried to call out, to warn his sister, but he couldn't speak.

Huge flames of lava spurted from the sun's molten surface, shooting past Elise's body.

Sebastian tried to move towards her, but the same force that was propelling Elise away from him was now pushing him back. Helpless, he watched fiery tendrils lash out and wrap around his sister's limbs. The hem of her dress ignited. Her hair crackled and sparked.

Elise burst into flames. All around, stars crumbled and imploded as she screamed in agony.

Sebastian snapped his eyes open. He was breathless, drenched in sweat. Bed sheets were twisted around his limbs like serpents. He struggled to free himself then sat up.

Next to him, Elise muttered and turned to face the wall.

Why am I in Elise's room? he thought.

Perhaps he'd crawled in here during the night. He'd done so many times before when he was younger, even more after their mother disappeared. Back then, Elise had never seemed to mind. She even welcomed the intrusion, wrapping her arms around his tiny frame, her breaths hot and comforting on the back of his neck.

Those had been strange and frightening days. Always feeling alone. Always waiting for the front door to open upon his tearful mother, distraught that she'd forgotten her children in the same way she'd sometimes forgotten to pay the bills or pick up some milk or lock all the windows before leaving the house. Even now, Sebastian sometimes found himself sitting at the foot of Nana May's stairs, wistfully watching and hoping, his heart aching so much he thought he might die. But the door never revealed anything more than the empty front yard.

At times like these, Nana May would sit down beside him, her joints creaking, and she would hold his hand in hers, would turn it over and trace the lines of his palm with a delicate finger.

'Some doors stay open,' she would say, 'and some stay closed.'

Nana May talking in riddles. It always brought a smile to his face. It always—

Sebastian tore back the sheets and leaped from the bed.

'Oh God!'

Elise stirred in her sleep but didn't wake.

'Oh God! Oh shit! Oh Christ!'

He had forgotten. Just for a few minutes but he'd forgotten all the same. The sudden remembrance hit him like a tidal wave, engulfing his body and spilling from his eyes in floods.

Sebastian ran from the room and kicked open the bathroom door. He lunged towards the toilet, pulled up the lid, and vomited.

When there was nothing left to come out, he slumped against the cold tiles of the bathroom wall, welcoming the tingling sensation they brought to his skin. He sat for what seemed like hours, panting and sobbing, rubbing tears from his eyes and snot from his nose, until the skin on his face was red, itchy, and raw.

Nana May was gone. What did that even mean?

"Dead" was the word Elise had used. What a terrible sounding word, he thought.

His grandmother was dead.

Not a single strand of pain he'd felt before could even compare.

Nana May was dead. And she was still outside. In the garden.

Sebastian sat up. His knees trembling, he stood and tore off a long strip of toilet paper, using it to wipe his mouth and dry his eyes. He moved over to the sink, turned on the tap, and drank handfuls of cold water.

What were they going to do?

Panic threatened to delve deep and find more nasty things to throw up. Sebastian turned his head towards the bathroom door.

Elise would know, wouldn't she? He nodded. Yes, she would.

Allowing a moment for his stomach to settle, he flushed the toilet then tiptoed along the landing. He heard the heavy rise and fall of Elise's breaths as he approached.

How could she still be asleep? He shook his head as he watched her from the doorway. People usually looked at peace while they slept, but not Elise. Maybe long ago. These days, she looked tired, asleep or awake. He wondered if it was because of the changes Nana May (his heart cracked a little more) had spoken about. The ones to do with growing up and becoming an adult.

His mind drifted back to yesterday's fight and guilt grew heavy in his chest. He decided not to wake her just yet.

Things that go wrong can always be put right, he thought. That was not one of Nana May's sayings, but one of his mother's.

When they lived with her, things always had a habit of going wrong. Sometimes the electricity went wrong and there'd be no television for days. Sometimes the telephone went wrong and there'd be no calls to Nana May for weeks. Sometimes even their mother went wrong, and she'd sit in her room for hours, perched on the edge of her bed smoking cigarette after cigarette.

Sebastian remembered little of these episodes but following their mother's disappearance Elise had made sure to refresh his memory daily.

"Going wrong," she informed him, was their mother's way of saying she had spent the bill money at the bar. "Going wrong" was when yet another one of her boyfriends had come to live with them for a week or a month, and then had left, stealing what little money or valuables they'd possessed. One loathsome individual had even taken their dog, Sparkles, which their mother had said was fortunate seeing as Sparkles had been just another mouth to feed.

As for their mother going wrong, Elise could never explain it. When Sebastian asked about her sitting on the bed and staring into space, when he questioned the drunkenness, or the viciousness that sometimes fired from her tongue like spiny needles, Elise could only look away.

'Don't ask me about that, Sebastian,' she'd whisper. 'I don't have an answer.'

He hoped she had an answer to the question plaguing his mind right now.

A low growl interrupted his thoughts and he clasped a hand to his empty stomach. Nana May would have been serving up omelettes by now. Chilled glasses of freshly squeezed orange juice would have been sitting on the kitchen table.

A whimper escaped the boy's mouth.

How would he and Elise survive? They would die of loneliness and starvation before anyone even noticed Nana May was gone!

He needed Elise to wake up and tell him everything was going to be fine. But he had a feeling that not a single comforting word or stroke of a hand could paint over an inch of the trouble they were in.

His stomach empathised with another undulating rumble.

Breakfast. That was a comforting word. It didn't have the power to make everything right again, but with full bellies he and Elise would be able to think clearly about what they should do. With full bellies, there was a chance they might make it to the afternoon without losing their minds.

'Can't make a chicken dance,' he said. 'Can't start a day without breakfast.'

It was his favourite of all Nana May's sayings.

Still in his pyjamas, Sebastian made his way down to the kitchen.

As usual, it took a moment for his body to become accustomed to the heat from the oven. In winter, when snow and bitter winds transformed the outside into an eerie, alien land, the kitchen was a warm embrace. In summer, it was stifling. But as Nana May would stress at least once a week, no fire in the oven meant cold food and even colder water.

Wrapping a towel around his hand, he pulled open the oven's furnace door and was greeted by glowing embers. His eyes began to sting as he reached for the small shovel in the coal bucket and placed a few of the black rocks into the furnace.

He stood, listening to the crack and fizzle of the burning coal, and soaking in the stillness of the room. It was as if he'd stepped into a life-sized painting; a photograph taken moments before the world woke up. The emptiness pervaded his thoughts as he turned to the back door.

She was out there. On the other side of the wall. Sitting in her rocking chair, shoes kicked off onto the grass. If she was left there, she would eventually rot away. The birds would peck at her eyes. Woodland creatures would come out at night to feast upon her flesh.

They would have to bury her. That was what happened to people when they died. They were buried. Or they were burned.

Sebastian shuddered. Suddenly, breakfast was the last thing on his mind.

Chapter 4

For a moment she was disoriented and afraid. Eyes the darkest of green looked down upon her with a tenderness that consumed her whole being. Soft pink lips parted to reveal a perfect smile.

'There you are,' the voice said, and it resonated with so much love she thought she might burst into tears.

Elise sat up and threw her arms around her mother's neck. She held on, fingers running through raven black hair. She held on for so long she became afraid to let go. Her mother took her arms and placed them by her sides.

She lifted a finger and motioned to Sebastian, who was curled up in the back seat, his favourite toy rabbit tucked under one arm.

Mother and daughter shared a secret smile. This was their time; a few minutes together when they were the only two people in the world. Elise didn't doubt her mother shared similar moments with Sebastian, but for now she revelled in having her all to herself.

'Are we here already?'

Through the windows, she saw the familiar tree-lined lane and the potholed road that was always such fun to drive over because it was like being tossed about on a fairground ride. Her mother nodded, and for a moment so brief that Elise almost missed it, her expression fell away into desolation.

'You were out all the way, sleepyhead.'

'Sebastian kept me awake all night. I wish I didn't have to share a room with him.'

Again, that look on her mother's face. Again, came the smile. This time, she fought to keep it there.

'It won't be for much longer. Soon as I get another job, things will be just fine.'

'And we'll get a bigger place? I can have my own room?'

Her mother stared into the trees, squinting as if she could see something in the shadows there. 'You'll have your own room and Sebastian will have his. Everything will be just fine.'

Elise had not had her own room since before Sebastian was born. The idea sent waves of excitement coursing through her. She could have friends over to stay. She could sleep at night without her little brother climbing into her bed, frightened by another bad dream. She wouldn't have to step over toy cars and robots, or find the heads pulled off her dolls ever again.

'Can my room be yellow?' she asked, her eyes sparkling and wide.

Her mother turned and any trace of sorrow was swept away. She leaned across the car to kiss her daughter on the cheek.

'It can be any colour you want it to be. Now let's wake up your brother or he'll miss out on the potholes. That boy could sleep through an earthquake!'

Elise giggled. 'I hope Nana's made chocolate cake again.'

In the back seat, Sebastian opened a sleepy eye.

'Wake up,' he said. 'I've made breakfast.'

Elise woke up.

Slowly, she sat up, blinking the dream away. Sebastian stood at the side of the bed, a tray in his hands.

'What is that?'

'It's an omelette!' Sebastian said. 'Just like how Nana May makes it.'

"Made," a voice whispered inside Elise's ear. Her eyes moved from the plate of blackened mess to the half-spilled glass of orange juice.

'I don't remember Nana's omelettes ever looking like that,' she said. 'You're supposed to cook on the stove, not inside the furnace.'

Sebastian stared at her. 'You look tired.'

'I'm fine.'

Their gazes crossed paths for a second, then went on their separate ways. Elise speared some of the omelette and forced it into her mouth. The taste was worse than the smell, but she tried her best to hide her disgust.

'Yum!' she enthused, scrabbling for the orange juice. 'Aren't you having any?'

'Not hungry.'

'Well, you should eat even if you're not hungry. You need to keep your strength up.'

Sebastian's face grew pale. 'What are we going to do?'

Elise looked from the plate of charcoal remains to the pallid form of her brother. A knot of anxiety pushed its way through her chest. Rubbing her temples, she winced at the pain that greeted her fingertips.

She had fallen, hadn't she? On the garden path. Her hair on that side was caked with dried blood.

After dragging an unconscious Sebastian up to her room, Elise had returned downstairs and cleared away the remnants of Nana May's leftover ingredients. She'd washed up the dirty pans, bowls and baking trays. She'd placed cakes and cookies into tin containers and stored them on shelves inside the pantry. Finally, she'd got onto her knees and scrubbed the flagstone floor with hot water and an old wire brush, until all traces of dirt were vanquished and her hands were red and her knuckles were scuffed and raw. Then she'd gone to bed, the injury she'd sustained lost under a blanket of exhaustion.

Sebastian was staring at her, waiting for an answer.

She shook her head. 'I don't know.'

'We should call the police. That's what Billy Tooms did when his dad got drunk and pushed his mum down the stairs.'

'No one pushed Nana down the stairs.'

'I know, but that's what they do on TV, isn't it? When somebody gets hurt they call the police. Or an ambulance. Do you think we should call an ambulance?'

'Ambulances save lives. Nana May is dead.'

The word hung between them like the smell of burned bread. For a long time, the air was heavy with silence.

Then Sebastian began to cry.

'Why is she dead?' she sobbed.

'I don't know.'

'Maybe she's just sleeping.'

'She isn't sleeping, Sebastian.'

'Do you think someone hurt her?'

'She was old. It's what happens to everybody.'

This new revelation plunged Sebastian further into the depths of despair. Shutting out his pitiful sounds, Elise picked up a spoon from the breakfast tray and flipped it over in her hand. An elongated reflection of her face stared back. She turned her head and her bloodied temple stretched out before her, a dried up crimson streak.

Sebastian sat down on the bed.

'Will we be in trouble with the police?'

'For what?'

'For leaving her out there in the cold.'

'I don't know. Perhaps.'

'I don't want to go to jail.'

Elise closed her eyes, exhaustion creeping back in. 'They won't put you in jail, stupid.'

'They might take us away, though. Billy Tooms had to go and live with another family when his dad got thrown in jail and his mum went crazy.'

'Has everything happened to Billy Tooms?'

'I think so,' Sebastian said.

'Grown-ups can't be trusted,' Elise muttered. Her face, which had been etched with a stony expression, momentarily betrayed her.

Sebastian choked on his sobs. 'What do you mean?'

'Forget it. All I know is we're not living with strangers. Not again.'

'What about Uncle Edward? We could live with him.'

Elise shook her head. 'I—he wouldn't want that.'

'Well, he could come here and take care of us.'

'He wouldn't do that.'

'Why not? He says we're his favourite nephew and niece.'

'We're his only nephew and niece you idiot! Besides, he only tells you that to keep you happy. All Uncle Edward cares about is himself. There's no chance he'd want us because he's too busy with his stupid job.'

Sebastian stared at the wall. 'What about Mum?'

'No! She didn't want us before so why would she want us now? Besides, do you know where she is because I bloody don't! No one does. We're on our own, Sebastian! We've been left all on our own!'

The words knocked the breath from her lungs. Her hands shot up to her mouth to prevent more seeping out.

Sebastian stood up from the bed then sat down again. He let out an unbearable, drawn-out howl.

'Please,' Elise begged. 'Please, don't do that.'

Something was happening to her. A collision of impenetrable rage and irreconcilable loss was bubbling and churning, threatening to erupt like the guts of a volcano. Her lips moved, yet no words came out. Her head made little jerking motions. Her fingers twitched. She looked down at her breakfast plate and pushed it away.

'I can't eat this.'

Pulling back the sheets, Elise rose on unsteady feet. Images of Nana May flooded her mind. Her knees buckled and she gripped the edge of the windowsill.

'Nana!' she moaned.

She'd never felt so alone. Not even when her mother had left.

The rush of blood in her ears became a deafening roar, a landslide burying all thought. She squeezed her eyes shut.

And then it was silent. Soft whispers caressed her ears and she savoured the heat of the breath that enveloped them.

'Hush now,' Nana cooed. 'The world's not burning yet.'

Elise sucked in a breath. 'But we're all alone now. And I don't know what I should do.'

'Don't fret, sweet thing. Don't cry. Time will give you your answer.'

'I'm scared, Nana. I don't want you to go.'

'Nothing to be done about that. Remember I'll always love you. I'll always be here.'

The words floated out through the open window and danced away over the trees.

Calm embraced Elise, washing over her like a summer tide. The world was quiet and the world was still.

Sebastian reached across and touched his sister's cheek. She looked up, a steely gaze hardening her features.

'I need to think.'

Elise sat down on the bed. Veins throbbed at her temples. Her eyebrows knitted together, then unravelled like balls of wool.

Outside, the day shimmered and wavered.

Finally, Elise looked up. Her eyes blazed with determination.

'I'll do all the cooking,' she declared. 'And not because I'm a girl but because you obviously don't know how. You can clean the house and wash the dishes. I'll take care of the laundry, but you can help me hang out the sheets.'

Sebastian nodded. A smile rippled across his lips. Elise knew it was because she was taking charge. She was deciding what to do. She would take care of him now because it was her duty. Because no one else could be trusted.

'We'll take turns feeding the cats. You can do them in the morning while I'm cooking breakfast, and I'll feed them at night while you're cleaning up after dinner. And we mustn't forget the stove. I'll keep it burning because I'm doing the cooking, but it can be your job to make sure the coal bucket is always full. Okay?'

'Okay,' Sebastian replied, there but not <u>really</u> there, his gaze fixed somewhere between reality and a dream.

'So, I'll make some food now, something we can actually eat. And you can feed the cats. Okay?'

Sebastian smiled again. 'Okay.'

Then his smile faded. His eyes grew wide and large.

'No! I can't! Please, don't make me!'

Elise frowned, her hands coming to rest on her hips. 'And why not?'

He stared at her. 'The cats get fed outside!'

'And?'

'She's still out there.'

Elise fell silent. The same thoughts that had visited Sebastian earlier now came to her, creeping through the trees on all fours and swooping down from the sky.

'She is, isn't she?' Elise said. 'We should do something about that.'

They began with a hearty lunch of eggs and sausages. Sebastian had lied about not being hungry. He'd been ravenous, but one taste of his omelette had almost sent him bolting back to the bathroom. The fact that Elise had decided to take on the role of cook pleased him immensely. At least he would be safe from food poisoning or starvation; two deaths he could strike from his list of ways to die now that Nana May was gone.

They ate in silence. When they were finished, Elise left the kitchen and Sebastian busied himself with washing up plates and pans. When the dishes were done, he moved over to the coal bucket and saw it was half empty.

His heart fluttered. The coal was stored in the outhouse, a small brick building that stood a few metres away from the side of the house.

He could hear the hungry mewls of the cats floating in through the kitchen windows.

Don't forget, he imagined the cats saying, she's out here waiting for you, and if you don't feed us soon we'll have no choice but to make her our meal.

Frightened, Sebastian left the kitchen and hurried along the hall. He stopped in his tracks.

Elise was standing at the foot of the stairs, a bed sheet draped over one arm and a length of thin rope coiled over the other.

'Where did you get that?' Sebastian asked, pointing at the rope. His knees trembled beneath him.

'The cupboard under the stairs.'

'But we're not allowed in there, you know that. There are sharp things. Nana May says—'

He fell silent. Elise stepped down onto the floor.

'We're going to move her,' she said.

'What?'

'She can't stay in the garden. We're going to move her.'

'But—'

'We have to.'

'Why?'

'Because . . . because she can't stay there.'

Sebastian wrapped his arms around his body and squeezed. 'Where are we going to put her? What if she wakes up?'

'She's not going to wake up,' Elise replied. 'She's dead.'

Sebastian looked up at her.

'But she might,' he whispered.

'What did Nana May say about what happens to people when they die?'

Sebastian shrugged. He felt suddenly very small.

'Think, Sebastian!'

'Heaven,' he choked. 'She said they go to heaven.'

'That's right. And that's exactly where Nana May is right now. So that can't be her sitting out there, can it? That's just what's left behind.'

'We can't move her!'

'Do you really think Nana would want us put into care again? Do you think she'd want us to get split up? Maybe never see each other again?'

Doubt filled Sebastian's veins.

'If we don't do this, then that's what will happen.'

Sebastian stared at his feet. His lower lip trembled.

'Everything will be just fine,' Elise said. She forced a smile onto her lips.

It was a lie, Sebastian knew, but it was what people said in troubled times, whether they meant it or not. It was what their mother had always said about everything.

Elise handed Sebastian the sheet.

'We'll wait until night-time. It will be cooler. And darker.'

Sebastian nodded. Darkness was good. It covered things up. It stopped you from seeing what you were doing.

'All right,' Elise said, her tone lightening. 'Let's watch some TV. How about cartoons?'

Sebastian swallowed. He glanced up. 'Can I choose?'

Elise draped the rope over the stair rail.

'Whatever you like,' she said.

Chapter 5

The Past

In the ten years that Catherine had made the city her home, her mother had visited exactly three times. The first was to attend Catherine's wedding to Mr Nathaniel Parker. He had proposed just four weeks after meeting her, and because he'd seemed like a decent enough man, Catherine had accepted. It wasn't until she'd stepped out of the registry office doors and brushed away the confetti that she'd realised getting to know a person might very well take an entire lifetime. The marriage had ended five weeks later.

Catherine's mother had known nothing about her first marriage—an eight-month stint with a man twice her age and keen on using his fists.

May Montgomery's second visit came two months after Elise was born. And what a surprise that had been considering she was unaware her daughter had even been pregnant.

'Who's the father?' May had asked, peering with round eyes at the sleeping bundle in Catherine's arms.

Catherine had only shrugged. 'Good question.'

May's third visit turned out to be a month-long haul. Catherine had thoughtfully remembered to inform her mother about her second pregnancy and was glad she had done so when labour came.

For thirty-six hours she screamed and wailed and pushed and moaned, until Sebastian made his way into the world. May stayed by her side the entire time, leaving only to telephone the babysitter to check on Elise, to eat a little something to maintain her strength, and to go to the bathroom to relieve herself.

Mostly, she sat at Catherine's bedside, squeezing her daughter's hand and whispering soft, velvety words into her ear. Words that calmed her when panic came. Words that let her know the pain would not last forever and that the pain meant her child was healthy and strong. A fighter.

'Think of the beautiful life you're about to create,' May soothed, as another agonising contraction caused Catherine to scream. 'Think about that beautiful face staring up at you when you hold him in your arms.'

Catherine tried to imagine holding her soon-to-be-born son against her chest. The pain began to subside until, minutes later, she felt nothing at all. And perhaps Sebastian had sensed that nothingness. Perhaps it had given him an indication of the kind of mother he would be getting—one that might not sit by his side and hold his hand and fill his head with lovely words. Perhaps that was why he had fought so long and hard to remain hidden in the darkness of his mother's womb.

Two days after the birth of her son, Catherine came home. Labour had left her far from well and with more stitches than her favourite pair of jeans.

'I'll stay for a while,' May announced, as she helped her daughter out of the cab. 'Just until you're able to get around.'

Catherine nodded in silence, while May picked up the carry-cot in which Sebastian slept. Elise crawled out from the back seat of the cab, her mouth stretched open in a yawn.

'I'm tired,' she complained. 'Aileen's house is too noisy.'

May paid the driver and pushed open the garden gate. She raised an eyebrow at the tumble of weeds choking the lawn.

This was her first time at the flat. Catherine had moved three times since her last visit, and while she'd been recovering in hospital, she'd insisted May stay with Aileen. Elise had been right about the woman's home—it was full of noise and people and dubious goings on.

After helping her daughter into bed and setting Sebastian down in the cot that was crammed into the corner of the bedroom, May took her suitcase to Elise's room. She stared at the tiny bed she was expected to share with her granddaughter. Something tugged at the side of her long blue skirt.

'Can we play?' Elise asked, clutching an old ragdoll.

Smiling, May bent down and pressed a soft hand against her granddaughter's cheek.

'You go ahead, my lovely. Your Nana's got some work to do.'

She spent the next hour picking up toys from the floor and cleaning up sticky stains on the carpet. Next, she wiped mould from the walls and dust from the furniture. Now that parts of the house were hospitable, she went to the kitchen to make some tea.

Dirty plates filled the sink, while a mountain of clean dishes lay on the drainer.

Shaking her head, May opened the refrigerator door. Rancid odours of rotting food burned her nostrils. She disposed of a litre of sour milk, a half-eaten block of mouldy cheese, and a plastic container holding some unknown horror inside. This left the refrigerator empty. She checked the freezer, found a tray of ice cubes and half a bottle of vodka.

She removed the lids of three ceramic jars sitting next to the kettle.

'At least there's some sense left in this house,' she muttered, spying tea bags.

'I hope you don't mind your tea black!' she called out to Catherine. 'Looks like the cow's gone and died on us.'

There was no teapot.

Tea without a teapot was like a horse without hooves. May tut-tutted and shook her head some more as she dropped teabags into cups.

'No father figures around,' she moaned, 'the place a mess. You should come home with me.'

'Don't start, Mother.'

May jumped out of her skin. Catherine leaned against the doorjamb, her face as white as the refrigerator doors.

'Are you trying to scare me to death?' May cried. 'I'm not ready for my grave just yet!'

Catherine brushed hair from her eyes. 'I'm not coming home, so don't even ask.'

'But—'

'I'm twenty-seven years old. I can take care of myself.'

May contemplated this as she poured hot water into the cups.

'You're not coming home, you say. Though you still call it home.'

'You know what I mean.'

'There's no food in the fridge. The cupboards are empty. What have you been living on? Fresh air? You've two other mouths to feed besides your own. You can take care of yourself, can you?'

Some colour forced its way to Catherine's cheeks. 'Don't . . . don't even—you've no idea how difficult it's been for me.'

May fell silent, thinking of a thousand different things to say: No, I don't have any idea how difficult it's been for you—I don't even know you. Why aren't you more like your brother? If only your father was alive to see you in this sorry state. But she said nothing. This was her daughter and she barely recognised her. There were few words to describe how that felt.

'There's a shop on the corner that sells milk,' Catherine said, her teeth snapping together. 'Don't worry about dinner. I'll phone for takeaway. We can shop for groceries tomorrow.'

May nodded. Funny food in foil cartons? What was the world coming to?

Over the next few weeks, she learned to navigate her way through the local streets, finding her way to the corner shop and the supermarket but never venturing beyond.

The hustle and bustle and pushing and shoving that constituted city living was unhealthy in her countrified opinion. There was too much noise. The air was toxic with exhaust fumes. But it was the people that unnerved her the most. There were too many of them, all scurrying by with dark scowls and hunched shoulders. All so forgetful about life as they rushed back and forth.

'What's the point?' May mused. 'You'd wake up dead before you knew it.'

She spent as much time as she could indoors. She did everything that needed to be done, tending to the house and her family.

Catherine stayed in bed for hours at a time. Sometimes May stood outside the bedroom door and listened to the muffled sobs coming from the other side. Sometimes she crept inside, only to see Catherine turn over and pretend to be asleep.

'Why is she always tired?' Elise asked one morning over breakfast. There was no kitchen table, so she sat on the tatty sofa in the living room while she ate a bowl of cereal and watched cartoons.

May sat in the armchair, giving Sebastian his morning feed. That was another thing— feeding the baby that artificial stuff. How was he expected to grow up healthy and strong if he was denied his mother's milk?

'Your mother's just had a baby,' she said. 'One day, when you grow up and have children of your own, you'll see how much it takes out of you. How tired it makes you feel.'

Elise frowned as she twirled her spoon between her fingers. 'I don't want babies.'

May raised an eyebrow. 'Why ever not? Having your own children is the most wonderful thing on earth.'

'<u>She</u> doesn't think so.'

May set the milk bottle down by her feet. Sebastian gurgled then burped up the milk he'd just swallowed. She wiped him clean and kissed him on the forehead.

'Come on now, you don't mean that. Your mother loves you very much.'

Elise shrugged her shoulders and crammed cereal into her mouth. She watched the cartoon that was playing—Road Runner and Wile E. Coyote. When her cereal was finished, she placed the empty bowl on the faded carpet.

May cooed over Sebastian.

'Nana?' Elise said.

'Yes, my dear?'

'I don't like it here. Can we come and live with you?'

'Your mother is happy to stay here,' May said, smiling as she adjusted Sebastian's blanket.

'She doesn't have to come. Just Sebastian and me. We could help tidy your house and do the gardening.'

May chuckled. 'Your place is with your mother. She needs more looking after than I do right now.'

'Then why don't you live here?'

She felt her granddaughter's eyes on her as she fiddled with the blanket, adjusting and readjusting it, even though Sebastian seemed content.

'Oh, you see now, me and the city are chalk and cheese,' she said at last. 'I like the peace and quiet.'

'But—'

'I'm too old to be living in a place like this,' May said. 'This place would be the death of me.'

Elise burst into tears. Suddenly, the sofa looked huge and ready to swallow her whole.

Chapter 6

The garden was silent and still. Light radiated from the kitchen window of the old white house and was met by the pale of the moon. Countless stars glinted like shards of glass across the night sky. In the undergrowth, crickets found their song and began to play a melodic sonata of chirps.

Nana May's cats were dotted along the lawn and whining to each other, bothered by the lifeless form sitting in the rocking chair. Red padded towards Nana's body, sniffing the air. The warm, heady scent usually so abundant in her presence was now gone, replaced by something sharp and unfamiliar.

He rubbed the side of his head against her exposed feet then backed away.

Elise stood, rooted to the doorstep, a thin coil of rope in her hands. Stepping into the garden at this late hour was like stumbling upon uncharted territory. All the flowers were transformed into wild, alien species. The surrounding trees became infinite in their stature, their branches reaching past the stars. Moonlight played tricks on the girl's eyes, making the trees appear to move towards her then take a lumbering step back.

Elise's appearance had caused a stir amongst the cats and now they moved towards her, a tide of bodies brushing against her legs as they mewled like hungry children. They hadn't been fed since yesterday, and although most were natural hunters and could catch their own prey if necessary, all had become accustomed to their twice-daily feed.

The girl turned her head in the direction of her grandmother's shadowy form. Then she looked away again, staring at trees, the stars, and the ground.

The back door opened and Sebastian appeared, a bed sheet draped over his shoulder. In the monochrome wash of moonlight, his face was as white as bones.

'Did you get it?' Elise whispered.

Sebastian nodded, holding up a key attached to a long piece of string.

'Good. Put it in your pocket.'

He did as he was told, and then held onto his sister's arm so forcefully that fingerprint bruises would be left come the morning. Elise winced. She drew in a deep breath.

Then she was stepping onto the garden path.

'No!' Sebastian's grip intensified. 'Please, Elise! I can't do it! I want to go and live with Uncle Edward!'

Elise turned to face him. 'We have to do this.'

Sebastian threw the sheet onto the ground. 'No!'

'I told you! If people find out what's happened we'll get put into care. We'll get split up! We'll never see each other ever again!'

'But Uncle Edward—'

'Uncle Edward has no time for us, you know that! He comes once a month and all he talks about is how much money he's making and how big his house is. Why do you think he never got married or had children? Because he doesn't care! He doesn't want a wife or kids because that would mean having to spend time with them and money on them and less on himself!'

Sebastian shook his head. 'You're wrong.'

'Am I? When was the last time he invited us to stay? When was the last time he said,

'Come on Sebastian, I'll take you fishing by the river', or, 'Come on everyone, let's go into town for a movie and an ice cream'? Never, that's when. And if you're stupid enough to believe that now Nana May is gone he's going to take care of you, then you're as crazy as our mother!'

Sebastian stopped his tears. 'Our mother isn't crazy.'

'Isn't she?'

'No, she's not!'

Now it was Elise's turn to throw the rope onto the ground.

'Leaving us here, abandoning us wasn't crazy! Getting drunk every night and crying all over the place wasn't crazy! That's your problem, Sebastian—you're too young to remember. And I wish you weren't so I didn't have to remember it all!'

The sound of silence was all encompassing. Even the crickets had halted their tune.

Aware the whole world was listening in, Sebastian dropped his voice to a whisper.

'It's not my fault that I don't remember. Maybe you got some of it wrong.'

Elise balled her hands into fists.

'Got it wrong? Why have we been living with Nana May for the last four years? Why has Mum never bloody-well come back to get us or been to visit once? Not one phone call, Sebastian. Not even a letter or a postcard to tell us she's all right, or to ask us how we're doing. We could be dead for all she cares. <u>She</u> could be dead.'

'She's not.'

'How do you know? How do you know she's not dead?'

The boy covered his ears. 'Stop saying that word.'

'Nana May is dead. Look over there. See! She's dead and her own daughter wouldn't even care if she'd died right in front of her!'

'Stop it!'

Sebastian flew at her, his tiny fists striking her shoulder and chest. She let him have the first two blows and then she grasped his arms and forced them down. Sebastian hissed and spat, baring his teeth.

'We're alone,' Elise said. 'Nobody's coming to save us. We need to stick together now, just you and me. All we have is this house and each other.'

Sebastian faltered. He leaned against his sister, breathless and exhausted, and she held him close.

'Someone will come,' he said.

Elise rested her chin on the top of his head. 'I know. But we need time to figure out what we're going to do.'

'But Nana May—'

Elise put a finger to his lips. 'Nana May is in heaven.'

She looked towards the body in the rocking chair.

'It's just a shell, Sebastian. Like the paper presents come wrapped in.'

Sebastian looked up. 'What presents?'

'Come on.' Elise bent down and picked up the rope. 'Let's do this as fast as we can.'

Sebastian stared at the rope, imagining a writhing mass of muscle and fangs. To his young mind, rope was used for climbing, or attaching to tree branches to make a swing. But he knew it was also used for tying things up.

He stooped down to pick up the sheet. Bed sheets were for putting on mattresses, for making sails, and for dressing up as Romans when you were bored and had nothing better to do on a rainy day.

Yes, his mind whispered, but sheets are also for covering up dead things.

'Are we going to bury her?'

Elise slid her arm through the coil of rope and hooked it over her shoulder. 'We can't. Not yet. The first thing we need to do is get it—her—out of the garden.'

'Why?'

'Because if we leave her here she'll—'

—stink and rot and decay, and her flesh will fall away and her eyes will melt like ice cream in the sun, and her guts will burst and spill out onto the lawn, and you'll need more than a piece of old rope and a bed sheet to clear up that mess—

'—be in the way.'

'Why can't we just bury her?'

'Because it would take too long and I don't know where we should bury her yet. People are supposed to be buried in the graveyard at the church.'

'Well, then let's bury her there.'

'Are you stupid or what? How are we going to get her up there? It's miles away.'

'Then where are we going to put her?'

'The outhouse. Why do you think I asked you to get the key, dummy?'

Nana May had never liked locking her doors. 'If I want to be a prisoner,' she'd said, 'I'll commit a crime.' She'd argued that they were too far out from the nearest town for thieves to come looking for homes to break into.

Then she'd caught a vagrant man trying to break into the outhouse and steal her coal. But instead of calling the police, she'd taken the man into the kitchen and given him a decent meal. Then she'd sent him away, but not without making him promise he'd never return.

After the vagrant had gone, Nana May had asked Mr Elliot to install a bolt and padlock on the outhouse door.

Sebastian shook his head at the thought of locking his grandmother in there. He tried to speak but no words came out.

'We can't put her in the house,' Elise said. 'It's the only safe place until we decide where to bury her.'

Sebastian wondered if his sister was right—that if social workers came, he and Elise would be separated. After all, it had happened before.

'It's dark in the outhouse,' he moaned.

'It's dark in the ground. Do you still want to bury her?'

The boy winced and risked the quickest of glimpses at Nana May's body. She was just a silhouette now. A shadow.

'What do we do?'

Elise extended her hand. 'Give me the sheet.'

He handed it over and watched as she unfolded it and held it up by the corners. She glanced over her shoulder and Sebastian saw terror ripple across her face.

Elise walked towards Nana May, arms outstretched, the sheeting hanging down and covering her view.

'Tell me when I'm there!' she said in a trembling voice.

Sebastian's heart crashed against his ribcage as he watched her shuffle forward and the cats leap out of her way.

She was getting closer. He heard her breaths getting faster, heavier.

'Nearly there!' Sebastian cried. He stumbled back, taking refuge on the doorstep.

Elise took another step forward. Then another.

'You're there! You're there!'

With a cry, she shook the sheet up in the air and it billowed like a sail. The sheet came down and draped Nana May's body. Elise staggered back, catching the rope as it slipped from her shoulder.

Covered in the sheet, Nana May looked like furniture ready for removal. It was easier to think of her that way, Sebastian thought—as an object, something that had never contained life or spirit.

Leaving the harbour of the door, Sebastian crept across the lawn and put a hand on Elise's shoulder.

'Are you all right?'

She nodded.

'She looks like a ghost,' he said.

'We have to tie her.' Elise began to unravel the rope. 'So she doesn't fall out.'

Handing Sebastian one end of the rope, she crouched down beside the chair.

'Something smells bad.' Sebastian said, covering his nose.

He watched Elise wind the rope around the sheet and the chair. It was difficult to believe that Nana May was under that sheet now, even though he had seen her in the chair just a minute before. In his mind, Nana May was no longer his grandmother at all, but a ghost they'd captured, and Elise was tying it up to make sure it never bothered them or spooked anyone else again.

A thought struck him. 'You think Nana May will come back and haunt us?'

Elise had finished tying the rope. Sebastian watched her reach under the sheet. For a second, he wondered what she was doing. Then he realised she was holding Nana May's hand.

Grief welled up from the pit of his stomach. Nana May would never hold his hand again. She would never brush the hair out of his eyes, or gently stroke his cheek, or playfully pinch his nose.

Elise gasped and recoiled in horror.

'She's stiff!' she cried. 'She's like a statue!'

Sebastian took the tiniest of steps closer. 'What do you mean? What's happened to her?'

'I don't know. Maybe that's what happens when you're . . .'

Elise glanced at Sebastian but said nothing more.

'Is it like when we found Thomas?' he asked.

'I guess so.'

Thomas had been the eldest of Nana's cats. They had come across him in the woods one afternoon. He'd been missing for three days. Nana had told them that Thomas had gone off to die because he was old and it was his time. Sebastian had poked Thomas with a stick and the stick had snapped in half.

Elise stood up. 'Still got the key?'

Sebastian nodded. Brother and sister moved around the rocking chair until they stood behind it. Their fingers wrapped around the back bars. Sebastian felt Nana May's body pressing up against him. Terrified, he glanced up at his sister.

Then they were pulling with all their might.

At first, the chair refused to move. The children pulled harder, clenching their teeth and grunting as if they were competing in a tug-of-war match on school sports day—a match they were losing.

'I can't!' Sebastian wailed.

Elise dug her heels deep into the grass. 'You can! You have to! Pull, Sebastian!'

The chair jerked towards them in one large movement and the children fell back onto the lawn. A strange sight greeted them as they sat up: a tied-up ghost, rocking back and forth in the middle of the garden. It was a strange sight, funny even—until on a forward rock, the sheet covering Nana May's face slipped down.

As fortunate as they were to be standing behind and only able to see the back of her head, the reality of what they were doing sent both siblings into throes of hysteria. Sebastian burst into a fit of braying sobs. Elise choked as her stomach churned and convulsed.

'D-don't look!' she stammered.

The children jumped to their feet and caught the chair in mid-swing. The weight of their grandmother's body dragged them forward, making their feet slide through the grass.

'Keep pulling, Sebastian!'

Whether it was sheer force of will or strength borne from terror, the children shifted the chair towards them once more. This time they didn't let go but used the rocking motion to their advantage, allowing the chair to roll forward before pulling hard as it swung back.

Nana May came up to meet them and then flew away, see-sawing in jerky movements as they hauled her through the garden. Sebastian stood on a cat's tail and the screech the animal emitted before darting away made the children howl like babies.

Elise's hands flew away from the back of the chair and Sebastian was lifted from the ground. Lunging forward, Elise regained her hold. Slamming her heels deep into the earth, she pulled back. Sebastian found his footing again. Then they were moving towards the outhouse once more.

At last, they rounded the corner of the house. Every inch of their bodies screamed with pain. Their lungs burned with each ragged breath. Grass gave way to gravel and the chair ground to a halt.

'It hurts!' Sebastian wailed. 'I need to rest!'

'We're nearly there!'

The muscles in his arms felt like stretched elastic. He looked around and saw the trees closing in on the left and the house looming over him on the right. Although darkness cloaked its position, he knew the outhouse was just a few metres away.

'Pull, Sebastian! Pull as hard as you can!'

He had no more strength, nothing left to give, but Sebastian pulled anyway. So did Elise.

They pulled too hard. Nana May lurched towards them. Elise slammed into the corner of the outhouse, her shoulder glancing off granite, sending her spinning like a ballerina into the shadows.

Sebastian was dragged forward, then backwards. He let go of the chair and fell to the ground. Nana May rocked wildly, gravel crunching under her weight.

Hurt and crying, Sebastian sat up. The palms of his hands were cut and bleeding. Tiny slivers of grit were embedded in his flesh.

Wrapping his arms around his ribcage, he wept as he watched Nana May slow to a halt.

Elise emerged from the shadows and loomed over him.

'The key,' she said.

He winced as his bloody palm rubbed against his pocket. Sebastian fumbled for the key. It wasn't there. He checked his other pockets to find them empty.

'I can't find it!' he squealed. 'It's gone!'

'Look again.'

He tapped at his pockets with the flats of his palms, snivelling with each stab of pain.

'It must have fallen out.'

'Damn it!' Elise spat the words out like poison. 'Well, don't just sit there, stupid! Find it!'

Sebastian jumped to his feet. Tears blurred his vision and stung his eyes. He sobbed and hiccupped.

'It's too dark!'

'Fine. Then you can sit out here with her all night until it's light enough to find it.'

'I'll find it!' he screamed. 'I'll find it!'

And it was as if the moon had seen enough and taken pity on him because a shaft of light shifted on the ground, and there was the key; a diamond in the darkness.

Sebastian picked it up and handed it over. Elise turned away and moved towards the outhouse. The key slid into the padlock.

By day, the outhouse was a harmless looking construct made of granite and slate, its interior small and nondescript. Now, the doorway was an open mouth with teeth and an insatiable hunger. It was an accusatory eye, a pointing finger. A bottomless hole in which to throw all guilt, all remorse, all goodbyes.

'Help me, Sebastian.'

With the final, pitiful shreds of their energy ebbing away, they took hold of the back of the chair and pulled. They no longer cared whether they could see Nana May's exposed head; exhaustion had taken hold of their limbs and was refusing to let go.

Nan May was in the doorway now. Sebastian let go and turned to face the impenetrable blackness of the outhouse.

'I don't want to go in there.'

'One more time,' Elise urged, reaching out to touch his face. She lowered her head and kissed his hair. She brought her lips to his ear. 'One more time and we're done.'

They took hold of the chair and pulled Nana May into the darkness.

Outside, the stars rippled over the treetops. Inside the outhouse, brother and sister stood for a long while, catching their breaths. Then, together, they stumbled out into the world.

Sebastian collapsed onto a stretch of moonlit grass. He panted and wheezed as Elise leaned against the doorjamb and stared into the night sky.

'I'm sorry,' she whispered to the darkness. She closed the door and slid the padlock back into place.

Sebastian watched as she lay down next to him. Their fingers found each other amongst the blades of grass. For a long time, their breaths were the only sounds in the world.

Chapter 7

Tuesday came and went. The weather succumbed to rolling, thunderous charcoal skies and rain that fell in heavy sheets. Occasional bursts of lightning lit up the dark day. Sebastian and Elise slept away the hours, their limbs swollen and aching from the previous night's exertions. When they woke, Elise prepared a dinner that neither of them had the appetite to eat.

Evening came. They moved into the living room, sitting on separate sofas to watch television. If they had been asked, neither of the children would have been able to name the shows they had sat through. They were watching but not <u>really</u> watching. Talking sporadically but without conviction. Cracks of thunder punctuated their empty words as the storm gathered momentum overhead. Rain on the windowpanes sounded like pebbles being dragged out on the ocean tide. Twice, the living room light flickered and the television lost its signal. Sebastian and Elise glanced at each other and caught their breaths.

At midnight, they returned upstairs. Elise pushed open her bedroom door and waited for Sebastian to step inside. His head hanging low, he continued along the corridor until he came to his own door.

'Goodnight,' he said, without looking back.

Elise stood still, listening to the rain skim the slates of the roof.

'Goodnight,' she replied.

Wednesday surfaced and was ill-prepared for the blistering heat that greeted it. The voluminous rain clouds that had been growing throughout the night had now evaporated back into the atmosphere. All around, plants and trees gasped for water, and animals dragged themselves into shadows.

Sebastian could hear the distant drone of a plane flying overhead. He wondered how much hotter it was up there, closer to the sun. He sat on the front step overlooking the yard, wearing dark blue shorts and the dirty white vest he had slept in. It was much too hot for shoes, so he left his feet bare.

He'd been awake for almost three hours now. The light had woken him, leaving him tired and waspish and glad that Elise was still asleep. Red sidled up and rubbed his head against Sebastian's thigh. He smirked as the fur tickled his skin, then scratched behind the kitten's ears, producing a loud and enthused purr. Sebastian liked the sound. It was the most contented sound he could think of.

'Better feed you,' he said. He gave Red's tail a playful yank and made his way to the kitchen.

He moved quickly, checking the furnace and grabbing an open sack of dried cat food and two tins of meat from the larder floor. By the time he returned to the front doorway he was panting and drenched with sweat. The kitchen had to be as hot as the surface of the sun. No doubt about it.

The sight of Sebastian carrying their morning feed sent a wave of delirium through the cats. Even though they were hot and cantankerous as hell, they were ravenous. Their lapsed hunting skills had so far produced two mice and an injured sparrow, and those that had killed were not akin to sharing.

The air filled with hungry mewls and hisses as each cat clambered over the next to be first in line to eat. Some rubbed themselves against Sebastian's calves in an effort to be noticed and favoured first. Others used their paws to club away the young and easily intimidated.

Sebastian looked down at the writhing mass of fur and claws around his feet. He pushed his hands though the feline bodies and retrieved their feeding dishes. Two of the cats pulled at the sack and he gave them a light kick to the flanks. They jumped back, spitting and complaining.

'Just for that, I'm going to take my time,' he said, not caring if the animals understood. He took the dishes inside then came back for the food. He shut the front door behind him, using his foot to push away some of the older felines who had decided that if the food was going inside then so were they.

The hallway was cool, and the boy took a moment to enjoy the drop in temperature. The fuss the cats were making only added to his bad mood. He pulled a tin opener from his pocket and flipped it over in his hand. The cats could sense the lids coming off, could smell the meaty odour wafting out from underneath the front door. Their din grew louder still.

'Shut up!' Sebastian yelled at them. They did. For a moment. He dumped the meat into the dishes, poured biscuits on top, and then used the end of the tin opener to mash the food together.

'Stupid cats,' he grumbled. 'Should bloody-well learn to feed themselves.'

Opening the front door, he was greeted by a wailing choir of begging voices. He smiled then, reminded of a week before Christmas last year.

The school music teacher, Ms Merrifield, had decided to show her Goodwill to Man and Woman by sending Sebastian and his fellow choristers to sing carols at the retirement home in town. The old folk were lined up in chairs in the day room, and the children had screeched their way through Silent Night and butchered Good King Wenceslas. After a group effort of transforming We Wish You a Merry Christmas into a different tune entirely, they looked upon their captive audience to find more than half of it fast asleep and snoring. Only one woman in the back row seemed to be enjoying the show. She sang along and clapped her hands and when the performance was over, she stood and asked if they would sing all the songs again.

When they returned to school after the holidays, Ms Merrifield couldn't wait to tell them about how their poor renditions had all but ruined her reputation, not to mention her Christmas holiday. As punishment, the eight-year-olds were subjected to hours of intense vocal training and rigorous rehearsal. Ms Merrifield, it transpired, was a big fish flailing in a dried up pond.

Pushing his way through the multitude of cats, Sebastian dumped the dishes on the ground and sat back to watch the ensuing frenzy. It was quieter then; the animals too busy wolfing down their food to keep up their noise.

Sebastian thought about school. Term started in just over four weeks. How were he and Elise going to survive until then? And if they did, what would they tell their teachers and friends when asked about their summer holidays? "Oh, we didn't get up to much. You know, the usual. Our grandmother died and we hid her body in the outhouse."

Even before school came along, what were they going to say to other people? To Uncle Edward? His visit was less than two weeks away. How were they going to explain it all to him? How would he react to the horror of what they'd done? Sebastian held his head in his hands. It <u>was</u> horrific. He wasn't going to win that argument with his conscience.

Sitting on the step, he wondered if Elise had been right about Uncle Edward, about all the reasons she'd given for doing what they had done to Nana May. He prayed that she was right because if she was wrong, they were going to be in terrible trouble.

'What are you doing?'

Elise came up from behind, yawning and rubbing sleep from her eyes. Her hair sprung up like springs from an old mattress. She wore a faded pink nightdress over scruffy looking jeans.

Sebastian avoided her gaze.

'Just fed the cats. They were really hungry.'

Elise sat down beside him.

'It's so hot already.'

Sebastian turned his hands palms up, examining the cuts. They were healing but still stung whenever he moved his fingers.

'Did you clean those?'

He nodded.

'Good. You don't want to get an infection.'

Silence. It grew between them like a wall of thorns.

Elise sighed and turned her attention to the yard, her gaze wandering from the squirming bulk of feeding cats to the disused pick-up truck, to the end of the yard where the trees closed in to form the winding, leafy lane that connected the house to the outside world. It was the lane their mother's car would come bouncing along, tyres running in and out of potholes, the growl of the engine startling birds from overhanging branches.

'Want to eat something?' she asked.

Sebastian shook his head as he continued to stare at the cuts on his hands.

'Well, I'm going to cook. I'll make enough for you in case you change your mind.'

Sebastian shrugged his shoulders and returned his gaze to the cats.

'Don't be sitting out here all day. There are things to be done. You should have a bath as well. You're starting to smell.'

Sebastian said nothing. Elise huffed and puffed.

'What's the matter with you?' she said.

'Nothing.'

'I can tell when you're lying.'

There was a long silence and then Sebastian said, 'I just . . . I mean . . . I don't know.'

But he did know. It was just that the words were hiding somewhere between his brain and his throat, refusing to come out, because if they did the truth of what he and Elise had done would be exposed to the world. It would be caught on the air currents and it would float over the trees and past the village, all the way down to the ocean. Everyone in its path would hear and they would come for the siblings with clenched fists and abhorrence in their eyes. Sebastian clamped his teeth together, swallowing the words down into his stomach.

Neither of them had uttered a word about Nana May since that night. Sebastian hadn't even cried. How long would this go on for? How long would it be before they felt normal again? He doubted they ever would.

'Let's do something,' Elise said. 'Let's go somewhere.'

Sebastian turned to her. 'Are you mad? We can't go anywhere.'

'I'm bored. I need to do something.'

'Have a walk around the yard.'

'I'm serious. We need to have some fun.'

Sebastian lifted his head at the mention of the word. Fun would be good. He couldn't remember how it felt to be happy and silly and carefree. Just the other day he'd been playing with his toy car, but now it was a memory stolen from some other, happier child.

'What do you want to do?'

'We could go up to the meadows. We could have a hay fight.'

'Boring.'

'Or a walk in the woods?'

'Maybe.'

'How about the river?'

Their eyes lit up.

Chapter 8

In the kitchen they gathered two apples, two oranges, a large wedge of blue cheese, a loaf of homemade bread and slices of ham, and they placed it all inside an old wicker picnic basket that Sebastian found tucked away beneath the sink. Next, they put in two plastic beakers, a large bottle of blackcurrant juice, and Elise put in a sharp looking knife.

'What's that for?' Sebastian asked, unable to avert his gaze from its shiny blade.

'To cut things, of course. You going to eat that entire block of cheese in one mouthful?'

'Oh.'

Taking a towel, he wrapped it around the blade and placed the knife at the very bottom of the basket. The last things to go in were two blue bath towels and a tatty grey blanket for sitting on. The basket was packed. The furnace was filled with fresh coal. Swimwear was being worn beneath shorts and T-shirts.

They left through the back door and made their way through the garden. They carried the basket between them, grasping a handle each. It was an old and worn basket, and protruding pieces of osier jabbed at their legs. Neither of the children spoke until they had cleared the garden and climbed through the broken wooden fence that separated their home from the woods. The garden was no longer a tranquil place of colour and light. It was now a reminder of Nana May, of what they had done to her.

Once they had cleared the fence, nature greeted them in all its magnificence. They made their way through the woodland, admiring the pallid bark of silver birch trees and staring in awe at the multitude of blue and purple flowers spilling from the undergrowth. Birds sang out in the canopies above. Shafts of dusty light lit up small clearings like spotlights on an open air stage. They passed thickets of green holly and spiky ferns, and they stopped to pick dark berries from bilberry bushes and blackthorn.

Not once did they stop to check their bearings. This was a journey they had taken a hundred times. The cluster of Davey's Elm told them to go straight ahead. The towering oak that stood alone in a marshy clearing indicated to head right. For Sebastian and Elise, finding their way through the woodland was as easy as navigating their way through the rooms of their house.

After a while, they came upon a labyrinth of fallen trees, knocked down like pins by winter storms. Weaving her way through,

Elise imagined an elephant graveyard full of giant white bones. Sebastian regarded the trees' upended roots, which were still intact but now dead and rotting, and for the second time that week was reminded of coiling serpents. He shuddered.

The ground was changing beneath their feet, grass and soil giving way to stone and rock. A rushing, bubbling chorus of voices greeted their ears and any trace of disquiet was lost.

'We're here!' Elise enthused.

They set the basket onto the ground and then removed the blanket and laid it out on a flat stretch of rocks. They sat down, allowing their aching muscles to recover, and stared in silent wonder at the river. It was deep and wide, and the water was clear enough to see the amber of the riverbed. Tiny minnows darted beneath the surface, pushing against the gentle current and disappearing where the river veered around a stony outcrop.

The woods spread out into the distance on the opposite side. The ground there was soft and marshy, the trees taller and older, their thick, leafy canopies weaving together to create an impenetrable umbrella.

Elise did not care much for what lay on the other side of the river. Her side was light and beautiful and filled with life. Sebastian regarded the other side with a wary curiosity. He had crossed the river once and taken a few steps into the sombre shade of the trees. Moments after, he had felt an inexplicable urge to turn back.

'Are you hungry?'

There was something about Elise today. Something of her old self sneaking through. Her movements were more animated. Her eyes sparkled. Sebastian comforted himself in her smile. If Elise could allow herself to forget, even for one afternoon, then he could allow himself the same pleasure. Standing, Sebastian kicked off his sandals and stripped down to his swimming shorts.

'I'll eat after,' he said.

Emitting a cry that startled the birds from the trees, he propelled himself into the air. A second later, he surfaced in an eruption of water, froth and flailing limbs.

'It's freezing!'

Laughing, he wiped away his mess of hair to see Elise standing on the riverbank, hands thrust on hips. Dark patches were spreading across her clothes. Droplets of water glinted like crystals on her face and in her hair. For a moment, her expression was one of stern annoyance. Then her face softened and her laughter resounded through the woodland.

They stayed for the rest of the afternoon, whiling away the hours by swimming in the deepest parts of the river and dousing each other with handfuls of icy water. When they were soaked and shivering, they wrapped themselves in their towels and warmed themselves on dry rocks.

When their energy returned, they made tiny sailing boats fashioned from twigs and leaves and fallen pieces of bark. They raced them down the river, running alongside until the boats sank or came apart in sodden pieces.

Returning to the rocks, they delved into their sumptuous picnic. When they could eat no more, the children scrambled up the nearest tree and edged themselves along its lowest branch.

'It feels like we're the only two people on the planet,' Elise said after a long while.

Sebastian looked down at his feet, at the ground below. He felt a sudden dizziness and gripped onto the branch with both hands.

'Maybe we are,' he muttered.

Through the trees they could see the sun passing by and a flurry of feathers as birds flew from the treetops in search of their next meal. The world felt infinite then. A million miles of woodland could have lain between the siblings and their home.

'Remember when we used to come here with Mum?'

Elise was surprised by her own question. It was Sebastian who talked about their mother. The only time she mentioned her was to say something derogatory or damning. But here by the river, nostalgia flowed in the current.

A memory came to her.

'I used to play here when I was your age,' their mother said, just a year before she vanished. They were sitting on the same stretch of rocks by the river. Nana May was there too, braving the trek through the woods to enjoy the river view and the children's antics.

Catherine looked radiant in a sleeveless white cotton dress that clung to her curves. Her hair was long then, tumbling past the front of her shoulder to reach her lap. She sat, twining elegant braids into its length as she spoke.

'I used to come here every day of the school holidays. Even when your grandma expected me to do chores. I would sneak out of the back door and run as fast as I could until I got here.'

'That you did,' Nana May chortled. 'And you felt the back of my hand when you came creeping home as well.'

Catherine laughed, and Elise thought it the most beautiful sound she had ever heard. She shifted herself over until she was snuggled into her mother's side. Sebastian was busy at the riverbank, attempting to ensnare turquoise dragonflies in a tiny plastic net. The dragonflies were too fast for him and too near the surface of the river to reach. He gave up, threw the net down and climbed onto the blanket to join his family. Jealousy flashed in his eyes when he saw Elise wrapped in his mother's embrace. He moved across, nestling himself between her body and the crook of her free arm. Then he and Elise glanced at each other, dreamy smiles etched on their lips.

'You're both just like me.' Catherine smiled and planted kisses on the tops of her children's heads.

This was a rare moment; the three of them huddled together, entangled and inseparable. It was the happiest Catherine had been in months, and her happiness was all encompassing, warming everything it touched.

The memory faded.

Elise stared down at the spot where they'd sat a lifetime ago.

Catherine had removed herself from their lives a year later (Elise would argue quite the opposite—that their mother had removed

<u>them</u> from her life), and any hope of revisiting the joy that lit up that day by the river had been packed in a suitcase, never to return.

'Come on,' Elise said, her voice low as she turned to Sebastian. 'Let's go home.'

The journey back was tainted with difficulty. Climbing over the fallen trees, Sebastian lost his footing and slipped. He came down hard on his knee, rolled, and struck his elbow against a protruding rock. Elise came next, unbalanced by Sebastian as he pulled on the basket. She fell forward with a cry, landing on her stomach. She turned over onto her back, wincing as she drew in each breath.

Minutes later, brother and sister were being poked and scratched by broken pieces of osier. Sebastian was close to tears. His knee stung. His elbow throbbed. He looked down with disdain to find the osier had scored long thin scratches on his bare legs. Now they stung, too. He looked up at Elise.

'Don't you dare!' she snapped. 'Don't make this worse by being a cry baby!'

'But it hurts!' he wailed. The tears came anyway.

Elise stormed ahead. Stupid Sebastian! Always crying at everything! Why couldn't he be more like her? Why couldn't he learn to just shut up once in a while and get on with things? Her stomach hurt. Her hands were bruised. Was <u>she</u> crying?

'You're going too fast!' he called out, the basket banging into his legs, the osier scratching deeper still.

'Good! Maybe I'll go so fast you'll get left behind!'

'No!'

'Then bloody-well stop moaning!'

'Then bloody-well slow down!'

Elise let go of the basket and Sebastian lurched forward, scraping his shins. He looked up, eyes filled with rage. His fists curled into tight balls.

'You little—'

'Quiet!'

Aware of a noise that didn't fit with all the other woodland sounds, Sebastian fell silent. It was low and rumbling, causing the birds to flap above their heads.

'Leave the basket,' Elise whispered.

She took his hand and then they were running towards the house as fast as they could. They came up to the broken fence that surrounded the garden.

The sound grew louder.

Elise veered away, following the perimeter of the dwelling, weaving between the trees. Sebastian followed, half-running, half-dragged along.

They stopped behind a sycamore tree. The front yard of the house was just metres ahead. A large pick-up truck was moving down the lane, its engine growling like an angry dog. It rolled into the centre of the yard, spraying gravel in all directions.

The late afternoon sun gleamed off its metallic red body. Thick black smoke curled out from the exhaust pipe and choked the air.

'It's Wednesday!' Sebastian breathed.

Elise said nothing. Her eyes were fixed on the truck. She knew it well. It had driven into the yard every Wednesday afternoon since before she and Sebastian had come to live here.

How could she have forgotten?

The engine cut off. The driver's door opened.

'Go inside,' she said to Sebastian. 'Go back through the garden. Go inside and stay there. Don't come out.'

He moved quickly. Elise watched him disappear through the hole in the fence. She sucked in a breath, held it, and exhaled. Then she stepped from the harbour of the trees and into the yard.

Chapter 9

The man was dressed in faded blue jeans, a dirty yellow singlet, and a worn pair of work boots. White hair sprouted from the tops of his brown shoulders.

'Afternoon,' he said, turning towards her.

'Mr Elliot. How are you today?' She smiled, flashing her teeth.

Mr Elliot had an outdoors face. It was tanned and leathery, reminding Elise of Nana May's handbag. It was a cruel description, she knew, but the most accurate one she could think of. When he smiled, five decades of working in fields under a hot sun appeared in deep grooves around his eyes.

Mr Elliot winked and ran a hand through thinning grey hair.

'Sure is a scorcher, don't you think?'

He took a soiled handkerchief from his back pocket and used it to dab the perspiration from his brow.

'Busy day?' Elise asked.

'As busy as the last one and the next.'

The old man stared at her through squinted eyes, then behind her at the trees.

'You been up to no good again?' he chuckled. It was cracked and rasping laughter, that of a man who had been smoking cigarettes for more years than he cared to remember.

On cue, he pulled one from behind his ear and sparked it up. He gave it a few puffs before sending smoke rings floating into the air.

The smell made Elise giddy. She shook her head.

'One of the cats is missing. I was just looking for her.'

'Cat, eh?' He took another drag, this time sending the smoke out in a steady stream. 'Let's hope damned foxes didn't get it.'

'Let's hope so.'

Mr Elliot puffed away on his cigarette, his eyes fixed on hers. He clenched the butt between yellowed teeth and smiled.

'Where's that scamp you call a brother? Thought he might like to give me a hand with your Nana's supplies.'

'He's out in the woods. Looking for the cat.'

'Not that kitten of his?'

'No, one of the older ones.'

'Probably gone off to die, then.'

Mr Elliot's gaze returned to the trees. He took one last drag on his cigarette then crushed it under the heel of his boot.

'Where's your Nana?'

It was the question Elise had been dreading. She swallowed hard and licked her drying lips. She took a step towards Mr Elliot and the truck.

'She's asleep.'

'At this hour?' The old man raised his eyebrows and half-coughed, half-chuckled. 'In all my days I've never known your Nana to be partial to an afternoon nap. Usually, she's standing on that doorstep right there, waiting as I drive into the yard. Not one for tardiness is your Nana. One time, I was an hour late due to a tractor turning over on the road, and the look your Nana gave me—well, I was never late again let me tell you!'

He exploded with throaty, phlegm-filled laughter, then hawked and spat onto the ground

Elise wrinkled her nose in disgust. Mr Elliot was an honest and hardworking man, who did his job well and even offered to help Nana May when things needed fixing. But there were times—like when she would turn around and catch him staring from the back of the church at Sunday service—that he filled Elise with unease.

It was that look he sometimes gave her—an expression that suggested he had things to say when nobody else was around. And Elise didn't know if this was a good thing or a bad thing, or if it was nothing.

'Nana never means to be rude,' she muttered. 'She just likes things a certain way, that's all. She's resting now. She's not been well.'

Mr Elliot was quiet, staring at her.

'I'll give you a hand if you like.'

It was the last thing she wanted to do because it would mean more questions for which she would need to invent more answers. But the faster the supplies were taken care of, the faster Mr Elliot and his truck would be out of the yard and away from the house.

Mr Elliot shrugged a shoulder then moved to the back of the truck. 'What's wrong with her?'

He handed Elise a large paper bag of groceries. She took it, shifting its weight until it sat comfortably in her arms.

'Nothing serious. Just the heat. It's been very hot.'

'That's certainly no lie,' Mr Elliot agreed. 'Can't remember a summer hotter.'

He picked up a sack of potatoes and hoisted it over his shoulder; old age had yet to catch up with his strength.

Elise hurried towards the front door, setting the groceries down onto the step.

'You want me to take this into the kitchen?' Mr Elliot poked the potato sack with his free hand.

Elise froze.

'No, thank you. I'll do it later. I don't want to wake Nana.'

'I usually take it in. Potatoes are heavier than they look.'

Elise dragged a box of tinned foods towards her and heaved it into her arms. Her muscles had still not recovered from their exertions of two nights ago, and they protested at the weight.

'I'll get Sebastian to help.'

'If you say so.'

Mr Elliot was watching her again. She avoided his gaze, shifting her attention to the box. There were tins of fruit in juice, tins of corned beef and ham, and tins of cat food. The labels jumped out at her, the colours dazzling in the sunlight.

'How's Mrs Elliot?' she asked.

Elise had seen Mrs Elliot at church every Sunday but had never spoken to her. Like Nana May, she seemed the type of lady who kept to herself. Not that she ever came across as rude the way that Nana May sometimes had. She smiled or said hello whenever she was greeted, and even made polite conversation, but she always appeared shy or put upon, as if she were somehow distanced from the other churchgoers.

In a way, this was true. Nana May had said it was because she was not from the country, and that sometimes people found it difficult to accept those who were not born and raised here. Elise couldn't understand why because Mrs Elliot had lived here for years.

She moved away from the truck and back towards the house, keeping her head low as she passed Mr Elliot.

'Beth is just fine,' he said. 'Now, I hope you have no objections to me taking the coal along to the outhouse. I don't want to be responsible for you breaking your back.'

The box slipped from Elise's hands and burst open on the gravel.

Chapter 10

Sebastian tore through the kitchen and slid to a halt in the hallway. As he caught his breath he strained to hear the muffled voices coming from the front yard. His legs quaked beneath him. Mr Elliot was going to find out what they had done. He was sure of it!

He sank back against the wall, tears skimming his cheeks and splashing on the floor. He and Elise would be taken away. They would never see each other again.

He thought about what kind of place he would be sent to—some kind of prison for children, where they would keep him until he was old enough to go to a prison for adults.

Unless Elise could stop Mr Elliot from finding out.

He wondered if she could do that.

Pushing away from the wall, he bolted upstairs. If Mr Elliot did find out, then maybe Sebastian could hide where no one would find him. Elise's bedroom was to the right, and just along from that was his own. But these would be the first places where they would look.

Down from the hall was the bathroom, where there wasn't even a shower curtain to hide behind.

Across from the bathroom was Nana May's bedroom. Neither of them had entered the room since their grandmother's death.

He pulled on the door handle.

Sunlight poured through two large windows and rebounded off white walls. Dazzled,

Sebastian shielded his eyes. When he could see again, he looked about the room for a hiding place.

The bed was the first thing to catch his eye; its sheets pressed and tucked in at the sides. A large white blanket was draped over them, its edges falling to an inch above the floorboards. He thought of hiding beneath the bed, then changed his mind—all kinds of horrors could be lying in wait under there.

Beside the bed, sat on a small white cabinet, a silver carriage clock ticked away with merciful quietness.

There were photographs on the walls. There was one of Sebastian and Elise, taken last year. Next to it was a black and white photograph of their grandfather, who stood in a grassy meadow, dressed in work clothes and rubber boots, thumbs hooked into the belt loops of his trousers, and amusement creasing his lips.

The third photograph on the wall presented a young girl sitting precariously on the top bar of a wide, wooden field gate. Her straggly hair had strands of hay entwined in its length and she was laughing hard, her eyes squeezed shut.

Sebastian touched the glass of the photo frame.

'Mum.'

A worried looking boy stood next to the gate. He was a skinny boy; his clothes hung from him like sheets on a washing line.

Voices filtered in through the open windows. Panic returned.

The bedroom overlooked the front yard. He could see the red pick-up truck parked in the middle of the yard. Elise was next to it, clutching a heavy looking box. Then the box was slipping from her hands and bursting open on the ground.

Sebastian leaped back from the window. Dizziness taking hold, he spun on his heels and his eyes fell upon a towering mahogany wardrobe.

* * *

Food tins hit the gravel and bounced off in every direction. One struck Elise in the ankle and she yelped with pain. Another rolled towards Mr Elliot, who caught it beneath the sole of his boot.

'Steady on, girl!' he laughed. 'You're going to do yourself an injury. Or me come to that.'

Cheeks flushing, Elise murmured an apology and bent down to rub her bruised ankle. She set about retrieving the tins, her heart threatening to burst right through her ribcage.

Mr Elliot stooped down and snatched up the tin he had stopped with his foot.

'Peach slices,' he said, reading the label. 'Old May going to make you a nice fruit pie?'

Elise carried the tins she had amassed to the doorstep and dumped them down. Mr Elliot brought the remaining tin over and balanced it on top of the others.

'Now let's see about that coal,' he said, heading back to the truck.

Elise remained where she was, staring at his back. A single image played over and over in her mind, until she felt sick to her stomach— Nana May, tied to the rocking chair, waiting in the darkness of the outhouse.

Mr Elliot was at the rear of the truck now. He leaned in and took the large sack of coal between both hands, grunting as he dragged it towards him.

'This thing's heavier than me,' he chuckled. Clenching his teeth, he bent his knees and manoeuvred the sack onto his shoulder.

Elise clutched at her T-shirt.

Mr Elliot was moving away from the truck, the sack of coal draped over his shoulder. He used both hands to balance it as he walked out of the yard and towards the side of the house.

'Wait!'

The sound startled him. The weight of the sack shifted and almost toppled him to the ground.

'Are you trying to send an old man to his grave?' he cried.

Elise shook her head. 'Sorry. I—we need the key.'

'Fine,' Mr Elliot grunted. 'I'll see you there.'

As soon as he was gone, Elise leaped over the supplies on the step, wrenched the door open and dashed inside. An oppressive hush had fallen upon the house and she felt it pressing down on her shoulders.

'Sebastian?'

She moved along the hallway, her footsteps silent against the carpeted floor. Reaching the living room, she peered in. It was dark in there—they hadn't opened the curtains in two days.

Elise waited for her vision to adjust to the gloominess. Apart from the old-fashioned furnishings and the array of brass ornaments that adorned the side cabinet and mantelpiece, the room was empty. She stepped back into the hallway.

'Sebastian!'

She grasped the stair rail as she listened. The only reply was the stalwart ticking of the grandfather clock. Elise raced into the kitchen. But Sebastian was not there, either.

Thoughts and sounds flashed by like train windows. She had to get Mr Elliot away from the outhouse and away from Nana May.

But how?

Her mind wouldn't focus! She couldn't think!

Why wasn't Sebastian here? Why couldn't he ever do as he was told?

Elise slumped against the kitchen wall.

'Not like this,' she moaned. 'Please, please, not like this.'

'Talking to yourself, girl? That's a sign of madness!'

Mr Elliot's frame filled the back doorway.

'Got tired of waiting,' he said. 'Got things to do.'

Chapter 11

He didn't know how long he'd been asleep, but when Sebastian woke he found himself in darkness. He sat up, groggy from his slumber. Things from above reached down to tickle his forehead and ears. Drawing in a sharp, shocked breath, he kicked out his legs and struck wood. For a moment, he wondered if he was dead, buried inside a coffin deep underground. But then memories of the afternoon forced their way into his mind.

With a sigh of relief, Sebastian pushed open the wardrobe door.

Nana May's bedroom was cast in a radiant orange glow. Moving to a window, Sebastian peered out.

The sky was bruised with magnificent streaks of blues, powder pinks and purples, and tinged with grey. The sun was melting on the horizon, setting alight to the treetops.

Sebastian stared in awe, briefly forgetting the events of the afternoon, wishing he could stand here forever, witnessing a never-ending sunset.

A memory danced before his eyes. He was in the garden, sat on his mother's knee as she rocked him back and forth in the rocking chair. With one arm wrapped around his chest, she pointed up at the evening sky and said, 'You know what sunset is?'

'Uh-uh.'

'It's all of God's angels putting out the sun with their tears.'

'Why are the angels crying?'

'Because the world is both beautiful and full of pain. For the angels it's too much to bear, so they douse the sun with their tears. Then the day goes and darkness comes.'

Sebastian hadn't understood what his mother had meant, and yet as he stood watching the wondrous sight before him, an aching deep inside his chest surfaced and grew heavy, threatening to drag him to the floor.

Tearing his gaze away from the skyline, he glanced down into the yard.

Mr Elliot's truck was gone.

Leaving the bedroom, he stumbled onto the landing. He fumbled for the light switch and flicked it on.

'Elise?'

Silence greeted him. He drifted past his bedroom, then his sister's, ducking his head into each doorway to find each room empty.

He reached the top of the stairs. The light faded into darkness halfway down.

'Elise? Are you here?'

He sniffed the air, hoping to inhale cooking smells, which would mean his sister was in the kitchen preparing the evening meal, and that the troubles of the afternoon had been abated. There was a faint, musty odour and that was all.

Sebastian crept downstairs, hitting the light switch at the bottom. He checked the living room and then opened the front door.

Supplies were piled up on the step. A breeze blew spirals of dust around the yard and sent shivers down the branches of the trees beyond.

Leaving the door open, Sebastian headed back down the hall towards the kitchen. Nine chimes sang out from the grandfather clock and resonated up to the ceiling.

He had never known the kitchen to feel so cold. In fact, he had never known it to feel cold at all. He moved over to the oven and used a towel to pull open the furnace door. A few dying embers sat in a mound of ash.

They had let the fire go out.

No. Elise had let the fire go out. She was responsible for coal duties in the evenings. She had said so a few days ago, hadn't she? Or had she been talking about feeding the cats?

A tight knot formed in the pit of Sebastian's stomach. Forgetting the furnace, he hurried to the back door.

The garden was ablaze with molten colours. Each blade of grass had been painted the deepest of reds. Even the cats, now springing to life in the coolness of the evening, had not escaped the brush.

Sebastian gasped in wonder. The trees really did look as if they were on fire and for a second, he wondered if they were.

His thoughts jumped back to Elise. She was gone.

Mr Elliot had found out. He had seen. Elise was probably at the police station right now, locked up in a cell with tall walls and windows on the bars. The detectives would be glaring at her and asking her confusing questions to trick her into a confession. They would have her in handcuffs. Her eyes would be puffy from crying.

Sebastian slumped down onto the grass. 'Shit.'

If Nana May had been alive to hear him say it, she would have grounded him on the spot.

A strange half-giggle, half-sob slipped from his mouth. If only they had called Uncle Edward. Perhaps they would be wrapped in his arms right now. Perhaps he would be kissing the tops of their heads and promising that everything would be all right.

If only Nana May hadn't died. If only their mother hadn't abandoned them like unwanted kittens.

Nana May was dead, and whether it was Uncle Edward showing up for his monthly visit, or Mr Elliot delivering the coal, or Mrs Seagrove, the post mistress, wondering why Nana May had not been by to pick up her mail, it was only a matter of time before someone uncovered what Sebastian and Elise had done.

And it was a vile, unspeakable thing that they'd done.

Sebastian's thoughts tripped over themselves. He sat up, his mind racing through the events of the past few days.

Elise had convinced him they were now alone in the world. Elise had told him there was no other alternative. Elise had been adamant that if nothing was done at that very moment, they would be torn away from each other.

Since the death of their grandmother, Elise had instigated every action. She had made every decision for them both. She had made him believe that there was only one choice.

Sebastian stood and turned in the direction of the outhouse. Concealing their grandmother's body was so far from a solution to their problems that they may as well have called the authorities themselves.

Elise had said it was to give them more time, but for what? To hide in their house and wait for the outside world to be wiped clean like dirty windows? To fail to think of a single, solid solution?

A familiar shudder of dread racked Sebastian's body. He turned the corner of the house and the garden gave way to gravel.

The outhouse stood ahead of him; a desolate and solitary building that contained something it was not supposed to contain— something that was beginning to look less and less like his grandmother with the passing of each hour.

Waves of guilt burst forth from Sebastian's chest to consume him. Responsibility had to be shared in equal measures because surely he'd had the power to say no.

They had committed this atrocity together.

Instead of the possibilities of living in the comfortable surroundings of Uncle Edward's home, or joining a new but soon-to-be familiar family (surely not all foster families were mindless and cruel), he and Elise would now live out their days in dank prison cells, with misery and remorse as their only companions.

Sebastian stared at the outhouse and it stared right back.

Dragging his feet against the gravel, he moved forward until he was standing just a few metres away from the door. In the fading light he could see a large sack of coal lying in the grass. He saw the bolt on the door was slid into place and the padlock was snapped shut.

If Mr Elliot had seen what was inside then he had made sure no one else would have to until the police came. But if Elise had managed to keep him from Nana May, where was she now?

A loud thud pulled him from his thoughts.

The sound had come from the outhouse.

Sebastian held onto himself as he listened. The evening breeze danced through the branches. A shrill cry of an unseen bird soared high above the trees.

'You're dead. You're in heaven,' he whispered.

The sound didn't come again.

He was going to lose his mind. That was what happened when people ran out of hiding places. It would begin with the tiniest of cracks, like the ones on the frozen surface of the river in winter. And the crack would grow. It would splinter and divide, until there was nothing left of him but countless pieces.

'Why, Elise?' he mouthed. 'Why did you make us do that?'

Perhaps, in her own deluded way, she had been trying to keep them both from harm. After all, they had endured a barrage of rejection for the best part of their wretched lives.

The only person to ever show them the slightest bit of interest was now gone.

Nana May had pulled them from the jaws of a hideous world and now, through no fault of her own, she had fed them to it.

And now Elise had lost her mind, and Sebastian knew that he was treading the same path, just a few steps behind.

Reality was slipping away.

As he headed back to the house, he wondered what it would be like when he was mad. Would he find everything he saw hilarious, and would he laugh until he cried? Or would he relive these past few days, over and over, until his screams became a virus that infected the world with torment?

Suddenly, it was clear to him why their mother had left them that day.

It was because her children were evil.

What they had done to Nana May was proof of that. And like most wrongdoers, they were going to get everything they deserved.

Chapter 12

The Past

They awoke early one Saturday morning in May, filling the house with excited chatter as they gathered clean clothes and toothbrushes, and comic books and puzzle games to fill the hours of journey time ahead. It was their first trip out of the city in nine months and so their usual banter was more electric than ever.

'I hope it's warm, I want to go swimming. Where's my swimming costume? And we can walk up to the village and get ice cream. Or we could ask Nana to make some like she did before, and then we can eat as much as we like in whatever flavour!'

Elise threw clothes from her wardrobe onto her bed. Sebastian was busy filling his pockets with plastic green soldiers poised in various stages of combat.

He smiled. 'Nana makes good ice cream.'

'I bet you can't wait to see the cats,' Elise continued without pausing for breath. 'You love the cats, don't you? I don't mind them but I'd rather Nana had a dog. You can't really take cats for walks. Have you packed all your clothes yet?'

'Uh-huh.'

'Because Mum says to pack extra clothes in case we get wet or dirty, and she says if we're good we might be able to stay for an extra day or two, which would mean missing school but I don't mind because I don't really like that school anyway. I liked the one before we moved. Anyway, I hope we do get to stay a bit longer because it's been ages since we saw Nana May or been to the countryside and I really miss the river.'

Sebastian looked down at the little blue suitcase lying open on his bed. So far, he had packed a pair of blue jeans with patches sewn on the knees, two T-shirts (one with blue and red stripes, one with a picture of a sailing ship stitched on the front), two pairs of socks, two pairs of underpants, eight comic books, two plastic racing cars, one rainbow-coloured slinky spring, and three musclebound, gun-toting action figures.

He frowned.

There was no more room for extra clothing and his trouser pockets were already full. Would it really matter if he wore the same clothes for a day or two longer? He pulled the suitcase lid over his toys and garments, snapping the lock into place. He glanced over at Elise, who had now packed so many clothes that she may as well have been packing for an around-the-world tour.

'Finished,' he said, watching his sister's eyes flicker from the folded clothes in her big red case to the adjacent pile of discarded items.

'I'm almost done.'

She exchanged a tattered blue cardigan for a pastel lemon blouse, then closed her case, pressing down with all her might.

'Right! Let's go wake up Mum.'

Catherine had been awake for several hours. Her clothes were packed and her suitcase sat in the boot of her car. She had been to the ATM two streets away and now a small bundle of cash was nestled at the bottom of her canvas bag, hidden beneath tissues and a folded magazine.

She had taken time to prepare sandwiches and drinks for the children. It was a long drive to her mother's house and they were going to get hungry. And if they were hungry and there was nothing to eat, they would become irritable, and Catherine so wanted this to be a pleasant journey.

Sitting down, she poured herself a generous glass of vodka from the bottle on the table. It was for medicinal purposes of course, she told herself as she swallowed it down. It was a nerve calmer, a relaxant. She reached for the bottle to pour another shot.

The thunderous din of her children coming down the stairs like a landslide stopped her in her tracks. She picked up the bottle and slid it to the back of the freezer. Then, patting down her blouse and trousers, she returned to the kitchen table. Her children came spilling in, gushing with noise and excitement.

'Mum! It's nine o'clock!' Sebastian cried.

'We need to leave now or we'll be late for lunch! Nana's cooking roast chicken and it's not even Sunday!'

Catherine gazed from one child to the other as they babbled and enthused about their coming weekend at Nana May's. She frowned and her features fell away into blankness. She watched their mouths open and close. She did not hear words but a series of wails and screeches and high-pitched clicks that hurt her ears and caused pinpricks of irritation to rile her tired mind.

'Do you think it will be sunny there like it is here?'

'Will Nana make ice cream?'

'Because I really want to go swimming. Maybe if it's really hot we can drive down to Devil's Cove and go swimming off the rocks!'

'And cookies. Do you think she'll be making chocolate ones or treacle?'

'Did you call my school to say I might not be in on Monday? We've been really good. Please can we stay an extra day? Pleeease?'

'But you didn't do your homework.'

'Shut up, Sebastian! I did do my homework, Mum, because I knew we were going to Nana's this weekend and I didn't want to be doing stupid homework there. See

Sebastian, you don't even know what you're talking about. Just because you didn't see me do it doesn't mean I didn't do it. You don't know anything anyway. You're five—you don't even get homework!'

'I do!'

'No, you don't. What? Drawing pictures? That's hardly homework. You draw pictures all the time!'

'I—'

'Go and put your things in the car. Now.'

Catherine slid the car keys towards Elise. Sebastian made a grab for them but his sister was quicker.

'I want to open the door!' he complained.

'Tough luck, I'm the eldest.'

And away they went, their relentless drone buzzing through the house and out into the street.

Catherine's fingers trembled.

Why did she feel like this? So irritated. So overwhelmed by her children. She knew it was wrong to feel this way towards them. She should have shown nothing but unconditional love and an unfaltering maternal instinct.

And she did, upon occasion. There were times when she brought her children close to her chest and wrapped her arms around them, submerging in their warmth and their smell and their love. Tears would form in her eyes and she would bring her children closer still, terrified they might somehow slip away from her, that somehow something terrible would happen to them if she let go even for a second.

There were moments when a look from Sebastian or a smile from Elise made her feel so loved, so important that suddenly nothing else in the world mattered.

Her children loved her, which meant that all the misjudged choices she had made, all the damaging words that had slipped from her serpent tongue, were forgiven.

Her children loved her. Her children understood.

And yet lately, she felt nothing but contempt for them. They were two flies trapped in her house, oblivious to the open windows and resistant to her swat. They buzzed about her day and night, flitting from room to room, spreading filth and disease, swarming about her until she wanted to scream.

Catherine moved over to the freezer and pulled out the vodka bottle. Ignoring the cold against her skin, she unscrewed the cap and took a hefty shot into her mouth. The liquid numbed her throat. Her insides ignited in a ball of fire. Through the window, she saw Sebastian and Elise scrabbling with the keys to the dark blue Datsun.

She looked beyond them, at the street of terraced housing, which was cloned and repeated in countless rows, one after the other; all red roofs and white bricks sullied by traffic pollution. All the same in all directions, on and on, until you drove yourself insane thinking about it or you drove fast enough to escape.

Drive in one direction and you would hit the city; a sprawling machine fuelled by urban chaos and relentless motion. Every inch of it moved and swelled. Every inch of it was capable of replication, repair and expansion. To her, the city was a once loyal dog gone mad. It barked whenever she came near. It showed its teeth whenever she sought to put on its leash.

Drive in the other direction and you would eventually come upon fields and trees, clean air and rivers. You could see the stars at night in the countryside, every last one, and the night was how night was meant to be: pure black, unspoiled by the man-made haze of electricity that cast nights in the city in mists of olive and tangerine.

Night in the country was so dark you could not see your outstretched hand reaching for a light switch. It was all encompassing. Nothing and no one could escape it.

Darkness was as inevitable as the light of day. And it was a good thing. And it was a bad thing.

Catherine replaced the cap onto the bottle, fished out a plastic bag from a cupboard beneath the dish-filled sink, and placed the bottle into it.

The children loved the countryside. They liked its freedom and its miles of open land waiting to be explored. They loved the diversity of trees and shrubs, and the abundance of birds and rabbits and badgers and foxes that roamed the woodlands. They grew excited about visits to the river and to the seaside, and about the horses in Mr Favel's fields. They loved the dew that formed on the grass at dawn. They loved the beauty of sunrise and the solitude of sunset.

Catherine had been as passionate once, but so long ago now that she was unable to remember how it felt.

The front door slammed shut, sending a wave of minute tremors through the walls of the house. Sebastian and Elise bounded into the kitchen, breathless and panting, squabbling over who would sit up front with their mother.

'We're ready!' Elise said, the fight instantly swallowed up by excitement.

Breaking into a grin, Sebastian nodded in agreement.

Catherine looked at her children. Two flies, she thought. How she would like to swat them, to squash them against a wall, to tear off their wings and press against them until they were bloody smears.

Streets dwindled behind them. Houses shrank away until they looked too small for even ants to inhabit.

Sebastian watched the familiar disappearing through the rear window of the car, his furtive eyes capturing every passing moment in detail.

Soon, they were driving along the motorway and an infinite black tongue of a road stretched out in front and behind. The painted lines that split the lanes shot past like lightning. Cars of all shapes and models surrounded their own, each vehicle transporting its passengers at breakneck speed.

Steep grassy embankments flanked the sides of the road. Sebastian looked to the top of them, counting the flimsy trees that grew there. Then the embankments were flattening and spreading out into forests and countless fields occupied by cows, sheep and horses, or bursting with crops that begged to be harvested and thrown into a delicious spring stew.

The boy sighed. Sometimes, just looking out of a window was enough to make him happy.

'Sit down, Sebastian. Put your seatbelt on.'

Sebastian did as he was told, sliding the silver key into the catch. He liked the clicking sound the action made. It was the safest sound he could think of.

'Thank you,' said Elise, watching him in the rear-view mirror. 'We don't want any accidents now, do we?'

Sebastian shrugged. He pulled open his backpack and took out a brightly coloured book. He read the title aloud: 'One Hundred and One Funniest Jokes.'

He'd purchased it second-hand for the diminutive sum of five pence from his school's summer fete last year. And although an advanced reader at the time, he'd been unable to grasp the meanings behind most of the puns.

Now, as a seasoned five-year-old, Sebastian felt he had finally mastered the art of telling jokes.

'What do you call a man with a shovel on his head?'

'Doug,' groaned Elise.

'All right then . . .' He skimmed through a few pages, deciding the jokes were not particularly funny, before reading out another. 'Doctor, Doctor! I feel like a pair of curtains!'

'Then pull yourself together. Really? Is that the best you can do?'

Sebastian closed the book and tossed it aside.

'Honestly, those jokes are older than Nana May.' Elise shook her head. Blonde curls fell into her eyes and she brushed them away.

'How long till we get there?' her brother called from the back seat.

She glanced at the plastic yellow watch strapped to her wrist. 'Another two hours.'

'Aww!'

All of Sebastian's good toys and books were packed inside his suitcase, which was now in the car boot. The only things he had brought along for the journey were the stupid joke book, a couple of old comic books he'd read five times already, and his pockets of plastic soldiers—and he couldn't play with those because he was now strapped in by the safety belt.

Letting out a long, low sigh, he looked at his mother's reflection in the rear-view mirror.

Her eyes were unblinking, fixed on the road.

'Mum, can we put on some music?'

Catherine didn't reply. Nor did she blink or move an eye or show any indication that she'd heard his request.

160

Sebastian growled in frustration.

'Mum! Can we—'

'Do what you like!'

The words shot out and the lips were sealed tight again, like two impenetrable gates.

Sebastian drew in a wounded breath. She had been listening after all. He looked into the rear-view mirror, deep into his mother's eyes. There was no emotion there, just a steely concentration that sought no interruption.

Flipping down the overhead passenger mirror, Elise caught her brother's gaze and coaxed it away from their mother.

'I'll look in the glove compartment, shall I? See what cassettes I can find. What did you do with that joke book? I bet you can't find a joke I haven't heard.'

They spent the rest of the journey taking turns reading jokes and not laughing at any of them, playing I Spy (which they found limiting trapped in the confines of a car), and counting the colours of the vehicles they passed by. They listened to Bob Dylan, The Carpenters and John Denver, all of their mother's favourites, although she failed to sing along to a single tune.

The car finally turned off the long stretch of motorway and found its way onto a narrow, snaking country road wedged in between fields.

Elise dug deep into the glove compartment, found the cassette she had been waiting to play, and popped it into the machine. Joni Mitchell filled the vehicle with her sweeping vocals, singing of pirates, seagulls, and cactus trees. Elise smiled as she sang along to Sisotowbell Lane.

Twenty minutes later, the children were laughing hard as the car bounced in and out of the potholes of the tree-lined lane that led to Nan May's house.

The snarl of the engine and the children's high-pitched screams sent birds flapping from the treetops.

Sebastian clutched his belly as he cackled, the rocking motion of the car mixing the contents of his stomach into a nauseating stew.

'I'm going to throw up!' he bellowed.

Elise laughed harder. 'You shouldn't have eaten all of the sandwiches!'

The lane twisted sharply. Reflections of trees and their canopies skimmed over the windscreen and dripped off the rear window. The yard and the old white house that sat at its centre came into view.

Nana's cats were sprawled on the gravel, their tails flicking up clouds of dust as they bathed in the early afternoon sunshine.

Catherine pulled up to the middle of the yard and killed the engine. There was an immediate hiss and a dull clanking from under the car bonnet. The cats looked up with expressions of mild disregard then returned to their napping.

'Beep the horn, Mum!' Sebastian called from the back seat as he squirmed out of the seatbelt.

Catherine's hands remained gripped around the steering wheel.

'Mum?' Elise gently nudged her arm. 'Everything all right?'

'Hmm?'

Catherine blinked and lifted a hand to her eyes. 'I'm fine. Let's get your things inside, shall we?'

Now free, Sebastian leaned forward and tapped his mother on the shoulder.

'Beep the horn!'

Catherine's hand hovered over the car horn. But Nana May was already pushing her portly frame towards the vehicle. Their eyes briefly met and they exchanged awkward smiles.

'Nana!' the children cried in unison.

Pushing open the car doors, they scrambled out into the yard.

May's face lit up, bright as the sun above her.

'Well, let's have a look at you both! Oh my, you've grown so tall! Your heads will be parting the clouds before you know it!'

Catherine watched her children wrap themselves around her mother, showering her with hugs and kisses. She stuck her head out of the side window.

'Grab your stuff from the car!'

Pulling away from their grandmother's sides, the children moved to the back of the car.

'Ouch! It's hot!'

The heated metal of the car burned Elise's skin. Opening the boot, she pulled out her suitcase and dumped it on the ground.

Catherine remained in the car, her gaze fixed on the dashboard. Her hands gripped the steering wheel so tightly that her fingers trembled.

'Coming out of there?'

She glanced up to see Nana May. Concern creased her mother's brow.

Catherine swallowed.

'Mum, you'll have to get your own case. It's too heavy.'

Catherine nodded. 'Okay.'

The children flew back to their grandmother's sides, their words tripping over each other in a torrent of excitement.

Nana May patted them both on their heads.

'Why don't you go on in? Take your bags upstairs. There's a treat for you in the kitchen when you come back down.'

Squealing with delight, the children picked up their cases and thundered towards the house. So dismissive only moments ago, the cats sprang to life and leaped out of their path.

Elise entered the house first, with Sebastian close behind. Their cases flew in all directions, slamming against the walls and floors. Minutes later, they were opened and unpacked, and clothes lay folded in drawers.

Sebastian and Elise galloped downstairs. They found Nana May standing in the kitchen, a multitude of baked wonders cooling around her. She held a tray in her hands that contained two gingerbread men. They wore blue icing trousers and white icing shirts, with raisin buttons done up to the collar. They smiled with red lips and winked with pink eyes.

'There you are!' Nana May exclaimed.

The children swayed in the doorway, intoxicated by the incredible smells flooding their senses.

'Your mother's just driven up to the village to get a few things that I need. She won't be long.'

She handed each of her grandchildren one of the baked men, paused to watch the delight in their eyes as they began to eat, then moved over to the stove.

'I hope you'll have room left for roast chicken!' she called over her shoulder. Sebastian and Elise's eyes widened even further.

'Always!'

'Of course!'

Nana May chuckled. 'Wash your hands once you've finished eating. Then we can sit at the table and you can tell me all about what you've been up to.'

Gingerbread men devoured and hands washed in the kitchen sink, the children flopped down on their usual chairs at the table.

'I hope Mum won't be long,' Sebastian said, his lips smacking together in anticipation of his grandmother's chicken.

'Well,' Nana said, her voice sounding strange. 'I suppose she'll be as long as it takes her.'

She moved away from the stove and joined them at the table. They talked about school and the city. They waited for Catherine to return. They waited until they were too hungry to wait anymore. They ate a lunch of delicious chicken. Then they waited some more.

Chapter 13

Pulling his handkerchief from his back pocket, Mr Elliot dabbed perspiration from his brow.

'Come on, slow coach,' he said, some humour returning to his voice. 'I got a thousand and one things to do before I get home to Mrs Elliot, and if I'm late there'll be more than tears before bedtime.'

All the air in the room had been baked dry by the oven. Elise struggled for breath as she stared at the old man's crooked shape in the doorway. She attempted to move, but it was as if nails had been driven through her feet and into the flagstones of the kitchen floor.

No words came to her rescue. Not one single thought offered her an alternative to telling the truth.

And once he was enlightened with the truth, what would Mr Elliot do?

He would call the police and no matter how many ways Elise might try to clarify the events of the past few days, not one person was going to believe the reasons for her actions.

No. Getting caught was as inevitable as sunset, as the ebbing of the tide, as growing old and dying.

How long had she expected to keep Nana May's body locked up in the outhouse? Elise's grandmother had not been the most sociable of people, but she was no stranger to the inhabitants of the village. And she was certainly no stranger to this man standing here.

How foolish Elise had been. How reckless.

She cursed her negligence. If only she had a few more days. Perhaps she would think of the perfect plan. Perhaps she would find a way to stop inevitability in its tracks.

Elise cleared her throat. The truth, then.

'Mr Elliot, there's something I need to tell you.'

Mr Elliot hawked and spat thick brown saliva onto the garden path.

'Whatever it is that's on your mind, girl, you want to grab that key? I got another two deliveries to make.'

Elise nodded. Her mouth as dry as tree bark, she turned to the key rack hanging next to the hallway door.

You can't tell him! her mind shrieked. You can't tell him that!

'Better just to show him,' she whispered, and the words were hot lead on her tongue.

-You're in terrible trouble now. And not just you. You should have called for an ambulance like Sebastian said to. You should have done a lot of things differently!

'Terrible things would have happened,' she moaned.

-Terrible things are happening right now. You locked your Nana in a dirty, dark shed. You didn't even check to see if she was still breathing when you found her in the garden. What if she'd still been alive? You could have saved her but you left her to die. You killed her. You left her alone, just like your mother left you!

'Stop it!' Her voice rose up to the ceiling, startling Mr Elliot.

'What in God's name?'

Her mind cleared. The voice had gone and she wished for it to never return.

'What's got into you, girl? You're acting like you got demons in your head.'

Elise avoided his gaze. 'I'm fine.'

'Glad to hear it,' he replied. 'Now, are you getting that key for me or will hell be freezing over first?'

The key.

Elise looked up at the rack. All emotion drained from her body. She turned towards Mr Elliot and then back to the rack, staring at the empty hook where the outhouse key should have been hanging.

'It's not there!' she gasped. 'The key's not there!'

Giving the sack of coal a childish kick, Mr Elliot grumbled under his breath.

'Well, unless you know where the thing is I'll leave this lot outside the outhouse, if you don't mind. I'm sure you and Sebastian can manage to roll it in between you when the key turns up. You hear me, girl?'

Unable to tear her gaze from the empty hook, Elise nodded. She had hung the key back on that hook the same night she and Sebastian had put Nana May in the outhouse. It had been there ever since, catching her eye each time she passed it.

A thought crept up on her: Sebastian.

Elise smiled, but only for a moment. Sebastian had acted quickly and instinctively while she had stumbled from the trees in a blind panic, thinking a smile and clever talk would send Mr Elliot on his way.

The man stirred in the doorway.

'You sure you're all right?' he asked. 'You're acting awful strange today.'

Elise nodded.

'Worried about your Nana? Want me to check in on her?'

'No.'

Mr Elliot crouched down and with a grunt, heaved the sack of coal onto his shoulder.

'Better get this moved. Tell your Nana she can pay me when I'm by next week.'

The old man gave her a wry nod and disappeared into the garden. Elise shuffled to the doorway. Warm sunlight bathed her skin as she watched Mr Elliot move around the corner of the house, pausing once to shift the weight of the coal on his shoulder.

When he was gone, the girl let her gaze wander over the colours of the garden. The scent of flowers filled the air, carried along by a breeze that teased the leaves of the woodland. The sputtering engine of a distant tractor droned behind lazy birdsong. Elise sat down on the doorstep, her head falling into her hands.

The world was still turning. Life was still going on. Mr Elliot coming here was proof of that. She looked up at the garden. The flowerbeds would soon need weeding. The lawn would need mowing.

Nana May's voice echoed in her head: "Life spins around like a bicycle wheel. Sometimes you need to pedal a little faster, sometimes you need to slow right down. Sometimes something nasty might spring up into your spokes, but things will be dandy so long as you keep—"

Nana May's shoes were still sitting on the lawn, one flipped over so its worn heel pointed skyward. They had been sitting there for days now, baked crisp by the heat and washed clean by the rain. Insects had made a home inside them.

Shocked by their presence, Elise got to her feet. Picking up the shoes, she clutched them to her chest as if they were made of glass.

Were they really all that was left of Nana May? It was too cruel to be true.

Mr Elliot was returning from the outhouse, distaste wrinkling his features.

'If I were you,' he said, coming to a halt beside her, 'I'd find that key soon as I can. Get up close and it smells like something's gone and died in there. Hope it's not that cat you've been looking for.'

He stared at the shoes in Elise's hands and waited for a response. When it didn't come, he nodded and said, 'Regards to your Nana. Hope she's feeling better soon.'

Elise followed him into the yard and watched him climb into the truck.

Seconds later, the air was disturbed by the engine growling to life. The exhaust pipe spat out thick grey fumes and then the vehicle was moving forward, crunching gravel beneath its tyres and spraying dust into the air as it headed out of the yard.

Silence fell so heavily upon the yard that even the cats felt it, rearing their heads and flicking their tails from side to side.

Elise stood still, watching the lane through hollow eyes. One after the other, the shoes slipped from her hands. She took a step forward. Then another.

She walked towards the lane, her pace gathering momentum. Her stride lengthened. Then she was kicking up as much dust as Mr Elliot's truck.

She ran through the yard and in between the potholes of the lane. Lines of trees streaked past in blurs of green and brown. The lane turned and she turned with it.

No thoughts passed through her mind as she pinned her gaze on the archway of light where the lane met the outside world.

She pushed herself onwards. The light was closer now.

And it was no longer just light. It was tarmac and hedgerows, and a vague hum of car engines and air tinged with traces of cut grass.

With a cry, Elise stumbled from the lane and onto the road.

Chapter 14

The road was narrow and winding. In one direction, it coiled around fields and pastures, heading into town. In the other, it rolled over a vast hill and descended towards the coastline, towards beaches and secluded coves once used by sea pirates and smugglers.

Elise looked in both directions. She stared at the hedgerow in front of her, at the myriad of wild purple flowers protruding from it.

Beyond the hedgerow a vast field of lush grass sloped upward to a copse of trees. A chestnut-coloured horse was cooling itself in the shadows there and Elise watched it swat flies away with its tail. She wondered if it ever got dizzy running up and down that sloped field. She wondered if it ever wanted to jump over the hedgerow and run free.

She looked up at the sky. Clouds painted pictures against a rich blue background. She stared down at her feet and felt the road beneath them. She wondered how long it went on for and where it stopped. Perhaps it didn't stop. Perhaps it circled the entire country and back again to meet at this very point.

She started walking.

The hill was steep and the muscles of her calves and thighs ached as she pushed against the incline. On her right, trees began to fall away. Soon, only their canopies were visible. Breathless and overcome by heat, Elise paused to rest. From here, the woodland looked more like an ocean, its many shades of green ruffled by the breeze. Nana May's house was down there somewhere, hidden away like a secret.

She pressed on, panting and puffing, until she reached the crest of the hill. The view was magnificent. Past the woods, a patchwork of fields was knitted together by wooden post fences, stone walls, and hedgerows. Each field was of a different shape and colour. Some were dotted with livestock. Others were brown and bare, their yield already harvested. Farmhouses sat in between the fields, each one solitary and lonely-looking, even in the warm glow of daylight.

Beyond the fields, villages and hamlets of tiny buildings huddled together in protective circles. Beyond them was the town. It rose and fell over the contours of the land, sparkling like crystal. It was no city, but it was large enough to send waves of anxiety surging through Elise's veins.

Sebastian was lucky, she thought. He still had the pleasure of the village school and its quiet classrooms and small cohort of students. Her school was spread across two sites. Children crawled over it like ants on ice cream. She had to take a bus every morning. She had to push her way through the already bustling high street to get to the tall grey buildings in which she sat, Monday to Friday, watching time slow down. When the school day was over, she would climb back on the bus and shut out the incessant chatter and squeals of the other country-living children, and she would wonder what mouth-watering surprise was awaiting her return.

Elise turned on her heels. On her left, she saw sweeping stretches of moorland peppered with patches of thorny gorse, its yellow flowers overshadowed by huge outcrops of black rock. Here and there, ancient stone circles grew out of the land and she wondered who had put them there and for what purpose.

Her eyes found the ocean. It lay in the distance, a hazy expanse of greens and blues that stretched out as far as she could see. From up here, it looked flat and still. She imagined herself walking on its surface. She wondered how long it would take to find an island, and if she might like to stay there and never come back.

The road was descending. Below her was the village where they attended church on Sundays and Sebastian went to school. From here, it was small and toy-like, made up of thatched roofs and cobbled streets and flowers in baskets hanging over doorways.

There was a butcher's shop, a bakery, and a post office that doubled as a general store, selling milk and eggs from local farms. The village square sat at its centre, formed by the old church and its small cemetery, a row of cottages, and a pub called The Journey's End.

At the centre of the square was a mermaid carved from stone. She was balanced on the tips of her tail, long hair covering her breasts. Her hands held a large stone bowl over her head. Water cascaded over its edges, spilling into the round trough in which she bathed. The early evening sun made the water sparkle and shimmer.

'Beautiful!'

It was the first word Elise had spoken in almost an hour. Quickening her pace, she entered the village.

Brightly-painted cottages flanked the narrow road. Each building sat back in a garden so immaculately pruned that Elise wondered if their owners had time for anything else.

As she approached a cottage with the name "Eden" scribed on the garden gate, Elise's heart sped up. She ducked her head and quickened her pace. Then a voice stopped her in her tracks.

'Good evening, Elise! How nice it is to see you!'

Mrs Thorn waved from a throne-like deckchair in her garden.

'Hello, Mrs Thorn,' Elise said, looking up. 'How are you? And Mr Thorn?'

'Oh, we're very well,' the woman said, fanning herself with a rolled-up magazine as she peered over her sunglasses. 'As a matter of fact, we've just had a new kitchen fitted. It's very modern. Very luxurious. I won't even tell you how much it cost!'

Elise forced a smile. She looked around the woman's garden. Her eyes fell upon life-sized figurines of Adam and Eve, standing naked beneath an apple tree.

'Adorable, aren't they?' Mrs Thorn said.

'Lovely.'

'You know, Elise, you really must visit Gemima one afternoon. Perhaps she could teach you to ride one of her horses. You've probably never ridden one before. That would be nice for you, wouldn't it, dear? To ride a horse?'

Elise nodded. 'Yes. It would.'

'Well, do say hello to that grandmother of yours.'

Elise smiled, waved goodbye, and was on her way. Two cottages down and her eyes were burning with fury. Riding horses with Gemima Thorn?

'I'd rather roll in cow shit!' she scoffed.

Gemima Thorn was one of the most despicable girls she had ever met. She was the kind of person who took the greatest pleasure in humiliating the quiet, the impoverished, and the supposedly strange. Whether her chosen victim really fell into those categories was irrelevant. If Gemima Thorn took a disliking to you, you were in for trouble whether you asked for it or not—and most likely you hadn't.

In the three months that Elise had attempted to keep a diary, she wrote the following entry:

Tuesday, 29th May

Dear Diary,

I want to die! Today at morning register, Gemima Thorn told Mr Samuels that my mum was a prostitute and that everyone knows it and that I was probably just the same and would try to sell him my body to get good grades!!! The whole class laughed and laughed and didn't stop all day! Gemima got a detention but that's not good enough! Everyone is calling me Mr Samuel's baby whore! Nana May said that Gemima Thorn has as much brains as a headless chicken but it's not her fault because like mother, like daughter. But Nana May doesn't have to go back to school tomorrow! I hate school, I hate my mum, and I hate, hate, hate Gemima Thorn! Please God, make her hair fall out and her teeth turn brown and her skin go all scaly!

PS. Just looked up "whore" in the dictionary. Words like that shouldn't be allowed. I'm never ever going to school again!

Other entries detailed further atrocities at the hands of Gemima Thorn and her gaggle of pre-teen, town girl worshippers. The hardest thing for Elise to digest was not the reasoning behind Gemima's delight in transforming school life into a waking hell, but rather why anyone could bear to be around the wretched girl. Yet, all the girls wanted to be her, and all the boys wanted to 'be in her'—as so delicately put in a later diary entry.

Elise hated Gemima Thorn with an intense passion. Perhaps she would accept that offer of horse riding lessons, and just as Gemima mounted her steed, which would no doubt have some ridiculous name such as Peaches or Princess, Elise would kick it hard in the flank, sending it into a rage that would throw her enemy from its back. Gemima's neck would break, killing her instantly. Or worse (and infinitely better), her spine would snap, leaving her paralysed and wheelchair bound.

Tell the world you're beautiful then, Elise thought.

She came to the end of the road and headed left. Mr Tonkin, the butcher, was just closing up for the day. He was a small, round man with large fleshy hands and a red face, and he reminded Elise of one of the slaughtered pigs hanging in his shop window. His wife was almost identical in appearance (with the addition of a mass of curly hair) and their three young sons always looked as if they were in constant fear of being devoured by the Big Bad Wolf.

'Evening, young lady,' the butcher smiled, flourishing fat fingers. 'How's that grandmother of yours? Tom Elliot just passed by and said she's not well.'

Elise froze. News travelled faster than lightning around here.

'She's fine,' she replied.

'What is it? Headache?'

'She'll be fine. I'm just running some errands for her now.'

'Anything I can help with?' Mr Tonkin asked.

Elise shook her head.

'Well, wait right here one minute,' the man chirped, disappearing into his shop. Moments later, he returned with a parcel of brown paper.

'Sausages!' he enthused. 'Tell your Nana I hope she's better soon.'

Elise stared at the package in her hands.

'Thank you,' she said.

She walked on, slipping past the post office and the bakery. Both shops were already closed for the day. A rumble of Elise's stomach reminded her it was past dinnertime. Holding the sausages in both hands, she turned a corner and found herself in the village square.

Elise sat down on a bench opposite the mermaid and let out a giddy breath as slivers of light danced in the fountain and shimmered on the ground.

Music and raised voices disturbed the air as the door to The Journey's End swung open. Mr Favel and his young farm hand, Davey, stumbled out. Elise watched as the pair staggered through the square, laughing raucously at crude jokes. Sighing, she hoped there would be someone sober enough back at the Favel farm to put the horses to bed.

'Elise?'

The voice startled her.

She turned to see a teenage girl with a shock of dyed black hair cut at savage angles and thick, black eyeliner spiralling out to her temples. She wore a torn black T-shirt with a faded picture of a zombie rising from the grave on the front, cut-off black denim shorts, and imposing army-issue boots.

'I thought that was you,' the girl said. 'What are you doing out here?'

Lamorna Brooke was fourteen years old and she was angry. The only thing village life had to offer her wistful and artistic temperament was blatant mediocrity. There was no inspiration here, no similarly-minded young people with whom she could convey her heartfelt grievances.

There was only boredom and inbred idiots, who avoided her like the plague.

The first time Elise had encountered Lamorna, she'd been sat at the front of church for Sunday service, waiting for the dreary organ music to end its assault on her ears. A ripple of shocked whispers had spread through the rows of churchgoers and Elise had turned to see a terrifying vision in white face powder, blood-red lipstick, and enough eyeliner to blot out the sky. Lamorna Brooke had stalked through the congregation like a lion, with her flustered mother trailing behind, a wad of tissues in her outstretched hand.

Nana May had told Elise not to stare, and, the tips of her eyebrows had almost touched her hairline. But Elise had been unable to do anything <u>but</u> stare. Until Lamorna had caught her.

'Fuck off!' she'd hissed, and the whole church had roared with disapproval.

Her second encounter occurred the following Friday, as Elise boarded the school bus home. There was just one empty seat and it was beside Lamorna Brooke. The other children watched with anticipation as Elise shuffled between the chairs and slid down next to her.

'I heard about you,' Lamorna said, staring out the window. 'Is it true your mum tried to sell you and your brother for drugs?'

Startled, Elise shook her head. 'No. She sold everything else, though.'

The bus pulled away from the kerb. Disappointed by the lack of confrontation, the rest of the children resumed their deafening banter. Lamorna turned and looked at Elise for a long time.

'Shit. You must really hate her.'

Lamorna asked question after question, and when the bus stopped and Elise got out, Lamorna followed.

'But you live up at the village,' Elise said nervously.

Lamorna fished out a pack of cigarettes and a lighter from her school bag. 'I feel like walking.'

She lit a cigarette, offered the pack to Elise, who shook her head.

'What's it like in the city?'

Elise raised an eyebrow at her newfound acquaintance.

'I told you.' Lamorna smiled. 'Everyone knows everybody's business around here. Even before you know it yourself.'

'Oh. Well, I hated the city.'

'How come?'

'It was too noisy. There were too many people and city kids were mean.'

'All kids are mean, Elise.'

'I'm not.'

'You ever call your brother a dirty word?'

'Only when he deserved it.'

'I know your Nana, too,' Lamorna continued. 'She's cool for an old lady, despite what some people might say.'

'What do you mean?'

Elise was shocked. Nana May was the kindest, most thoughtful person she knew. Who had been saying bad things about her?

'It's nothing,' Lamorna said, smoke spiralling from her nostrils. 'Just that certain people say she's cold and unfriendly and more than a little rude. But what do they know, right? People around here are so full of shit it's bound to come pouring out their mouths sooner or later.'

She flicked the cigarette butt off into the distance.

'See you at school,' she said.

And so began the strangest of acquaintances. On Monday lunchtime, Elise witnessed hurried steps and disgraced faces as her new older friend barked insults at the other girls, ridiculing their town fashions and "tragic hair". On Tuesday, she delighted in watching Gemima Thorn reduced to tears and threatened within an inch of her life if she ever came near Elise again.

Friendship blossomed as they spent every lunchtime together, alternating between sites so that Lamorna could have her pick of the latest teen queens and their superiority complexes. For a while, Elise found herself beginning to enjoy the school day instead of dreading it.

Of course, her friendship with Lamorna had been kept secret from Nana May. Instead, it was confined to school lunch hours and subtle nods and winks across church pews. Sometimes, Lamorna would sing psalms off-key and at deafening volumes. Elise would cement her lips together and pray the laughter bubbling in her throat would not burst free. Sometimes it did, and Nana May would shoot her with a scornful glare. Lamorna would sing even louder, much to the embarrassment of her weary parents.

Then one lunchtime, Lamorna was gone. Elise waited at their usual meeting place, in the narrow lane halfway between the two school buildings, until the electronic bell rang. Deflated and anxious, she made her way to her form room, wondering what had happened to Lamorna Brooke. She returned the next day and waited some more, forgetting to eat her lunch and avoiding the hopeful glares of Lamorna's victims.

On the evening of the third day, she waited until Nana May had gone outside to sit in her rocking chair, then picked up the telephone and dialled Lamorna's number.

'Elise? Hi! How are you? What are you doing?'

Lamorna's energy caught her off guard.

'I, um, are you sick?'

'What? No! Why would you think that?'

'You haven't been in school.'

'Yes, I have.'

'But I've been waiting in the usual place.'

There was another voice in the background. A deep, masculine voice, muttering incomprehensible words. Lamorna giggled, putting her hand over the receiver.

'Sorry, Elise. What was that?'

'I said I've been waiting for you.'

'Oh. Right. Sorry. I've been busy with stuff. You haven't been waiting your whole lunch time for me, have you?'

Elise lied. 'No.'

And there was that voice again, smooth as chocolate, deep and syrupy as treacle.

'Sorry about that,' Lamorna said. 'Listen, I have to go. Catch up soon, okay?'

'Okay.'

The line went dead before she could say anything else. Standing in the downstairs hall, the grandfather clock chiming in the hour, Elise came to a sudden and depressing realisation. Lamorna Brooke had discarded her anger and replaced it with boys.

She felt betrayed. Lamorna had been her only friend. They'd shared stories and secrets. Elise had opened up to her. And for what?

To be tossed aside like yesterday's newspaper.

It wasn't long before news of Elise's abandonment swept through the school like a tempest. Everywhere she went, she was followed by taunts and laughter and pointing fingers. Gemima Thorn danced and sang in her retribution.

Which was why, as Elise now sat on the bench in the town square, sunset dancing over the fountain water, she glared at Lamorna with such intensity that the girl took a step back.

'What?' Lamorna said. 'Why so cold?'

'Fuck off,' Elise hissed.

Then she burst into tears.

Chapter 15

Ten loud chimes resonated through the house. Darkness emerged from the trees and swept over the yard. Slipping under the front door, it stalked through the house, stealing the light from every room. In the kitchen, the very last embers of coal lay dying in the hearth of the stove. They crackled and fizzed and then, darkness took them too. Sebastian sat at the kitchen table with his legs pulled up to his chin. One word played over and over in his mind until it found its way to his lips.

'Nana. Nana. Nana. Nana.'

Normally, the dark frightened him. Normally, it harboured all manners of horrors that fed from his imagination like ravenous animals. Tonight, the dark embraced him. It mingled with his blood until it coloured his veins black. It blinded him. It lied to him in all kinds of ways.

It wasn't your fault, it said. She made you do it. She didn't give you a choice. You wanted to call for help and she stopped you. Why did she do that? Why doesn't she want you to be happy? To be safe? She did a wicked, wicked thing and she's given you half the blame. She'll give it all to you, Sebastian. She'll lie. She'll tell them it was your idea because she doesn't care about you anymore. And poor Nana May. Locked in that awful place, tied to her rocking chair. Remember when she read you stories from that chair? Remember how she rocked and rocked until she nearly tumbled out of it? How you laughed and laughed.

Sebastian startled the air with wild laughter. Then his voice broke into a low, undulating wail.

-Don't cry, Sebastian. Don't cry. I'll take care of you. Darkness is good, remember that? Darkness hides things. It covers things. It stops you from seeing what you're doing. Let me help you. Will you let me help you?

Sebastian wiped away his tears. He nodded.

-Good! That's good. I will help you, Sebastian. But before I can, there's something you must do.

'What is it?'

-There's a man outside. He wants to talk to you. Will you let him in?

Sebastian spun around in his seat to face the door. A hulking shadow spread across the panes of glass.

Let him in for a little while, the darkness whispered. He has something to tell you.

The shadow moved closer. It pressed its face against the glass. Sebastian stared in horror as the door handle began to turn.

* * *

'Drink this. It will make you feel better.'

Lamorna's kitchen was an altogether different affair compared to Nana May's. It was cramped and cluttered, with chequered linoleum flooring and harsh fluorescent lighting that induced headaches if you sat beneath it for too long. All of the appliances were shiny and modern. There was a toaster and a microwave, and a lever on the refrigerator door that when depressed produced ice from a hole.

The table where they sat was small and round and covered with an unpleasant plastic tablecloth patterned with flowers. There was no room for a table in such a small space, but what was a kitchen without somewhere to sit and drink tea and talk away your troubles?

Elise dabbed her tears with a towel and eyed the steaming cup in front of her with mounting suspicion.

'Don't worry,' Lamorna smiled. 'It's plain, old-fashioned camomile tea. Mother swears by it.'

Elise wrapped her fingers around the cup handle.

'Oh. Thank you.'

She brought the cup to her lips, enjoying the burning sensation that trailed down her throat and into her stomach.

'So,' Lamorna said, curiosity etching her features, 'I know I've made a lot of people cry in my time, but I don't think from just saying hello.'

Elise turned the cup between her hands.

'I mean I've had people running away at the sight of me but . . . it's because of Greg, isn't it?'

Elise looked up. 'Greg? That's who you're going out with?'

Cheeks flushing, Lamorna smiled. 'Everyone thinks he's weird. But then everyone thinks I'm mentally unstable. So I guess we're well matched!'

'I guess so.'

Elise thought about Greg and his wardrobe of black army trousers, big boots and torn black T-shirts. She thought about his skeletal frame and straggly hair that masked his features. He was perfect for Lamorna in every way.

They could vent their anger upon the world together. Perhaps they could even find some peace through it.

Elise's acknowledgement did not stop her from feeling cast aside and, as if Lamorna had read her thoughts, the girl cleared her throat and said, 'I'm sorry I haven't been around lately. It doesn't mean I like you any less. It doesn't mean we're not friends.'

'What does it mean?' Elise asked.

Lamorna thought about it. 'I don't know. Not many people like me. They sure as hell don't understand me. But Greg, he understands what it's like to realise you don't fit in. That maybe sometimes you'd be better off dead than to live in a place where people would sooner spit on you than say hello. That's why we found each other I think. That's why we love each other.'

Elise shifted on her seat. 'Oh. That's nice.'

'It's not nice!' Lamorna cried. 'How would you like it if everywhere you went people pointed their fingers and said things about you? I'm sick of it.'

'Maybe if you were kinder to people they would be kinder to you.'

How quickly Lamorna had forgotten everything Elise had confessed to her. Insulted, she slumped back in her chair and folded her arms across her chest.

'It's not about being kind to people,' Lamorna insisted. 'It's about people needing to leave each other alone. Forget it, Elise. You're not old enough to understand.'

Elise bit down hard on her lip. She'd just about had enough of being left alone by people. And she did understand. She understood more than Lamorna Brooke could ever hope to.

'One day, when you grow up, you'll see that —'

'When my mum tried to kill herself, she waited until me and Sebastian were asleep, then she took a bottle of sleeping pills and walked out of the front door.'

Lamorna stopped in mid-sentence, words tripping over each other in her mouth. She tried to look away but Elise caught her gaze in an iron grip.

'That was after she burned Sebastian's back with a hot iron. He was making too much noise. She had a hangover. So you see, I do understand, Lamorna. And you're wrong. People shouldn't leave people alone because when they do, all sorts of terrible things can happen.'

Sebastian jumped up from the chair and slammed into the kitchen door. He lunged for the key, twisted it and heard the lock snap into place.

Taking a step back, he watched as the door handle moved up and down, and then was still.

The shadow at the door remained unmoving.

'I know your name,' it said. 'I know what you've done.'

* * *

The two girls sat at opposite ends of the table, one filled with secrets, the other with dread. All traces of the day had been stolen away by the coming of night. The kitchen light flickered. Lamorna broke the silence.

'I'm sorry.'

Terrible things had happened to this girl in her kitchen, and as much as she loathed the banality of her life, she was suddenly exposed to a magnitude of comfort and warmth that she had been denying for years.

'I'm so sorry.'

She extended her hand across the surface of the table. Elise took it in her own, intertwining their fingers. There was so much more to tell. To expel every sad story from her body would leave her clean and whole and free. She looked deep into Lamorna's sad eyes. Could she really tell this girl everything? She trusted her once, and even though they had since grown apart, Lamorna still kept Elise's secrets to herself. Even if Lamorna did disappear from her life again, did it matter? What mattered was that she would be free of all of her secrets. What mattered was that she might begin to feel normal again.

As she thought, words formed an impatient queue. Which story should come first? And how much of each story should be told? All of it? Was that really fair? And what about Nana May?

'Elise?' Lamorna squeezed the girl's fingers. 'Why are you out here so late? Has something happened?'

Questions. There were too many. Sometimes Elise thought about questions. How many questions were there to be asked in the world? Why was there a question for every answer but not an answer to every question? Why did thinking about questions only lead to more questions?

'Should we call your Nana? Did you have a fight? Is that it?'

Elise opened her mouth and a multitude of words clambered over each other, tumbling and knotting together until they formed sentences that made no sense.

'A stupid thing . . . in the city . . . her shoes are still out there.'

Lamorna pulled her hand away and gripped the edge of the table.

'I told him, we left the basket in the woods and the coal has to keep burning! She said we were no good! No good!'

Lamorna looked about the kitchen.

'Perhaps I should wake up mum and dad.'

'And crying all the time. So sad! Crying all the time because of him! Why did he do that? Sebastian! He doesn't even know what he did!'

'Sebastian? What did Sebastian do?'

Elise fell silent. The kitchen light continued to flicker above their heads. Darkness crept into the corners of the room.

'Nothing,' Elise whispered. 'It's okay. We had a fight. It's okay now.'

'Are you sure?' Lamorna's eyes were wide, her skin more pallid than usual in the artificial light.

'I was upset. I'm fine now.'

'But—'

'I'm fine now. I should go home.'

She stood and took her empty cup to the sink. Lamorna watched as she stared out of the window, into the night.

'Elise? Are you sure you're all right?'

The girl nodded.

'Well you can't walk home in the dark. I'll get my dad to drive you. Maybe you should call your Nana too.'

'She's sick.'

'I know. But she'll get better. I'll go wake up my dad.'

When she had been left alone, Elise thought about the lies she'd been telling people about Nana May. She thought about Sebastian. She had left him alone for hours now. Her own words echoed in her head: "people shouldn't leave people alone. All sorts of terrible things could happen." This she knew was true. The churning of her gut, the fluttering of her heart, and the darkness closing in on her knew it too.

Chapter 16

This was how Sebastian remembered his mother: tall but not too tall; slim but not so that she was underweight; long, waves of raven hair that tickled his face when she bent down to kiss his nose; eyes so green and voluminous that he was easily lost in them for hours; a smile so radiant that the room lit up with the parting of her lips. He remembered her voice most—rich and melodic and as warm as a summer tide. When she spoke, the birds would cease their song. Passing strangers would stop and turn. And when she sang him to sleep, it was as if all the angels sang as one through her.

This is how Sebastian remembered his mother. But it wasn't an accurate remembrance. From his memories he had plucked out the wickedness that could roll so easily from her tongue. He had removed the lashings from her upturned hand. Gone were the drunken bouts and the unremitting tears. Gone were the unshaven men staggering from her bedroom doorway. The angry red scar forever etched into his back was now attributed to an accident in which he'd toppled the ironing board and brought the iron down upon himself.

So ingrained was this image of his mother that any attempt made by Elise to instil truth to the matter was met by stoic disbelief and swept from his mind, along with every other unwanted memory.

As for his abandonment, Sebastian concocted the idea that his mother had been deeply upset by something and needed time to feel better again. The fact that it had taken four years so far had been put into a box and marked "never open" and hidden in the darkest recesses of his mind.

Yes, he missed her. Yes, he thought about her every day. Yes, he waited and waited for her return. But not once did he utter a harsh word against her. Not once did he ever think she was lost to him.

It was different with Nana May. She had died, and although his mind was too young and naïve to comprehend her death, he knew she would not be coming back. He had cried oceans of tears for her and barely grazed the surface of his grief. Yet, there was a strange comfort at the middle of it all. He couldn't understand why it was there but he clung to it like a shipwrecked sailor clinging to driftwood, hoping it would carry him back to shore.

He held on to it now as he sat in darkness beneath the kitchen table, shaking with fear as the shadow spoke to him.

'Will you let me in?' it rasped. 'There are things I need to tell you. Things you need to know. You've done a terrible thing, Sebastian, but I won't tell anyone if you let me in.'

Sebastian shook his head. He covered his ears with his hands. The back door rattled in its frame as the shadow took hold of the handle.

'You're a wicked boy,' it said. 'What you did to your grandmother! The devil will be coming for you and your sister.'

'Go away!' Sebastian whimpered. Tears burned his cheeks. He choked on his sobs. The shadow moved closer until its lips kissed the glass.

'Do you think Elise really cares about you? Do you think she cared about poor Nana May? She's left you alone for hours and hours. Do you think she's coming back? Perhaps she's run away just like your mother. It seems everyone leaves you, sooner or later, one way or another. I wouldn't leave you, Sebastian. I would take good care of you if you let me in.'

'I can't.'

'Yes, you can. You see, I have secrets. There are all sorts of things I could tell you. Things you've always wanted to know about your mother. I could tell you something now if you like. Then it would be our secret. Something between you and me. Something Elise would never know.'

Beneath the table, Sebastian caught his breath.

'Like what?'

'Well now,' the shadow laughed. 'Got your attention, have I? What could I tell you about your mother? Let me see . . . ah, yes. Here's a little something for you. The day your mother left you here, she drove as fast as she could, all the way to the end of the lane. And then she stopped. Hit the brakes hard she did. Almost slid right into the trees.

She sat behind the wheel for a long time. It was almost as if she was waiting for something to happen. Then, just for a moment, a look came over her, which suggested she was about to change her mind and come back to get you. But it was just for a moment. She drove out onto that road as if she were being chased by the devil himself. The horses in the field were scared silly by the engine and they reared up on their hind legs. She was gone. Vanished. Not even a trail of breadcrumbs to track her down.'

Sebastian's eyes were now very much accustomed to the dark. He looked up at the shadow to see that it was no monster. It was a man. A towering, crooked man with ragged breaths and a head filled with secrets.

'Who are you?' Sebastian asked. 'How do you know that?'

'I've watched you for a long time,' the man rasped. 'Such a sad life you've led and you've barely set foot in the world. Don't you see,

Sebastian? You're not even ten years old and there's nothing left for you. Nothing but this falling down house that you and your sister hide in, an uncle you never see and who wants nothing from you, and a mother who should have drowned you at birth because this life she's given you has hardly been worth the trouble.'

Quiet sobs seeped out from beneath the kitchen table. The man pressed his cheek to the glass.

'It hurts,' he whispered. 'But I can make it stop. I can make it all go away.'

'How?' Sebastian stammered.

'By taking care of you. I could do that very well. And you'll need taking care of now that Nana's gone and Elise has left you. Why don't you let me in?'

The boy remained where he was. This man, as frightening as he was, knew so much about the children's lives that Sebastian could not help but find a wanton curiosity teasing his fear. He swayed under the table. Where was Elise? He wondered if she had really left him. He imagined a life without her, and it was a life filled with darkness and thorns and nothing else.

'She'll be back soon,' he said. 'She won't leave me.'

The man at the door snorted. 'Your sister? She's gone Sebastian. She's left you.'

'No. She'd never leave me. She'll be back soon.'

'You're wrong.'

Sebastian shook his head. 'Leave me alone. I'm not supposed to talk to strangers.'

The man pulled away from the door. He was motionless for a long time. Then he moved so close that Sebastian thought he would come through the glass.

'I never said I was a stranger.'

He laughed and it was an unpleasant, gargled sound that made the hairs on the back of Sebastian's neck spring up.

'Perhaps I'll force the door open,' the man said. 'Perhaps I'll huff and I'll puff and I'll blow the house down. Or perhaps I'll come through the front door that you've left unlocked. We could wait for your sister together. That would be nice, wouldn't it? The two of us together, sitting at your Nana's table.'

Sebastian shot out from beneath the table. He tore through the kitchen and ran down the hallway to the front door. Both locks were stiff from lack of use but fear gave him the strength he needed. The bolts slid into place and the boy slid down to the floor. He waited for the sounds of breaking glass, or the crunch of gravel under foot, but all he heard were the cats mewling for their dinner and his own breaths, deafening in the quiet.

'Elise!' he whimpered. 'Please, come home!'

Chapter 17

It wasn't long before Elise heard footsteps and curious whispers descending the stairs of the Brooke household. She linked and unlinked her fingers, aware that she was about to tell yet more lies. She stood up from the table and then sat down again. She tucked her fidgeting fingers between her arms and her sides. The kitchen door swung open and Lamorna bounded in, followed by her mother. Mrs Brooke gave her a warm smile.

'Hello, Elise. How are you? Everything okay?'

'I'm fine, thank you.'

Standing at a little over five feet, Mrs Brooke was a petite woman. She had thin lips and sharp cheekbones, and a nose that was large and beak-like. A nest of short red hair dishevelled by an hour's sleep crowned her bird-like appearance. Despite such sharp features, Mrs Brooke had a kind face, softened by deep blue eyes that sparkled when she smiled. And she smiled a lot, which Elise thought was a good thing. There were too many people walking the earth with glum faces and heavy hearts and Elise, as she would be the first to admit, was one of them.

'You'd never think summer nights could bring such a chill!' Mrs Brooke chirped, taking a seat at the table and pulling the folds of her dressing gown together. Lamorna wedged herself in between. With three people at the table, the kitchen appeared to shrink to half its size.

'Dad's putting on some clothes. He'll drive you home,' Lamorna said.

'Oh. Thank you. Sorry.'

'How's your Nana?' Mrs Brooke asked. 'I hear she's not very well.'

There it was. That question again. Elise felt as though she had heard it a thousand times and lied a thousand times in return. She had lied so many times now that it was almost easy to believe in the stories herself.

'She's a little under the weather.' The words sounded strained and all too familiar. 'It's nothing to worry about.'

Mrs Brooke nodded. 'You know people around here, they like to turn molehills into mountains. I'm sure she'll be right as rain come the morning. She's made of strong stuff, your Nana.'

Elise tried to smile, gave up and found a spot of spilled tea on the tablecloth. Mrs

Brooke's smile widened. She looked at her daughter with questioning eyes.

'Do you think you should call your Nana to let her know where you are?' The conversational torch was passed to Lamorna. 'She's probably worried.'

Mrs Brooke agreed. 'Yes, it's quite late. And it's dark. You can use the phone in the hallway if you like.'

Elise's heart thumped in her chest. She looked from Lamorna to her grinning mother and back to the tablecloth. She thought about counting all the little flowers printed on the plastic.

'I'll show you where it is.' Lamorna waited a moment. 'Earth to Elise? Do you read me?'

'What?'

'The phone?'

Elise got to her feet.

'We don't want your Nana worrying, do we?' beamed Mrs Brooke.

Elise followed Lamorna out of the kitchen.

'You're acting really strange. Is there something I should know about?' Lamorna whispered when they were alone in the hall.

'I'm fine.'

An array of family photographs hung from the red painted walls. There were pictures of family holidays, weddings, christenings, the children at different ages. Every photograph contained a happy memory of some kind. Staring at each one, Elise understood why Mrs Brooke had so much to smile about.

'I'm fine,' she repeated.

'So you keep saying. Well, the phone's right here.'

Elise nodded, lost in family memories that were not her own. How unrestrained they all looked. How loved. How together. Her eyes found the telephone. Lamorna watched Elise fumble with the receiver. Strands of hair fell over the girl's face and she swept them back, exposing the scab where she had struck her head on the gravel path. Had that really been just a few days ago? To Elise, it felt like months. Turning away, she cleared her throat and managed to say, 'I'm trying to remember the number. It's been a long time since I used it.'

Lamorna raised an eyebrow. 'Right. I'll leave you alone then.'

She brushed past Elise and made her way upstairs. When Elise was certain she was alone, she pretended to dial Nana May's number, waited a few seconds and then spoke to the droning dial tone.

'Hi Nana. It's Elise. I'm at Mr and Mrs Brooke's house . . . because of . . . I know, I'm sorry. How are you feeling? Mr Brooke is going to drive me home now. Okay. See you soon. Bye.'

She slammed the receiver into its cradle and while she waited for her cheeks to return to their normal colour, she drew her gaze back to the photographs hanging on the wall. One in particular caught her eye. It was Christmas time in the picture and the Brooke family was gathered around a pine tree so heavily decorated that Elise couldn't see the branches. Each person was smartly dressed; Lamorna too, if you ignored the black lipstick and smudged eyeliner. Mr and Mrs Brooke and their son, Nathan, held glasses of wine in a toast. Lamorna held her baby sister in her arms, cheek pressed to cheek. Even the family dog was full of festive cheer, its tongue lulling from the side of its mouth.

Elise brushed her fingers against the glass of the photo frame. As she made her way back to the kitchen, she burned the image onto her mind. In her version she and Sebastian were sat at Lamorna's sides, their arms filled with presents and their smiles as radiant as those of their newfound family.

Mrs Brooke stood in the centre of the kitchen, holding a tray on which sat a cake smothered in thick chocolate, dark cherries and frothy whipped cream. Elise gasped. For an instant, she was back in Nana's kitchen and it was Nana May standing before her, showing off her latest culinary creation.

'Here. Take this home for you and your brother. I made it fresh today but with Nathan moved out and Lamorna fading away on another one of her diets, I'm afraid it will go to waste.'

Elise's stomach embarrassed her with an intrusive grumble.

'Thank you,' she said. 'It certainly won't go to waste at our house.'

'Not by the sounds of things!' Mrs Brooke chuckled. Elise laughed with her and her laughter felt clumsy and unfamiliar. Mrs Brooke placed the cake into a plastic container and pulled the lid down tight.

'Hold it carefully in the car. You don't want all the chocolate coming away from the sides.'

'I will.'

'Now, you tell your Nana from me that I hope to see her on her feet and at Sunday service. Otherwise, her voice will be missed.'

Elise frowned. 'But Mrs Brooke, Nana can sing about as well as I can fly a plane.'

Mrs Brooke raised her eyebrows.

'Elise Montgomery!' she cried, and they both fell into fits of giggles. Then Elise was moving across the kitchen and wrapping her arms around the woman's waist.

'Thank you,' she whispered.

'Whatever for, dear?' Mrs Brooke asked, the embrace taking her by surprise. Elise tightened her hold.

'I don't know. For being nice.'

'Elise? Are you ready to go?'

Lamorna and her weary father stood in the doorway. Elise stepped away from Mrs Brooke, bowing her head until her hair fell across her features.

'I'm ready,' she replied.

Chapter 18

Night had descended upon the countryside. With it came a chill that slipped beneath the clothes of the Range Rover's passengers and teased goose bumps to the surface of their flesh. A waning moon cast fields and meadows in a silver-blue wash, which Elise observed with enthralled unease, picking out strange shapes and shadows that she knew would transform into the ordinary come the light of day. The night was a frightening and magical place.

On her lap, she held the plastic container with Mrs Brooke's cake inside and balanced on top of that was the parcel of sausages Mr Tonkin had given her. Lamorna sat up front. Her father concentrated on the road. Nobody talked for those first minutes of the journey. Then, as the vehicle approached the steep hill that took them out of the village and towards Elise's home, Mr Brooke changed gear and asked, 'Are you enjoying the holidays, Elise?'

He glanced at the rear-view mirror and saw darkness emanating from the back of the car. Elise stared out into the road, captivated by the white lines that cleft the road into two and fired past her like phosphorescent bullets.

'This one seems to be making the most of them,' Mr Brooke continued. 'We've hardly seen her all summer.'

Lamorna nudged her father on the knee. 'And you're complaining about this?'

'Who said anything about complaining?'

She slapped him hard on the thigh. Father and daughter both giggled. Mr Brooke cleared his throat.

'Was your Nana angry when you called?'

'A little.'

'I'm sure she'll just be glad to see you. She would have been worried, that's all.'

Silhouettes of hedgerows rushed past like train carriages. The Range Rover's engine hummed a repetitive rhythm as it climbed to the top of the hill. Elise looked out to see clusters of lights dotted around the dark landscape and the distant, effervescent glow of the town. Then, as they made their descent, each light was snuffed out, each star above them stolen away, until darkness was all encompassing.

Unnerved by Elise's reticence, Mr Brooke shifted behind the wheel. He had never been adept at handling adolescent mood swings, and when it came to girl problems, well, his wife was always much better at that sort of thing. She had a way with words that quietly amazed him, and he wished she was here right now, ready and able to appease whatever pains were troubling the girl sitting in the back seat. But Mrs Brooke was not here and so, for now, he would have to fill the quiet with the first words that came to his mind.

'Heard from your mother lately?'

Immediately, the air grew thin, leaving Elise struggling for her next breath. Lamorna sprang up from her seat, a look of sheer disbelief lost to the night.

'Dad!'

Mr Brooke shrugged.

'Sorry! Just making conversation. There's no need to scream at me like that, Lamorna. If you hadn't noticed, I'm behind the wheel of a moving vehicle!'

'So shut up and drive then! Jesus Christ!'

'Don't blaspheme!'

'Don't put your foot where it doesn't belong!'

'Okay, fine! Here I am, just driving!'

Lamorna slumped back in her seat. Her father muttered something under his breath, then offered his full attention to the road. Letting out a long, steady breath, Elise relaxed her grip on the plastic container.

'Sorry about that,' her friend called from the front. 'My father isn't the most subtle of people.'

'I'm sitting right here!' Mr Brooke complained.

Elise pitied the man. He seemed like a kind and decent person. In fact, both of Lamorna's parents seemed loving and responsible and utterly put upon by their daughter. How could someone be so ungrateful for the gift of a stable upbringing?

'I haven't, by the way,' Elise said, her voice reaching out of the shadows.

Lamorna cocked her head. 'You haven't what?'

'Heard from my mother.'

'Oh God, you don't have to talk about that!'

'I don't mind. There isn't really a lot to talk about anyway.'

'I remember when your mother first came to the village,' Mr Brooke told her, and because Elise had allowed the conversation, Lamorna was silent, curious even. Elise leant forward.

'You do?'

'I remember because of the stir her arrival caused among the boys.'

Lamorna shook her head. 'That's sick.'

Elise swallowed hard. How many times had she witnessed her mother's almost preternatural displays of sexuality towards mankind? She had seen her charm, seduce, outwit and humiliate more men than she cared to remember, and the moments that she did remember were indelible stains. She assumed most children (not all; surely she could not be the only child to have had such a wayward upbringing?) would grow up to remember their youth with warm, wistful nostalgia.

But that was not for Elise.

She would reach adulthood and what she would remember of her early years would be this: sitting up in bed at night, keeping a watchful eye on her sleeping brother as she listened to the drunken laughter, loud music and curious sounds her mother would make while her latest companion heaved his weight on top of her. She would remember trying to sleep. She would remember not being able to until she was sure her mother was resting and her guest was gone.

But sometimes the guests didn't go. Sometimes they stayed until morning. Sometimes they stayed for a day, maybe two. Sometimes they stayed longer and turned into boyfriends, but never for more than a few weeks. When they did leave, Catherine would lock herself in her room and Elise would listen to her sobs or watch as her mother dragged herself into the kitchen to fix another drink. Sometimes, Catherine would catch her looking, and her face would twist grotesquely as she screamed terrible things.

"What the hell are you looking at? Do something useful you little whore! You're no good! Take that bastard baby and get out of here!"

Other times, she planted herself down on the sofa to wrap her arms around her daughter and cry.

'Don't be like me,' she would wail, her alcohol breath smothering the air. 'Don't be like me!'

Elise would hold onto her, confused and terrified and awash with pity. To hear Mr Brooke speak about her mother and boys in the same sentence led to memories that were diseased.

'Oh yes, when your mother turned up for her first day at school, the boys were practically fighting one another to say hello.'

'You remember that?' Lamorna asked, faintly surprised by her usually redundant father.

'Ask any man who was at school then,' he said, his eyes ablaze in the darkness. 'They'll tell you the same story. Catherine was the prettiest girl they'd ever laid eyes on. She turned up that day, fourteen years old, long black hair falling past her shoulders, her uniform immaculately pressed. She walked into the school with that uncle of yours, and the whole place fell silent. The girls stared in awe and envy, and the boys literally fell at her feet. She stared back with the greenest eyes we had ever seen and then, she smiled a smile so dazzling that the whole playground lit up.

'School was never the same after that. There would be fights among the boys, fights among the girls, who all were determined to be her best friend. Teachers would stumble over their words as she entered the classroom. She had the entire school utterly bewitched. And you know the funniest thing? She barely said a word to anyone. Try as they might, not one girl could have called her a friend. Try as they certainly did, not one boy ever came close to dating her. She simply came to school, attended all her classes and went straight home as soon as the day ended.

'You'd imagine the kids would have something to say about that. That she was cold and unfriendly and stuck up. But she wasn't any of those things and we all knew it. The minute you caught her eye she would have a smile for you. If you said hello, she was only too happy to ask how you were. But beyond that . . . your uncle was quizzed daily but kept tight-lipped. Forgive me for saying this, but he was considered more than a little strange—following your mother wherever she went, never talking to anyone and, to be honest, looking like he might strangle the life out of anyone who dared speak to her.

'It was no surprise when she eventually left the village. She was destined for greater things. Or so it seemed. When we all heard what had become of her, of how she left you and your brother, well, nobody expected that.'

Mr Brooke fell silent. In the back seat, Elise's mind raced over and over the man's story. It was as far from what she had expected to hear as the sun from the moon—her mother had not always been bad.

They had reached the lane that led to Nana May's house. Ahead of them lay a tunnel so black and infinite that not one of the vehicle's passengers, not even Elise, was happy to be heading into it. As the vehicle rolled forward, trees on both sides were caught in the dusty beams of the headlights.

The Range Rover ploughed on, cutting through the swathe of darkness, its tyres running in and out of potholes.

'I hope I didn't say too much.' Mr. Brooke risked a quick glance into the shadows of the back seat. Next to him, Lamorna shook her head.

'I think Mum would say you've said quite enough.'

They came to the bend and the lane widened and spread open into the front yard. Mr Brooke slowed to a halt but left the engine running.

'Here we are.' The embarrassment in his voice was now so audible that his daughter covered her ears. Elise unbuckled her seatbelt. A cold rush of air streamed in as she pushed open the door.

'None of the lights are on,' Lamorna observed.

Elise looked up at the house. 'She'll be round back. In the kitchen.'

'What's all that stuff?'

The groceries were still sitting on the doorstep. Cats were gathering in front of the house. They watched the car with unease, their eyes glinting gold and green in the headlights.

'Delivery,' Elise murmured.

Pulling herself from the back seat, she stepped into the yard. The cold cut through her shorts and T-shirt, nipping at her skin.

'Thank you for driving me home.'

Mr Brooke gave a half-hearted wave.

'Want to meet up tomorrow?' Lamorna asked, but Elise was already closing the door.

She walked a few steps towards the house and stopped in her tracks. The day's events hit her like the swell of a wave. She had left

Sebastian alone. Mr Elliot had almost discovered Nana May in the outhouse. Nana May! How simple it had been to walk away, to pretend that none of it was real. What she hadn't realised was that it would all be waiting for her return, and now that she had returned, it came at her from all sides.

She fought the urge to run back to Lamorna and her father. The cats padded towards her, their eyes gleaming with accusation and blame.

'Move!' Elise hissed at herself. 'Walk!'

Nana May floated in front of her eyes. She was tied to her rocking chair, her face rotted away. Then came her mother, naked and drunk and screaming obscenities. Then Uncle Edward. Then Sebastian, hiding in darkness, crazed with fear. Elise propelled herself forward.

Behind her, the Range Rover reversed and turned back towards the lane. Elise hurried through the body of cats, stepped over the groceries and reached the front door. It was locked.

The girl shook her head. She had been cast out, trans-formed from humble dweller to unwelcome guest.

Curling her hand into a fist, Elise rapped on the front door and waited for Sebastian to come.

'Sebastian! It's me! It's Elise! Let me in!' she cried, pressing her ear to wood. The cats gathered about her ankles and rubbed their bodies against her skin, whining with hunger.

'Sebastian! Please let me in! I'm cold!'

'Elise? Is that you?'

'Of course, silly!'

Metal scraped and bolts thudded. The front door swung open, and Sebastian peered up from the darkness with wide, haunted eyes.

'You left me,' he moaned. His lower lip trembled and then was still. Elise opened her mouth to utter an apology, then snapped it shut again. She stared into the darkened hallway. Sebastian retreated into the shadows.

'I've got cake and sausages,' she offered. 'It's chocolate cake with cream and strawberries.'

'You're letting the cats in.'

Elise looked down to see the elder felines had pawed their way into the house and now sat at her feet, emitting guttural complaints and cutting the air with flicks of their tails.

'Out!' She pushed them away with her foot. The cats stopped still, pricking up their ears. Underneath the night-time sounds, there was a charge gathering. It crackled like electricity, singeing the air. Dropping their tails, the animals returned to the yard.

Sebastian brushed past his sister and stood in the doorway. He stared out into the night, looking across the yard and to the sides of the house. Shutting the door, he slid the two locks back into place. The sounds of them slamming home were like firecrackers exploding in Elise's ears.

'The supplies,' she breathed. 'We should bring them in.'

Sebastian was silent. Darkness folded around Elise in an unwanted embrace.

'I'm sorry, Sebastian. I don't know why I left. I don't know what happened but I'm sorry. You know I would never leave you on purpose, don't you?'

'The oven's gone out,' the boy said, ambling away from the door. 'There'll be no hot water.'

Elise shook her head. 'Once won't hurt. I'll fix it.'

'Nana said to never let the fire go out.'

'Sebastian . . .'

'Once won't hurt,' he mused. 'If you say so.'

Brother and sister stared at each other in the darkness, both sensing the charge they had created as it sizzled above their heads.

'I can't do this now,' Elise murmured. 'It's been a long day and I'm tired. Let's bring in the supplies. Then we can have some cake and some milk and go to sleep.'

She moved towards the kitchen. Sebastian sprang from the door like a crazed dog. He grabbed her arms, almost knocking the container from her hands.

'Don't go in there!' he hissed.

Elise tried to pull herself from his grip, but her body was drained of all reserves. Sebastian shuddered with bolts of adrenaline.

'Let go of me! What's wrong with you?'

'Don't go in there!' her brother repeated and this time, his voice quaked with fear. 'Someone's there!'

Elise stopped struggling and looked towards the kitchen door. 'What are you talking about? Let go! You're hurting me!'

Sebastian released his hold on her. He backed away until he hit the stair rail.

'There's nobody in there. How could there be?'

The boy was silent, shaking his head from side to side. Elise found herself enticed by the closed door. There were lots of things to be frightened of in the world, Nana May once said, but a closed door was not one of them.

'There's no one there. I'll prove it.'

Marching towards the kitchen, Elise swung open the door and stared into vast darkness. Reaching her hand along the wall, she scrabbled for the light switch and was encompassed by harsh, electric light.

It was icy cold and filled with ghosts, but no one else was in the kitchen. Elise took a few steps inside and began to shiver. It was an odd sensation; one she had never associated with this room. Setting down the cake and sausages, she looked over her shoulder. Light from the kitchen spilled into the hallway, illuminating bookshelves, pictures and the old grandfather clock. Sebastian hung back by the stairs.

'I told you,' Elise called to him. 'Now, will you help me with the supplies?'

They worked quickly, transporting boxes and tins from the front yard to the kitchen table. As they dragged the sack of potatoes in together, Elise watched with concern as Sebastian's gaze swung about the yard and searched out the shadows that lay at the woodland's edge. When they were done, he closed the door and pushed the bolts back into place once more.

Elise busied herself with storing the new supplies in the larder. When this was done, she took out plates and a large knife. As she worked, she blew into her hands and rubbed her palms together and stamped up and down to keep warm. It was freezing in here! As if summer had come to an untimely end.

Soon, there were two generous portions of chocolate cake sitting on plates next to two tall glasses of milk. His empty stomach allured by the prospect of food, Sebastian edged his way to the kitchen door. He peered around the room before taking a small step inside. He tiptoed over to the back door and tried the handle.

Satisfied the door was secure, he pulled back the curtains and risked a look out into the garden. He saw flowers, streaked with moonlight and tossed about by the night-time breeze. He saw prodigious silhouettes of trees. He saw two yellow eyes glaring at him from the dark.

Sebastian drew in a sharp breath as the eyes grew a long snout and jaws brimming with gleaming, needle-shaped teeth. The creature emerged from the foliage, its large paws flattening the grass, and moved towards the kitchen door.

Reaching the centre of the garden, it dipped its head, sniffing the ground before it. Then, it was looking at Sebastian again, its luminous eyes burning holes into him. Both fascinated and afraid, he watched the fox turn from the garden and slink away in the direction of the outhouse.

Elise watched her brother with rising concern. Being left alone had affected him in ways she could not imagine. Guilt hung around her neck in chains.

'Come and eat your cake,' she said. 'It's really good.'

Sebastian backed away from the door and sat at the table. He stared down at the cake and across at his sister.

'Try it,' she coaxed. She smiled and rubbed the tops of her arms. 'It's so cold. Aren't you cold?'

Sebastian ate a mouthful of cake. He picked up his glass and drank a mouthful of milk. He swallowed it down.

'I don't know,' he said.

'Well, I'm freezing,' Elise replied, ignoring her brother's unsettling behaviour and the shards of guilt it embedded in her chest. 'I'm going to light the oven.'

She pulled herself up from the table and moved across the kitchen. The coal bucket was empty. She remembered her encounter with Mr Elliot that afternoon. He had left the new sack of coal leaning against the door of the outhouse. And what had he said? "Smells like something's gone and died in there."

Elise felt the ground pulling away from under her feet. All she wanted was to be asleep in her warm bed, tucked up in dreams where Nana May was still very much alive, and her mother was full of love, and she and Sebastian lived lives so normal, so mundane, that they were the happiest children in the world.

Wiping tears from her eyes and fighting back more, the girl picked up the coal bucket. She turned towards the back door, using the very last of her energies to drag her stone-heavy feet, one in front of the other.

It didn't matter how much chocolate cake a person could eat, no matter how many strawberries it had on it or how much whipped cream it was smothered in. You could eat a whole bunch of chocolate cakes, but all you would be left with was a sick feeling in your stomach and the same problems you had to begin with.

'What are you doing?' Sebastian's voice was shrill, his back arched like a cat's.

'Have to get more coal,' Elise droned.

Sebastian flew from his chair.

'Don't go out there,' he pleaded. 'We'll do it tomorrow, in the daytime. I'll help you. Please.'

A tear spilled from Elise's eye and danced down her cheek.

Sebastian fell asleep first, curled up like a baby and gone from the world. Elise lay beside him for a long time, watching the rise and fall of his chest, waiting for each breath to be expelled. He turned his back to her and, caught in moonlight, she saw the iron-shaped scar tattooed in the centre of his spine. She traced its lines with her finger, awful memories replaying in her mind.

Eventually, she fell into a heavy, dreamless slumber. They lay together, her body sheltering his, until daylight put out the stars and sent the moon on its long journey home.

Chapter 19

The Past

Nana May sat next to a crackling fire in the living room, a half-made winter scarf trailing down her lap as she rocked back and forth, each motion of the chair punctuated by a soft wooden creak. Colourful Christmas decorations hung from the ceiling in ribbons and plumes. Shiny baubles clinked amongst the tinsel of the evergreen standing in a bucket of earth in the corner. They all sparkled and danced in the firelight.

'Nana? Why did our mother leave us?'

The clack of Nana May's knitting needles came to an abrupt halt.

'Oh my,' she said. 'Now, that's a question and a half.'

Perched in the windowsill, Elise watched thick flurries of snow twirl about the disappearing yard. It had been snowing since the middle of the night and with the grandfather clock chiming in the third hour of the afternoon, it showed no signs of relenting. The disused pick-up truck was already half buried. Woodland trees had transformed into scaled down icy mountains. All of Nana's cats had, for once, been permitted inside the house and were now sprawled out on a large red rug, basking in the heat of the fire. A symphony of contented purring floated on the air.

A shrill wind whistled past the house. Elise felt the chill through the draughty windowpanes.

'It's been almost four years,' she said. 'She's not coming back, is she?'

Nana May rested her knitting in her lap. 'Come away from that window, girl. You'll catch your death sitting there.'

Slipping off the sill, Elise padded over to the armchair next to the fire and dropped down into it, pulling her knees up to her chin.

'Feet!' Nana scolded.

Elise dropped her feet from the chair to the floor. The old woman picked up her needles, re-counted the stitches she had cast, and set off knitting with expertise. She spied on her granddaughter as she worked.

'Goodness! You got a face on you like a wet weekend!'

'I want to know what you think,' Elise pressed. 'About why she left.'

May puffed out her cheeks and fixed her gaze on her knitting.

'That snow keeps up and we'll be buried here for days. Good job we got supplies in.'

Elise sat forward in her chair. 'Nana! Answer me. Why do you think she left us?'

'Well, really! Is that any way to talk to an old woman? Your own grandmother no less!'

The girl bowed her head. 'I'm sorry. But I'm fed up with feeling like this, Nana. If she's not coming back I'd like to know about it. That way I can just forget about her and get on with things.'

'You wash your mouth out!' Nana barked. 'You don't know if she's never coming back. Only she and God know that. Your mother has her fair share of problems true enough, but she don't deserve to be forgotten.'

'Me and Sebastian didn't deserve to be dumped off. We didn't deserve all the times she left us alone, and Sebastian didn't deserve what she did to him. So tell her to wash her mouth out because we didn't do anything wrong!'

Nana May missed a stitch and dropped her needle on the floor. She bent over and picked it up. She wrapped the unfinished scarf around both needles and set the knitting down on top of a large basket of wool.

'I want to know what you think,' Elise demanded. 'I want to know why she left us.'

Nana May regarded her with a steely glare. She shook her head.

'Where is Sebastian?'

'In his room.'

They glowered at one another from their chairs.

'Good,' said Nana May. 'Before we go ahead and talk about this, there are three things I want you to remember.'

'What?'

'The first thing I want you to remember is I'm about as far from happy as can be being made to have this conversation, but seeing as you've deemed yourself old enough and wise enough for such business, who am I to pass judgement? The second thing you need to remember is, no matter what she said or did to you, your mother still loves you.'

'But—'

'That's not up for debating. You can believe it or not, that's up to you. All I want you to do is remember it. The third thing you need to put in that brain of yours is your mother also happens to be my daughter. It pains me every day to see the hurt she's put upon you children, and it breaks my heart knowing she's been out there for four long years, suffering a hundred different kinds of sadness. And there's not one thing I can do about that, apart from take care of you and your brother best I can till she's good and ready to come back home.'

Elise absorbed Nana's words with grim fascination. She refused to believe her mother possessed any kind of love for her or her brother—was it love that had burned into Sebastian's back? But she saw that Nana

May was so full of love for her daughter and her grandchildren that her heart had cracked into pieces for them, and for this Elise felt undying humility. Yet, there were questions that desperately needed answers.

'Why did she leave us, Nana?'

May clasped her hands together and stared into the fire.

'Your mother was very sad,' she said.

'I already know that.'

'Sometimes, people get to a point where sadness is all they know. It takes over everything else. It gnaws away at them like a dog at an old bone. People get so sad they can't see straight. They stop believing. They forget to take care of themselves and the children they dearly love. They slip away till they become like ghosts. Their life becomes a dream, or a memory. Something that once was but isn't any more. You understand me, girl?'

Elise nodded.

'Your mother got like that. It's why she said the cruel things she said. It's why she lashed out sometimes.'

'Like with the iron?'

'Yes, but she never meant none of that. Probably didn't even know what she was doing most of the time, she was so drunk. You see, people try to hide from their sadness. They get drunk or take nasty pills, but the medicine soon turns to sickness and that dog is chewing on its bone again.'

'But she hurt us so much.'

'And that's exactly why she left you with me. She was losing sight of herself. After what she did to Sebastian, she thought she might be capable of doing worse.'

Elise frowned, confused.

'She was scared she was going to hurt both of you. Really hurt both of you. That's why she left. She loved both of you so much she couldn't see any more harm come to you. At least, that's my opinion on the matter.'

Elise's eyes filled with tears. 'She wanted to kill us?'

'Don't be daft,' Nana said, shaking her head. 'She was trying to stop you from getting hurt.'

'But she's our mum. She's not supposed to hurt us.'

Nana May sighed. 'See now, this is exactly why I wasn't wanting this conversation with you. You're not as old as you think, Elise. Yes, you're clever beyond your years but this is adult talk. I never should have said anything.'

'You knew, didn't you?' Elise sobbed. 'You knew she was going to leave us.'

Nana May shifted in her chair. She shook her head, over and over.

'I think this conversation needs to have its end right about here.'

'Tell me!' Elise cried. 'Did you know?'

A terrible silence fell upon the room. The cats hushed their purr. The fire softened its crackle. Nana May looked out of the window. The blizzard had grown stronger and all she could see was a white sheet that shut out the world. A large gust of wind blasted the house. It rattled the windows. It gushed down the chimney and battered the flames of the fire.

'Yes,' she said. 'That I did.'

'Why don't you go on in? Take your bags upstairs. There's a treat for you in the kitchen when you come back down.'

The children squealed in delight, picked up their cases, and thundered towards the open doorway of the house. When she was certain they were gone, Nana May stared at her daughter for a long time, then asked, 'You sure you want to do this?'

Catherine nodded without hesitation.

'Where are you going to go?'

'I don't know. Somewhere. Anywhere.'

'How long are you gone for?'

Catherine shook her head. She didn't have the answer to that question. Laughter rang out from the upstairs window of the house. Mother and daughter turned their heads.

'What will you tell them?'

Nana May heaved her heavy shoulders. 'Still working on that one.'

'Tell them . . .' Catherine's voice fell away.

'It won't matter much what I tell them,' Nana said.

Catherine nodded. 'I suppose not. I should go.'

'Wait!' Nana lurched forward. Pulling a small bundle from her apron she placed it in her daughter's hand.

'It's not much,' she said, 'but it should help you along the road.'

Catherine pocketed the money and replaced her hand on the wheel.

'One more thing,' Nana said. Catherine looked up and Nana saw a terrified child at the wheel of the car.

'Be brave,' she said to her daughter. 'Brave enough to not come back for those kids until you're good and ready.'

Catherine hit the accelerator and balls of dust burst into the air. Nana May stood rooted to the ground like a sad old tree. She watched the car head into the lane. She watched the dust settle on the ground. She walked back into her house and towards the kitchen. She heard the excited chatter of her grandchildren floating down from upstairs. She picked up a tray on which two gingerbread men sat, smiling up at her.

'Treats for both of you,' she said, and waited for the children to come.

* * *

Elise leaped up from the chair. Tears streaked her face and burned her skin.

'You lied to us,' she said, glaring. 'We waited for hours and hours and you kept saying 'she'll be here soon, she'll be here soon'. But you knew she wouldn't be.'

Nana May rocked in her chair. Alarmed by the sudden discord, the cats reared their heads from blissful slumber.

'Why didn't you tell us the truth?'

'Because you weren't old enough,' Nana May said. 'You're barely grasping it now. You tell me how an eight-year-old is going to understand why their mother had to leave them behind and disappear.'

'I'm not bloody stupid, you know!' Elise raged. 'I could have understood.'

Nana brought the rocking chair to a halt.

'That will be enough of that nonsense! I won't be shouted at in my own home!'

Elise's face flushed scarlet. She sat back down in her chair.

'The thing you have to understand is people are a lot like trees,' said Nana May. 'The older you get, the more rings you'll have around your trunk, and I'm not talking about these great tyres around my waist, neither! The older you get, the wiser you'll become. You love her. That's why you got so much anger. You might not understand the meaning behind your mother's behaviour now, but you will eventually.'

Elise was quiet for a long time. Anger flashed across her features like lightning. Clouds of confusion rolled in and grew heavy with tearful rain.

'I guess I'll have to wait and see,' she finally said.

Nana nodded. 'That you will. Now let's see if we can't make this all taste better with a batch of chocolate caramel cookies.'

She pushed herself out of her rocking chair and picked her way between the feline bodies lying on the floor.

'Nana?' Elise called.

'Yes, dear?'

'Do you know why our mother was so sad?'

Nana stopped in her tracks.

'I really couldn't tell you.'

Elise looked at her grandmother. 'I know why.'

'You do? Why ask me then?' A little colour left May's face.

'Because I know <u>why</u> she was sad, but I don't understand why it made her hurt us.'

'What is it that you think you know, girl?'

'It's a secret,' Elise whispered.

Nana May stepped away from her granddaughter and stalked towards the door.

'Secrets are secret,' she muttered. 'Best you keep them that way too.'

A few moments later, Sebastian flew downstairs and burst into the living room. He saw Elise sitting in the armchair, looking as pale as the snow outside.

'I heard shouting. Are you in trouble?'

Elise did not reply.

'Do you think Nana will let me go into the garden? I want to make a snowman.'

Elise looked at her brother as he twitched with excitement.

'Go outside and you'll <u>be</u> a snowman,' she said.

Sebastian giggled and even though it was a joyful sound, Elise could not find her smile.

Chapter 20

Gentle rays of sunlight seeped in through cracks in the curtains and danced in patterns on the bedroom floor. Birdsong, sweet and playful, rode in on the back of the slightest of breezes. Woodland scents and flower smells perfumed the air. Elise sighed. After what seemed like the longest night on Earth, daylight was a welcome visitor.

Pulling back the covers, she sat up and stretched out her arms. An enormous yawn escaped her. Beneath the sheets, Sebastian rolled over in his sleep. Elise turned and watched him for a while.

'Poor Sebastian,' she whispered. Memories of yesterday forced her onto her feet. Why did the bad things in life always have a habit of sneaking up on you when you were least aware? Good things never did that. She had a lot of making up to do for yesterday's disappearing act, and a lot of explaining to do as well. The latter was going to be more difficult because she was still trying to understand the randomness of her actions herself. Nevertheless, she could begin making peace with Sebastian by dishing up a mouth-watering breakfast of eggs and sausages, courtesy of Mr Tonkin, the butcher. At least her inexplicable behaviour had not been entirely fruitless.

Leaving Sebastian to sleep, Elise made her way out into the upstairs hall. Stopping outside Nana May's bedroom door, she reached out and felt the wood's grain against her fingertips.

The bathroom light was harsh and discomforting, the tiles beneath her feet icy cool. Elise looked at her reflection in the mirror. Dark shadows circled her eyes like hungry sharks. Her skin was pale and drawn and unhealthy looking.

So much for well rested, she thought.

Her gaze dropped down to her flat chest and boyish body. She had not yet started her period and although she was happy about this (the thought of bleeding for days at a time, each month for the bulk of her life, was something she looked towards with unbridled terror), she could not help but wonder when she would develop the curves and breasts that other girls in her school possessed.

Nana May had explained that getting her period was a sure sign of Elise entering womanhood. The other physical changes that signified becoming a woman were never too far away from menstruation. The fact that from the head down she could still be mistaken for a boy was not as bothersome to her as the fact that she had started to care about such things.

Shrugging off her angst, she turned on the bath taps. She ran her fingers under the cold water as she waited for it to heat up. A memory sprang into her thoughts. Sebastian had let the oven go out. There would be no hot water until it had been lit again. The coal to fuel the oven was leaning against the door of the outhouse. Nana May was on the other side of that door. "Smells like something's gone and died in there," Mr Elliot had said, and the look on his face had told her it was no joke. Elise switched off the bath taps and slid down to the floor. How much more was there to do?

'This isn't working,' she moaned. The words shocked her—she had not meant to say them aloud. But they had somehow escaped and were now airborne, free to float on air currents, to whisper her confession in the ears of listeners.

And the words spoke the truth. Elise's plan was not working at all. She had not foreseen the trials and tribulations of adult living. She had underestimated the fearsome speed at which news could travel through a community bred on the banal. She had little knowledge about the decay of a dead body. She had seen its work on the corpses of dead birds, rodents and occasional roadkill, but it was something she had never attributed to human beings. After all, human beings were different from all the other animals, weren't they?

Mr Elliot's words echoed in her head and she shook them out. Too many questions were being asked. Too many mistakes were being made. Things as they stood would have to change. Elise got to her feet. Breakfast and a hot bath would help her think.

'Can't make a chicken dance,' she said. 'Can't start a day without breakfast.'

She moved out of the bathroom and headed downstairs.

The heat in the garden was suffocating, and she leaned against the house for a second, allowing her body to acclimatise.

High above her, the sun was burning an enormous hole in the sky. On its surface, explosion after explosion fired fountains of magma out into space, retaliating against the previous night's chill. Elise felt the metal bucket heating up her fingers. Pushing herself off from the wall, she took a giddy step forward. Heat and rising nausea were concocting a nasty feeling in her stomach. She made her way through the garden and breaking through the heat waves was like breaking through hurricane winds.

Get to the coal, fill the bucket, run back to the house. The words played over in her head. She left the garden and stepped onto gravel. Beneath the flower scents, she could smell something foreign, something sickly. The outhouse came into view and Elise gripped the handle of the bucket so tightly that her knuckles popped.

Horrible images of Nana May flashed before her. Maggots crawled from her grandmother's mouth and eyes. Worms bore into her ears and burrowed into her flesh. Strings of fat intestines pushed out of her swollen stomach to land in steaming piles on the ground. All the while she rocked back and forth, back and forth, a witness to her own stink and rot. The bucket slipped from Elise's hands and clattered on the gravel.

The smell was like raw chicken left out to fester in the heat of the sun. It was dying flowers. It was ditch water. It was the stench that rose up from old farmer Favel's septic tanks to stink its way through the woodland when the wind was blowing in the wrong direction. It was all of these smells, made all the more horrible by the knowledge of what was causing them.

Elise swallowed hard, pushing down a flurry of torturous thoughts. Her gaze moved from the bucket, towards the sealed sack of coal leaning against the outhouse door, and then to the door itself. A pulse of energy emanated from there. It rippled out in widening circles, thickening the air, silencing the creatures of the woodland. Elise felt it push through her torso, delving icy fingers into her flesh. It shot tiny shocks through her brain. It crushed her chest so she could not breathe. Then, it was moving on behind her, and she dragged in a ragged breath and pushed it out with all her might. Her eyes fixed on the sack of coal, Elise stepped forward. Another pulse of energy rippled out, squeezing the air from her lungs. And then came a voice.

'Help me.'

Elise stopped still.

'I don't belong in here'

It's not her, the girl told herself, as she ploughed towards the outhouse. It's just you going mad, that's all.

She was by the door now, and the stench seeping out from under it was so relentless

283

in its onslaught that she clamped both hands across her nose and mouth. Tormented whispers filtered through the door slats.

'Why did you put me in here, Elise? How could you do that to your grandmother? It's dark in here and I'm afraid. Won't you let me out?'

'Shut up, shut up!' Elise cried, clamping her hands to her ears. Then she was lunging forward to grab hold of the hessian sack. Digging the heels of her feet into the ground, she pulled as hard as she could. The sack jumped forward an inch. She heaved again and it jumped another inch. A better idea came to her. Changing positions, she pushed her weight onto the sack until it fell flat onto the ground. Now, turning her back on the outhouse, she bent down, placed her hands close to the ground and pushed upwards. The sack of coal rolled over. Grunting, Elise repeated the action. The sack was heavy but she managed to roll it over again.

'You put me in here!' the voice shrieked behind her. 'Tied me up and threw a sheet over me and put out the lights. I'm frightened Elise! Your Nana's frightened!'

Quaking with terror, Elise pushed with all her might, turning the sack over and over, bringing it closer to the house. Behind her, the voice reached a high-pitched frenzy.

'I'll get my hands on you, little bitch! I'll get my hands on you and when I do, you'll see what it's like to be put in the dark!'

Panting hard and soaked with perspiration, Elise cleared the corner of the house and rolled the sack into the garden. She rolled it on and on, until she had it propped against the stove in the kitchen. Her arms ached. Her heart thumped. Yet she felt an unexpected calm embrace her. The coal was in the kitchen. She would never have to go to the outhouse again—or at least not until next

Wednesday, when Mr Elliot would return with more supplies and problems for her.

* * *

Soon, fat black rocks of coal were burning in the hearth and while she waited for the oven to heat, Elise set about feeding the cats. She watched from the front door as the animals partook in their usual territorial skirmishes, pushing and shoving one another to get to their food. Today, they were more fervent than ever.

A while later, eggs and sausages fizzed and popped in the frying pan. Tantalising food smells wafted through the house, snaking out in tendrils that travelled upstairs. With the table set and breakfast cooked, Elise turned to see Sebastian standing in the doorway. He was dressed in the same shorts and T-shirt he had fallen asleep in. His hair stuck out at awkward angles. His skin was a lifeless grey. His eyes were puffy slits and the shadows beneath them looked out of place.

'How long have you been standing there?'

Sebastian was silent. He stared at Elise with an expression so lacking in character that she could not tell if he was still angry with her or if he was even awake. She forced a smile.

'I've made breakfast,' she said. 'Eggs and sausages. Go and sit down. I'll bring them over.'

Sebastian remained where he was, his gaze fixed on his sister. He blinked once, lowered his head, and then shuffled over to the table. Sitting down, he stared at the tall glass of orange juice and the empty place mat in front of him. Elise brought over two brimming plates.

'Tuck in,' she urged, picking up her knife and fork. Sebastian's arms remained hanging at his sides. He stared at his sister as she chewed up some sausage and swallowed it down.

'Eat your breakfast, Sebastian,' she said, concern now overriding guilt. 'It will go cold.'

'You're all dirty.' His voice was flat, his gaze expressionless.

Elise looked down at her pyjamas and saw black smudges of coal.

'And you smell funny.'

She shrugged her shoulders.

'The water will be hot soon. You better eat up so you can have a bath.'

Sebastian looked down at his plate.

'I'm not hungry.'

'But you hardly ate a thing yesterday. You must be starving.'

'I'm fine.'

Elise put down her fork. 'I know you're angry with me, Sebastian, but you have to eat. If you don't you're going to get sick and that's the last thing we need.'

'If I get sick will I die like Nana May?'

Elise pinned him with a shocked glare. 'Don't say things like that.'

'If I die will you put me in the outhouse too?'

Returning colours faded from Elise's face.

'What did you say?'

Sebastian picked up his knife and twisted it around with his fingers. He picked up his fork and began to eat, swallowing down every morsel with a curious creasing of his brow.

'The sausages are good.'

As he ate, his complexion grew less ashen. The shadows beneath his eyes retreated a little. He looked more like Sebastian again, rather than some undead imitation.

'I've been thinking about yesterday,' Elise said, when her plate was empty. 'About when Mr Elliot was here.'

Sebastian nodded. His appetite had returned and he was now finishing off the remaining food on his plate. He picked up his orange juice and took two large gulps.

'We were both stupid. We both forgot he was coming. We both know he always comes Wednesday afternoons. You always help take things from the truck and I always help Nana —I always help to put them away. We have to be more careful, Sebastian. Or that will be it for us. We'll be put in care.'

Having finished the last of his breakfast, Sebastian was now collecting grease from the plate with his finger.

'And we can't let that happen, can we? We'll never see each other again. We'll both end up living with people who just want the money they'll get paid for looking after us, and they won't even look after us properly.

Or worse, we'll get put into children's homes. You'll go to one for boys and I'll go to one for girls. And I've heard things about those places. There's no way I'm going to end up in one of those places.'

Sebastian finished the last of his orange juice and looked around the kitchen.

'Is there any cake left?' he asked.

Elise narrowed her eyes. 'Are you listening to me? I'm being very serious, Sebastian. We almost got caught yesterday and you're acting like you don't even care.'

'I thought you had,' he said.

'Had what?'

'Got caught. I thought Mr Elliot had found out and taken you away. I thought that was where you'd gone.'

Elise looked away. 'Well, that nearly happened. It probably would have happened if you hadn't taken the key.'

'Me?'

'Yes, you,' Elise replied, cheeks burning. 'If you hadn't taken the key then, well, we wouldn't be sitting here at the table right now.'

Sebastian frowned. 'But—'

'It was more my fault than yours really.' Elise's face was now the colour of claret. 'I'm the oldest. I should be thinking of ideas like that. I don't know what happened. I was so stupid.'

Sebastian stared at her. 'Where did you go? Why did you leave me on my own?'

Elise knew that she owed him an explanation. 'After Mr Elliot left, I—I don't really know. I remember running. Running and running, down the lane until I got to the road. And when I got to the road it seemed like a good idea to just keep going.'

She risked a glance at Sebastian, who stared straight back with unblinking eyes.

'I walked up the hill and ended up at the village. I saw Mrs Thorn, and Mr Tonkin gave me those sausages, and then I bumped into Lamorna Brooke. Everyone was asking about —about Nana May. Mr Elliot told people she was sick. Everybody was wondering if she was all right.'

'What did you tell them?'

Elise hung her head low until her hair covered her features in a sheet.

'That she was a little bit under the weather. That it was nothing to worry about. Then Mrs Brooke gave me that cake, and Mr Brooke drove me home.'

Both children were silent for a long time. Elise looked up to see Sebastian's face flooded with tears. They flowed from his eyes in streams and pooled onto his empty plate.

'I want Nana,' he sobbed.

Elise bit down hard on her lower lip. 'I know.'

'I want her to come back!'

Elise reached her hand across the table. Sebastian didn't take it.

'I miss her so much!'

'I miss her too,' Elise said, her fingers extending towards her brother.

Sebastian stopped crying. His eyes grew dark.

'Do you?' he asked, and the tone of his voice sent chills through Elise's body.

'Of course I do!' she cried. 'Do you think I'm glad about all this?'

Sebastian pupils had grown so wide and black that his irises were almost invisible.

'I would do anything to get Nana May back, but there isn't much anyone can do about that and you know it!' Elise sobbed. 'We don't have any choice about what to do now. If Mum was still around, if she hadn't been the way that she was, then things would be different. But she's gone and now Nana's gone, and I know this isn't working but I need more time.'

'To do what?'

'To figure out what we're going to do. We can't live like this for much longer. People are asking about Nana May. Someone will come soon, and when they do we're going to be in so much trouble!'

'With the police?'

Elise shook her head. 'I don't know. But we'll be put into care and I'd rather run away than do that.'

Sebastian's eyes softened. 'It might be all right in care.'

'No!'

'Why not?'

'Because you can't trust grown-ups! Not ones you don't know and sometimes not ones you do know. If anything happened to you, Sebastian . . . you trust anyone that gives you a smile. You shouldn't.'

'Why not?'

'Sometimes grown-ups seem one way but they're another. Sometimes they seem kind and nice but all they really want to do is hurt you.'

Sebastian shrugged, confused. 'Why would they want to hurt me?'

'Doesn't matter. All you need to know is that if we get split up, I won't be there to protect you from people like that.'

'But we might not get split up.'

'I'm not taking a chance.'

Frightening images pulsed through Sebastian's head; images of darkness and a man made of sin and shadows lumbering towards him. "Let me in," the shadow man had whispered at the door. "I'll take good care of you."

'What about Uncle Edward?'

Elise buried her head in her hands. 'I've told you. He won't want us.'

'But how do you know?'

'I just do.'

'But how?'

'Just leave it! I don't want to talk about Uncle bloody Edward.'

'I'm going to call him. I'm going to ask if we can come and live with him,' Sebastian declared. 'Nana says if you don't ask you'll never find out anything.'

'Don't.' Elise leaned back in her chair, her eyes flashing. 'Don't even think about doing that.'

'Why not?'

'Because—'

'Because what?'

'Because—'

'Because <u>what</u>, Elise?'

'Because if he didn't mind us coming to live with him before, he will when he finds out what we did to Nana May. She was his mum. You helped to do what we did. You helped to drag her all the way from the garden and into the outhouse, and if you call him I swear I'll tell him everything.'

Sebastian sat back, aghast. In his mind, the shadow man whispered to him. "She'll lie. She'll tell them it was you. She'll tell them you planned it all."

'It doesn't matter anyway,' Sebastian said. 'Uncle Edward will be here soon. Next Saturday is the second of the month.'

Taking his time, he stood up from the table. The feet of his chair scraped against the flagstone floor. Elise, who had been stunned by this new revelation, was startled by the sound.

'Where are you going?'

'To feed the cats.'

'But I've already fed them.'

Shrugging his shoulders, Sebastian walked towards the kitchen doorway.

'Where are you going now?'

'Away from you.'

'I think we should stay indoors today!' Elise called after him. She heard bolts being pulled back. The door was opened and then slammed closed, the impact sending shock waves through the house. Things rattled and clinked. A ladle jumped from its hook and clattered onto the kitchen floor.

Elise remained perfectly still. Sebastian was right. Uncle Edward would be here in just over a week. Then, nothing would matter. She ran trembling fingers through her sticky hair. The urge to bathe was suddenly so paramount that everything else was forgotten. Leaving the breakfast dishes on the table, she ran upstairs to the bathroom.

Chapter 21

Sebastian slammed the door and the house shuddered as if it were made of paper. He threw his body down onto the front step and thrust out his lower lip. Breaths came fast and heavy. Veins popped at the centre of his forehead. He had never felt so angry and the feeling had a frightening will of its own— tearing about his body, shooting from his brain where it painted nasty pictures, to his mouth where it deposited vile curses, to his limbs where it threw punches at the air and kicked gravel about the yard.

'Elise!' Sebastian growled through clenched teeth. 'Elise! Elise! Elise!'

She had been telling him what to do for days now. She had taken charge and planned everything. She had forced him to help put Nana's body into the outhouse, and then yesterday, she had abandoned him. (Had she tried to run away? Was that what she had been trying to do?) Now, Elise was threatening to betray him to the one person who had the means to remove them from such a terrible predicament.

'Stupid bloody bitch!' Sebastian cursed. 'Stinking bloody whore!'

Elise had caused the trouble they were in and she was keeping them stuck in it too. But why? Why was she doing this? How could she know that Uncle Edward would not want to take care of them? Did she think him heartless enough to turn his back on his only living relatives? He would never do that!

The cats had sniffed out Sebastian's presence and were now crowding around his calves, rubbing their warm bodies against his skin. She's jealous, Sebastian thought.

She's jealous because I'm Uncle Edward's favourite and she's not. Uncle Edward's always nice to me. He tries to speak to her but she's always rude to him or says she's busy helping Nana. She's never liked Uncle Edward, but I have. Me and Uncle Edward play games together. He tells me jokes and stories, and he doesn't do any of that with Elise. That's why she doesn't want me to call. She doesn't want to be the one that's not important.

Another thought struck him. It didn't matter if Elise told Uncle Edward about what they had done because he was going to find out anyway. Elise had made it clear that someone would uncover the truth, and sooner rather than later. The police or the care people, or whoever, would inform Uncle Edward of their actions. He was the only family they had left (their mother would be discounted) and he would have to be told. That was what happened in TV shows. They called people like Uncle Edward 'the next of kin', and it was always the next of kin who was told the bad news first.

Perhaps then, Sebastian thought, it would be better if Uncle Edward heard it from his nephew or his niece, rather than a complete stranger. After all, bad news was always better told by someone who knew you because they could give you a hug. They could kiss the top of your head and make it all go away. If Sebastian and Elise could admit what they had done to Nana May, perhaps Uncle Edward wouldn't be so angry with them. Perhaps he might understand how frightened they had been. How confused. If he was to hear about it from strangers, he might wonder why his nephew and niece had not had the courage to tell him themselves. And that would make him angry. Very angry indeed.

'That's what we have to do,' Sebastian told the feline faces staring up at him. 'We have to tell Uncle Edward. He might get mad, but he'll calm down, and then we can go and live with him.'

He searched through the cats for Red.

'And Nana wouldn't mind about what we did because we would have told the truth, and we would still be with our family.'

Thoughts of his grandmother quietened him. He pictured himself as a young child, sat in her lap as she read to him from books of fairy tales. He remembered her drying him down with a towel in front of the fire on cold winter nights after hot baths. He remembered her laughing and laughing, her eyelids squeezed together as she rocked back and forth. A deep black hole opened in the pit of his heart, and it grew wider and wider, until all feelings, all emotions were swallowed into the void.

Red was not here. Sebastian looked about the yard, calling to the kitten. Other cats appeared from the sides of the house and from the foliage. Sebastian frowned. Red always came to him. He only ever needed to call his name once. Standing up, he took a walk around the side of the house.

'Red!'

He looked into the trees. Spots of sunlight dappled the ground there, but he could not see the kitten. He walked on, gravel crunching under foot, until he turned a corner and came to the garden. There were more cats here, dozing in the flowerbeds and taking refuge from the heat in the shade of bordering oaks.

'Red! Here boy! Come on cat!'

Ears pricked up and feline heads turned in Sebastian's direction.

'Red! Come here, you stupid cat!'

He tried to recall the last time he'd seen him. It had been yesterday, just before he and Elise set off for the river. He'd been sitting on the step and Red had come up to him, mewling and in want of affection. Sebastian looked about the garden. Yesterday was a long time ago. Anything could have happened to the kitten since then.

The shadow man slithered into his thoughts. Perhaps he had taken Red to punish Sebastian for not letting him enter the house. The boy shook his head. There was no plausible way that could be true because the shadow man wasn't real. He was from a bad dream, crafted from darkness and patched together with fear. The shadow man did not exist.

A breath of wind blew up from the woodland. Flowers danced on its current. Sebastian's mop of hair lifted from his forehead and fluttered like sails. He made his way through the garden, towards the outhouse. There was a strange, unpleasant odour hanging at the edge of his senses. It twisted and curled about him, pricking his nostrils with sharp, repugnant stabs. Sebastian stopped in his tracks. If Red was near the outhouse, he would have heard the boy's calls and come running.

The boy backtracked to the centre of the garden. Where was that stupid cat? An unpleasant feeling was growing inside his chest. The shadow man lingered in the recesses of his mind. Perhaps he was real after all. And if he was real, what did that mean for Sebastian and Elise? Looking towards the kitchen door, he pictured the events of the previous night. The shadow man had stood right there, his face pressed against the glass, looking in.

A sound from the woodland caused him to turn on his heels. It was the sound of a cat calling. A young cat. Sebastian paced towards the wooden fence and scanned between the trees. The foliage was thick there. Large, leafy ferns covered the ground.

'Red? I'm here boy!'

The cat called back. He sounded close by, somewhere up ahead and to the left.

Sebastian cocked his head. 'Come here, Red! Come here boy!'

The cat called out again, and he sounded further away. Clucking his tongue, Sebastian pulled himself through a gap in the fence. He planted his feet on spongy soil and began walking in the direction of the cat's mewls.

'This way, silly cat!'

The sound changed direction, moving into the trees rather than out of them.

'You're going the wrong way.'

The sounds stopped. Sebastian ploughed forward, twigs and old bark snapping under his feet. Thick, moss-covered trees loomed over him like giants. He picked his way through bushes and brambles, calling to the kitten. Red did not reply. Sebastian stopped and turned a full circle. The woodland had fallen silent. Birds sat mute on branches. Insects froze on leaves. Animals stood motionless, catching strange scents in the air. Rustling up ahead spurred Sebastian onwards.

'Red?'

The cat answered with a frightening, prolonged growl.

Elise sat in a bath of hot water, a tide of foamy bubbles floating on its surface. Wisps of steam spiralled about the bathroom. Her hair had been washed and scrubbed, and now it hung like damp rags behind her ears. The graze on the side of her head didn't hurt so much now, but there was still some swelling and a blue-green bruise the size of a coin.

As she bathed, Elise thought about Sebastian. She had never seen him look so angry and she didn't know what to do about that. Perhaps if she waited a little, Sebastian would calm himself enough to succumb to her way of thinking. Perhaps then he would forget about calling Uncle Edward. She brought up her knees and rested her chin on top of them.

Why would Sebastian forget about that?

A sob escaped the girl. He won't forget about Uncle Edward because he doesn't know what he's really like! she thought. I should tell him. Then he'd forget about him for sure. Elise lay back in the water, her face floating just above the surface.

But would it change anything? Uncle Edward would be here in just over a week and there was nothing she could do to stop him from coming. If she told him that Nana was sick, he would come anyway. If she told him they were going to be away he would never believe it because the only time Nana May had ever been anywhere was to visit them in the city.

No, Uncle Edward was coming—maybe tomorrow if Sebastian called him, or next week as he was supposed to. Sebastian knowing the truth about his uncle would not change a thing. Her heart fluttering in her chest, Elise held her breath and sank beneath the water.

Chapter 22

He had lost the cat's trail. Red had fallen quiet, and all that Sebastian could hear was the breeze skimming the branches.

'Red!' he yelled as loud as he could. 'Here puss! Here boy!'

It was unusual for the cats to stray so far from the house and the hunt-free food they were provided. There were dangers camouflaged by the trees, predators that could tear a kitten into pieces before it could cry out for help. Such as the fox he'd spied in the garden last night. Its jaws had been large and salivating, its teeth many.

And its claws—long and curved and barbed like rose thorns.

'Red! Come on cat! Where are you?'

Somewhere, far in the distance, Red called back. The boy moved towards the sound, cutting through small grassy clearings and working his way around swamps of thick mud. He called the cat and the cat called back. He was getting closer, but how Red had travelled so far ahead of him was a mystery; for an animal of Red's size and burgeoning agility the dense woodland floor was a formidable challenge.

The trees were beginning to thin out, making room for large boulders that pushed their way out of the soft soil, transforming the ground into solid, ancient rock.

Rushing river sounds flooded Sebastian's ears. He stopped still, surprised by how far he'd travelled. The river snaked sideways in front of him, its clear waters travelling southwards through the trees. This was a different place to where he and Elise had set down their blanket. There were no dragonflies hovering at the water's edge. There were no minnows darting in the current. The vegetation growing here was frugal and scant.

Across the river, the bank was muddy and waterlogged and rose towards a platform of thick firs, which flanked the river's edge like a fortress wall. It was dark in there—the first rows of tall trunks were visible, but beyond that lay infinite blackness. And it was still. Not one needle stirred on its branch. No insect buzzed. No bird flew.

Sebastian called to the cat, fixing his gaze on the other side. Even the river seemed to arch away from it, bending and twisting from its bank in an unsuccessful bid to pull free.

Red called back. Sebastian shook his head in disbelief. The cat's cry had come from the other side of the river.

Stepping over rocks, the boy made his way to the edge. There was a short, sharp drop down to the water and he could see no visible stepping-stones that might provide a safe passage across.

If Red had come this way he would have had to leap into the river and swim to the opposite bank.

Could cats swim? As far as Sebastian was aware they couldn't and were even afraid of the water.

Crouching down, he scanned his surroundings. Something was wrong. He could sense it in the stillness. He could taste it in the back of his throat.

From the other side of the river, Red let out a high-pitched, frightened mewl, and the sound pierced through the quiet. Sebastian stood, following the river's edge until he cleared a bend and a new stretch of water became visible.

The distance between ground and river was higher here. Rock gave way to a steep, muddy incline, where clusters of tall, barren trees grew at warped angles. The other side of the river remained flat, but the firs grew thicker there, and the darkness that lurked between their trunks curled its fingers and dipped them into the water.

Red cried out once more, and this time, it was a strangled shriek.

Then came new sounds. Footsteps, crunching through the foliage.

Sebastian whirled around, his panicked gaze flitting between the tree trunks. The footsteps were moving in slow, careful succession, drifting closer and closer.

Perhaps it was Elise, playing one of her nasty tricks. Perhaps it was the fox, scavenging the woodland for food. Perhaps it was the ghost of Nana May.

The footsteps came to a halt just up ahead. Sebastian's nostrils filled with the stench of rot and decay. Then a voice, deep and cavernous, filled the air: 'There are no doors between us now, Sebastian.'

Darkness stepped out from behind a great oak.

Sebastian screamed. Then he ran.

The shadow man chased after him, extending long, sinewy limbs from a mass of black rags.

'We have so much to talk about!' he breathed on the back of Sebastian's neck. 'So much indeed!'

Chapter 23

Now clean and dressed in denim shorts and a plain white vest, Elise stood in the doorway of Nana May's bedroom. She hadn't been inside since her grandmother's death. Even when her grandmother had been alive, it was a rarely visited place. This was Nana's private haven; the one room of the house where the children were not allowed to dominate with their noise and drama. Quiet reigned here even now, enveloping Elise as she stepped onto the floorboards.

All the other rooms in the house felt as much a part of her as her own skin. In the other rooms, she could close her eyes and find her way around without bumping into a single object. Although this room belonged to Nana May and was filled with her things, it had an unfamiliarity that made Elise feel like an intruder. She moved towards the bed. Faint scents floated up from the sheets to fill her head with thoughts of Nana's soft skin. Tears brimmed at the edges of her eyes and she wiped them away.

Dropping to her knees, she reached under the bed and pulled out the small, round suitcase that had lain untouched for four years; that one long ago morning had been filled with Sebastian's toys and clothes.

Pushing the case behind her, she fished under the bed once more and pulled out a second, larger case. A thick layer of dust coated its lid and she swept it off onto the floor.

A hundred different thoughts collided in her head. Should she pack all their clothes or just a few? Were two cases going to slow them down? And what about things like food and toiletries—should she pack them as well, or pick some up along the journey? There were so many things to think about and so little time to make the right choices.

Elise looked down at the cases. She imagined Sebastian stumbling and complaining and struggling with the weight. One will have to do, she thought. She pushed Sebastian's case back under the bed and hoisted her own into the air.

Back in her room, Elise dumped the case onto her unmade bed and pulled open her wardrobe doors. Light, airy dresses hung to the left. Summer was reaching its last quarter, and then autumn would come, quickly followed by winter. Dresses would not keep Elise protected from its frosty descent.

A handful of tops and sweaters hung to the right. She chose a bright green zip-up jacket and a navy-blue jumper that Nana had knitted for her the previous year, and she threw them onto the bed. Trousers lay folded in two piles on the shelf above.

Elise reached up and took down faded blue jeans and a worn pair of chocolate corduroys. She moved over to the chest of drawers and removed two pairs of shorts and two T-shirts. Finally, she pulled open the top drawer, took out several pairs of socks and underpants and added them to the mounting pile of clothes on the bed.

'Right, Sebastian,' she said, heading out of her room. 'Your turn.'

Chapter 24

The birds were screaming and springing from their branches to fly in black, twisting droves through the woodland.

Sebastian ran between the trees. His eyes bulged in his head. His mouth hung rigid in a silent shriek. His muscles pleaded for respite, but Sebastian would not stop.

The shadow man was close behind, tearing through the vegetation, leaving holes in the ground. He drew closer, his fingertips inches from the boy's head.

Sebastian pelted forward. Trees stood in his way at every turn. He wove between them, ducking his head at the last second when low hanging branches threatened to knock him to the ground. Not once did he dare look back to catch a glimpse of his pursuer.

'No need to run, Sebastian!' the shadow man called out. 'For I am everywhere.'

Tears came and they shot behind the boy like bullets. He imagined them hitting the shadow man's face and hoped that they burned.

The ground dipped ahead of him, and he knew this meant he was nearly home. He pictured Elise sitting in the kitchen, waiting for his return. He pictured Nana May rocking in her chair, motioning for him to hurry. He fixed these images in his head and stormed forward.

'Got you!'

Icy fingers wrapped around the back of Sebastian's neck. He screamed and his knees buckled. His face slammed into the ground and then he was rolling down the bank, earth and air swinging about him, over and over, until he came to a halt.

Gasping for breath, Sebastian scrambled to his feet. Pain shot from his ankle and up through his thigh. He fell to the ground again. Behind him, the shadow man was descending the bank.

The boy hauled himself back up. He ran on, screeching with agony each time his foot impacted on the ground.

Nana May called to him. 'Run, Sebastian! Run as fast as you can!'

'I am Nana!' he wept. 'But it hurts so much!'

'It won't be long now. You're almost there. Just keep running and don't look back. You hear me, boy? Keep running!'

Sebastian kept running. The pain in his ankle began to subside. He felt a surge of energy burst through his veins.

He ran on, faster and faster.

Trees whistled past him. Sebastian lowered his head and sprinted towards home. The fence came up to meet him and he threw himself over it in one, fluid movement.

Elise had just returned to her room, carrying armfuls of Sebastian's clothes, when she heard screaming from downstairs. It was such an unnatural, terrifying sound that she threw the clothes onto her bed and thundered down to the hallway.

Sebastian was at the front door, slamming bolts into place. He spun on his feet to face her and Elise gasped. His face was ashen and streaked with dirt and blood. His T-shirt was torn at the shoulder. His knees were bloody and bruised.

'What happened to you?' she exclaimed.

'He's outside! The man from last night is outside! He tried to get me but I ran away just like Nana always told me to if I was in trouble! II ran away but he chased me and now he's outside in the garden!'

Elise froze. 'But there was nobody there last night. Remember? I checked and there was nobody there.'

'But there was! He wanted to come inside but I wouldn't let him and he told me things! He took Red and now he's outside. Don't let him take me, Elise! Please don't let him take me!'

Sobbing, Sebastian fell to the floor. Elise turned and walked down the hallway towards the kitchen. She pushed open the door and stepped inside. The door swung closed behind her and she heard Sebastian cry out.

'Don't go out there, Elise! Please! Don't go out there!'

Moving across the kitchen floor, she fixed her eyes on the back door. Through the glass she saw grass and flowers, and honeybees sauntering through the air.

Leaves fluttered on tree branches. Birds sang out from the canopies.

Sebastian had locked the door, and although bolts and locks had felt out of place last night, they now brought welcomed feelings of security.

Elise pressed her face to the glass and peered out. There was no one in the garden. There was no one hiding in the trees. She moved to the kitchen window, stood on the tips of her toes and peered out. No one was there.

Backing away from the door, Elise hurried out into the hallway. Sebastian had pulled himself into a corner and was now rocking back and forth and moaning incoherent words.

'Sebastian?'

His head jerked from side to side. His fingers drummed on his knees. Elise took his shoulders in her hands and shook.

'Stop this!' she shouted. 'Stop it now!'

Their gazes locked. Sebastian stopped rocking.

'Red's gone,' he said. 'I think he took him. I think he's hurt him.'

'Who, Sebastian? Who did you see? Who took him?'

'The shadow man.'

'Who's the shadow man?'

'I don't know.'

'What did he look like?'

'I don't know.'

'You're not making any sense. Are you talking about a real man or someone you made up in your head?'

'He's real!' Sebastian yelled. 'He was outside last night! He wanted to come into the house. He knows what we did with Nana May and he's taken my cat to get me back for helping you!'

Elise stared at her brother. He seemed to believe in what he was saying but that did not stop doubt filling her mind.

'How could he know what we did?'

'He said he's been watching us for a long time. He said Nana was gone and our mum was gone and yesterday he knew that you had gone away too. He said he wanted to take care of me, but he lied.'

The boy lowered his head and exposed the back of his neck. Thin red scratches scored his flesh.

Elise fell back against the wall, a hand clamped over her mouth.

'Did you see his face? Do you know who he is?'

Sebastian shook his head. 'I was too scared to look. I just ran.'

'What else did he say?'

'He said he knew me and what I've done. He said you would blame me, that you would tell people it was all my idea. You won't do that, will you? You won't do that, Elise?'

She shook her head. 'Of course not. What else did he say?'

'He said he knew things about our mother. He said he wanted to come in the house and take care of me. I didn't let him, Elise. I didn't let him. I told him I wasn't allowed to talk to strangers, and he said he wasn't a stranger.'

'Not a stranger?' Elise shivered. 'Who could he be?'

'I think he wants to hurt me.'

'Whoever he is, he's gone now. And I'm never ever leaving you on your own again, I promise.'

'What if he comes back?'

Elise fell quiet. Her eyes grew round and wide.

'Sebastian, where's the key to the outhouse?'

Confusion swept over Sebastian's features.

'The key,' she repeated. 'Yesterday, when Mr Elliot came, you hid the key so we couldn't open the outhouse. Where did you put it?'

'I don't know what—'

'Think, Sebastian. It's really important that you remember where you put it.'

'I didn't take the key,' he said. 'When Mr Elliot came I hid in Nana's wardrobe. I went to sleep and then you weren't here.'

'You must have taken it. You had to have taken it because it's gone.'

Sebastian shook his head. 'I haven't touched it.'

'The hook is empty,' Elise said, panic gripping her voice. 'That key's been hanging there since—and I haven't moved it. You stopped Mr Elliot from opening the outhouse, remember? You took the key. You must have.'

'I didn't.'

Elise had turned the colour of cement.

'What's wrong? What is it?'

'He's taken the key,' she whispered. 'He's been inside our house.'

Both children jumped to their feet, icy prickles jabbing their spines. The house creaked and groaned about them and they winced at every sound.

'He can't get in now,' Elise whispered. 'We're locked in with the keys on the inside. He can't get in.'

Sebastian reached for her hand and squeezed it. Outside, the cats began to mewl. Some hissed and spat while others let out low, defensive growls.

'We need to call Uncle Edward,' Sebastian urged.

'No,' Elise said. 'We're going to run away.'

'What?'

'You heard me. I've chosen some clothes for both of us.'

'But I don't want to run away! I want to call Uncle Edward. I want to tell him about Nana May. I want him to come and make the bad man go away!'

'He can't help us, Sebastian. We're in a lot of trouble, more now that someone knows what we've done. We have to run away.'

The boy wrenched free from her grip. 'No! I thought about it and Uncle Edward will be sad for a while because his mum died, but we're his family and he'll look after us. He loves me. He's kind to me. He'll take care of me.'

Sebastian moved to the bookshelves and found the telephone sitting on top. He lifted the receiver from its cradle. The dial tone hummed through the hallway.

'No,' Elise said. 'You're wrong. He's not going to take care of you.'

'Yes, he is.'

'No, he's not.'

'Why not?'

'Because he's the reason we're here and our mother isn't.'

Sebastian glared at her, his fingers poised to dial. 'What are you talking about?'

'I never wanted to tell you,' Elise replied. 'But you're not giving me a choice. Put the phone down.'

Sebastian remained where he was. 'Tell me what?'

'Put the phone down, Sebastian. If you still want to call Uncle Edward after I've told you, then I won't stop you.'

Out in the yard, the cats wailed and screeched and whined. Sebastian looked down at the telephone. The dial tone buzzed in his ear.

'Put the phone down,' Elise said.

Sebastian put the receiver back in its cradle.

'Tell me what?' he repeated.

Chapter 25

The Past

The street was dark and quiet. Cars lined both sides, their owners now deep in slumber. Cats stalked beneath the vehicles, baring fangs and arched backs as they staked out their territories. Wintry breezes picked litter from the ground and batted it between the tenements. Trees grew up from the concrete, their branches bare against the green night sky. Pinpoints of light twinkled as a hand full of stars struggled to make their presence known amid the polluted haze.

A loud sob pierced the hush. Catherine Montgomery had returned home.

She was drunk again and her co-ordination had left her alone at the bar hours before. Now, she made zigzag patterns along the pavement and muttered half-formed words. Her hair tumbled over her face in a tangled mess. Make-up was smeared and smudged. The heel of her left stiletto had snapped minutes before, which made walking a more arduous task than it had been when inebriation was all she had to contend with. Making it halfway up the street, she stumbled to a halt in front of a neglected-looking tower block. Managing to locate the third floor, she saw her living room was lit up like a beacon. A weary silhouette leaned out of the window. Elise.

'Have you got your key?' she asked, her voice sleepy.

Catherine squinted, attempting to focus. She swayed from side to side and the street lamps swayed with her. She slapped the empty pockets of her jacket, then reached for her handbag.

'Shit!' She stared up at the figure in the window. 'No bag. No keys. No nothing.'

After finding the lift out of order yet again, Elise hauled her mother up three flights of stairs and into their cramped two-bedroom apartment. Now, she was busy making coffee.

It was almost four in the morning. Sebastian had fallen asleep in front of the electric heater hours ago. Elise had woken him up and sent him off to bed, then she'd sat up, waiting for her mother to return, passing the time with late night television shows and drinking cold glasses of cola to keep herself awake.

Now, the rich aroma of coffee filled the kitchen as Elise poured hot water into a large mug. She added milk and sugar, then carried the cup into the living room and set it down next to a pile of yellowing magazines on the coffee table. Catherine was slumped on the sofa.

'What's that?' she asked, waving a finger at the cup.

'It's coffee. You should drink it.'

'I don't want any fucking coffee.'

Catherine lurched forward and somehow managed to pull herself back onto her feet. Tottering on her broken heel, she righted herself and staggered into the kitchen. Elise heard the hum of the freezer, followed by cupboard doors opening and slamming shut. A moment later, her mother returned with a half-empty bottle of vodka and two glasses, then she proceeded to pour out two generous shots. Alcohol spilled over the table and splashed onto the magazines. She pushed one of the glasses towards Elise.

'Here. I made you a drink.'

The girl stared at the contents of the glass and pushed it back towards her mother.

'I'm not allowed to drink. I'm eight.'

Catherine swallowed her shot down, then picked up the glass her daughter had rejected.

'Suit yourself.' She swallowed that shot down too.

Elise watched her mother pour out another drink, this time filling the glass almost to the brim. Catherine looked up.

'What? Don't like your mummy drinking? You should be used to it by now.'

She emptied the glass and refilled it.

'I'm going to bed,' Elise sighed, rising to her feet.

Catherine shot out a hand.

'Don't I get a goodnight kiss?'

Elise stood, glaring.

'I see,' her mother slurred. 'I'm not good enough for your kisses now. Is Mummy too much of a drunken old slut for even just one?'

Elise shrugged her shoulders.

'Don't be pissy with me, El. I've had a bad day and an awful fucking week. I don't need you giving me one of your looks.'

'You shouldn't swear. Sebastian will pick up bad words.'

'Yes, Officer. No, Officer. Three bags fucking full, Officer.'

'Goodnight, Mum.'

'Wait!' Catherine's voice became a girlish whine. 'Come and sit with me for a second.'

'No.'

'Please? I won't bite, you know. I'm your mother.'

She pulled on her daughter's arm. Elise resisted for a moment, then perched herself on the edge of the sofa. Catherine patted her hair, leaned in and planted a kiss on her cheek. The cocktail of alcohol and cigarettes on her breath was nauseating.

'Can't even give your mother a hug,' Catherine complained, her mood darkening. She pushed Elise away with one hand and reached for the bottle of vodka with the other. 'Go on. Go to bed then. You've got school in the morning.'

Elise stood up. 'It's Saturday tomorrow.'

'Well go to bed anyway. You're always in my way you are, breathing down my neck like my bloody mother. Well, I'm the bloody mother around here, not you. It's about time you remembered that, little girl.'

Catherine reached for her bag, remembered it was no longer in her possession, and cursed. 'Fuck! My cigarettes.'

'There might be some in your room.'

'Would you get them for Mummy? Please?'

Elise strode through the living room and pushed open her mother's bedroom door. A stale, airless odour wafted out. Switching on the light, she saw dirty clothes lying in heaped piles on the floor. Bed sheets were crumpled and stained. Mugs containing mould and old coffee sat on the bedside table. Beside them was an ashtray overflowing with cigarette butts and used tissues. Another astray had been spilled onto the carpet.

Scanning through the mess, Elise spotted a packet of cigarettes lying next to the bed. A lighter sat on her mother's pillow.

'One day, you're going to burn in your sleep,' the girl sighed under her breath. Shaking her head, she returned to the living room.

Catherine was crying. Fat salty tears coursed down her skin and splashed into her drink. Elise stood, watching the way her brow creased and the way her lips contorted into grotesque shapes. She watched how her whole body trembled with each intake of breath. It was such a miserable sight that Elise couldn't help but absorb her mother's sorrow. She held out a cigarette like a nurse dispensing medicine and Catherine took it between quivering fingers. Elise sparked the lighter. Cigarette smoke choked the air and burned her nostrils. Catherine wiped tears away with the back of her hand.

'It's not my fault,' she sobbed. 'I wasn't always such a mess.'

Unsure of what to say or do, Elise stared at the carpet. She'd watched her mother cry countless times, and helplessness had pervaded her on each occasion. Sometimes she would try to embrace her mother only to be batted away like a bug. Other times she would slink off to her room, forcing herself to become lost in storybooks. For now, she waited for the tears to stop, or for sleep to take hold, whichever came first. Neither seemed in a hurry to make an appearance.

'I try my best, you know. I do. I try my best and look where it gets me. Nowhere, that's where. And you can stand there for as long as you want, judging me. Looking at me like that! Like I'm nothing. And you're right. I am nothing. Useless nothing! Can't even get drunk any more without making a scene.'

'Maybe you should go to bed,' Elise said.

Catherine glared at her. 'Yes, miss. I'll go to bed now, shall I? So you don't have to listen to your sorry excuse for a mother cry about how awful her life is. Well, I'm sorry but my life is fucking awful. It's been awful for years —even before you kids came along and made it a whole lot worse.'

The words were like fingernails tearing at her flesh, but Elise had grown both accustomed to these outbursts and evermore determined to deny her mother the satisfaction of seeing her cry.

Shutting out Catherine's voice, she turned her thoughts toward the television shows she had watched earlier that night. There had been a crime series she followed, and a documentary about obese children with obsessive compulsive disorder, whatever that was. The late-night news had reported about warfare in some country she had vaguely heard of, but she had turned over halfway through, finding an old black and white movie starring actors who looked twenty years older than the characters they were portraying.

'I can't even remember the last time I was happy.' Catherine whined. 'Isn't that terrible, to live your life that way? I bet you want to know why it's turned out so bad. I bet you wonder what terrible things your mother did to deserve such a shitty life, don't you?'

Elise looked away. 'I need to go to bed now.'

'Don't you?' Catherine repeated, choking on her tears. 'Come on, be honest. I will if you will. I bet you think I did something really fucked up, don't you? I bet you think your mother is a first class, nasty little bitch, who's earned this misery because of all the terrible deeds she's done.'

Elise channelled her concentration into the carpet. She counted all the bald spots and then the stains, differentiating between the ones made by coffee, ash, and alcohol.

'Well, I'll tell you what I did,' Catherine cried. 'Nothing! I did nothing wrong! But here I am, year after year, still living a life you wouldn't wish on a dog. Still making a mess of things because of him.'

Elise looked up.

'You want to blame someone? You want to point the finger at someone for the reason you have such a fucking head case for a mother? Well, you can blame him. He's the reason I'm like this. He's the reason why all of you wish I'd just disappear.'

'Who?'

Elise had heard her mother's self-pitying, drunken monologues countless times before, but she had never heard her speak of the reason for her anguish. Until now, she had only to endure it. Catherine emptied her glass in one shot and filled it up again, splashing the last of the vodka onto the table and the carpet.

'Who, Mum?'

'Who?' Catherine mimicked and let out a strange, strangled peal of laughter. 'Who? I'll tell you who! My own fucking brother, that's who! He hurt me, Elise. I don't mean like when you and Sebastian have a fight. He really hurt me. He put his hands around my throat to stop me from screaming. He put it inside me. He pushed so hard I bled for days at a time. I was twelve years old, just a baby. He didn't stop until I was fourteen.'

And there it was, as simple as that. Except it wasn't simple at all. Forced down by the horrifying words spilling from her mother's mouth, Elise sank down to the floor. Catherine lurched forward onto her knees, pushing the coffee table away so there was only empty space between herself and her daughter.

'But nobody needs to know about that,' she smiled, sweeping the girl's hair from her face. 'Secrets are secret, and this one is yours to keep.'

'Mum,' Elise gasped. No other words followed.

'It's funny about secrets though,' Catherine said. 'How they eat you up like a disease.'

She fell asleep soon after. Elise sat on the floor until the sun came up. Then, she climbed to her feet, found a blanket to drape over her mother, and made her way to bed. Sebastian purred like a kitten above her head. Twelve hours later, he was writhing on the living room floor, screaming in agony, with an iron-shaped blister burning into his back.

Chapter 26

She had expected a surge of relief to pulse through her body. She had expected the removal of such a heavy burden to leave her feeling as light as the air itself.

There was only emptiness where the secret had been. A gaping hole.

Elise clutched at her chest as she stared across the hall.

Sebastian stood rigid beside the bookshelves, his expression flickering between confusion and shock, and then settling on disbelief.

'You're a liar,' he spat. 'Uncle Edward never did that.'

Elise nodded. 'Yes, he did. He hurt her. He made her go crazy.'

'No.'

'Think, Sebastian!' his sister pleaded. 'Why do I never talk to him? Why do you think I disappear whenever he comes around? What he did to our mother makes me sick, and there's no way I'm ever going to let him do that to me. Or to you.'

Tiny synaptic explosions blew in Sebastian's brain. His hand lunged out for the telephone. It jerked back again.

'Why are you saying this?' he cried.

'Because it's true.'

'He's never hurt us.'

'He would never have dared, not with Nana May around.' Elise's voice shuddered with foreboding. 'Nana isn't here anymore, Sebastian.'

'But Nana would be angry with him if he did those things. She'd never let him come and visit. She'd be cross with him for making Mum go away.'

'I don't think she knew. She couldn't have. She knew Mum was leaving, she told me so. But she couldn't have known why.'

Sebastian's mouth fell open, hung there as if on broken hinges. 'Nana didn't know Mum was going to run away.'

'All that matters,' said Elise, 'is that we are stuck inside this house with someone watching us. And if whoever it is doesn't get us first, you can bet Uncle Edward will get us second.'

'You're making it up.'

'I'm not.'

'I don't believe you! You're just saying those things because you're jealous.'

His hand shot out for the telephone again and this time collided with it, knocking the receiver from its cradle. His left eye fluttered like a butterfly wing.

Elise watched the telephone receiver swing on its wire and clatter against the bookshelves.

'You're saying those things because you won't be the favourite anymore. You're saying those things because you're going to get a real telling off. You'll try to blame me but Uncle Edward will never believe you! You'll get put into care and I won't because this is all your stupid, stinking fault!'

'I'm saying these things because Uncle Edward raped our mother!'

Shocked by the reality of her own words, Elise drew in a horrified breath. Across the hall, Sebastian began to cry.

'I didn't want you to know,' Elise moaned, her voice breaking. 'Secrets are secret Nana says, but you gave me no choice. Call Uncle

Edward if you still don't believe me. Tell him what we've done. Tell him we're all alone with no grown-ups to protect us. Then you can wait here to see who's going to get you first. Either way, I'm leaving tonight, with or without you.'

Elise stormed towards the stairs.

'You promised you'd never leave me again!' Sebastian wailed.

'You'd better come with me then, hadn't you?'

She cleared the stairs in seconds, flew into her bedroom and threw herself down onto the bed, knocking piles of clothes onto the floor. Tears came fast and heavy. She cried for the loss of her grandmother. She wept for her mother's anguish and the hopelessness of living. She felt the emptiness that filled the space where her secret had lived, and she let it devour her. Tears ceased to flow. All light faded from her eyes. Sinking nails into her flesh, she felt nothing. This was how she needed to be.

Elise looked at the clothes strewn on the floor. She looked at the suitcase sitting next to her and let out a helpless sob.

'No crying!' she hissed, twisting skin between thumb and finger. A jolt of pain made her wince. She twisted again and felt the embrace of nothingness.

Turning her attention to the suitcase, she unclasped the lock and pushed up the lid.

Elise found herself staring at her mother.

In the photograph, Catherine leaned against white painted railings. An endless expanse of calm ocean waters spread out behind her. The sky was clear blue. The sun shone down.

Catherine wore a light summery dress and she was barefoot. She smiled and Elise could see it was a truthful smile. Her hair was shorter than her daughter recalled. She looked healthy. She looked strong.

Picking up the photograph, Elise flipped it over in her hands. There was a date printed on the back. The photograph had been taken last summer.

Her heart skipped up and down inside her chest. Forgetting the clothes, Elise turned back to the suitcase. A small pile of opened letters stared up at her. Each envelope was addressed to Nana May, scribed in Catherine Montgomery's handwriting. Dizzy with disbelief, Elise sifted through them, studying the postmarks stamped on the envelopes to find the names of six different towns and cities. From the postage dates she saw the most recent letter was just five months old.

The room spun about her in feverish circles.

'This isn't—' she breathed. 'This can't—'

She could scarcely believe what she was seeing, yet the letters felt as real to the touch as the bed, the floor, her own body.

She picked up the photograph again. Her gaze returned to the post dates on the envelopes.

"Secrets are secret," Nana May once said. But she had kept the greatest secret of all.

With trembling fingers, Elise took out the oldest of the letters, unfolded it, and began to read.

Monday, 13th October

Dear Mum,

It's been a few months. I expect you've been wondering if I'm alive or dead. I think for a while I was wondering the same, but I'm here and I'm still breathing.

A lot has happened since I left.

At first, I drove for a long time. I passed through towns and cities, not wanting to stop in any. People were not what I needed then. I know you always say talking shares the load but I think I've burdened enough strangers with my troubles for now.

Anyway, I kept on driving until I ran out of road and came to the seaside. It's nice here. It's quiet.

The view from my window is of the ocean, which is grey-green, and the sky is charcoal and full of clouds and gulls. I don't think the sun reaches this far north, but then winter is not far from the door.

If you're wondering what I'm doing here, I can tell you I spend my time reading and thinking. In the mornings I go for long walks on the beach, which help to clear my head after nights of terrible dreams.

Yesterday, as the tide was going out, I saw something shining in the surf. It was a bottle with a letter inside!

Can you believe it?

The letter said, 'If you are reading these words you are truly blessed, for they have travelled the world to find you. Good things are coming your way.'

I'll write again soon.

C.

Elise clutched the letter to her chest. How was this possible? She examined the handwriting. It had been a long time but there was no mistaking her mother's unkempt scrawl.

Everything else was forgotten now. Uncle Edward, the shadow man; even Nana May was momentarily put to one side. She read through the letter again and it was like finding a missing piece of a well-worn jigsaw puzzle. She moved onto the next letter.

Wednesday, 21st April

Dear Mum,

It's been a long time since I said I'd write again. Winter has come and thankfully gone and now springtime is upon us. I'm not having the easiest time. I think I was at the seaside when I last wrote. It's difficult to remember. I know that I moved on from there after a while, staying in towns and places with names I'd never heard of. But they were too small and I couldn't breathe. I'm back in the city for now. I'm not at my old place so it's no good writing there. I thought maybe I should give you an address you can reach me at, but the truth is I'm finding it difficult to stay in one place for long enough.

I sold the car last month. I didn't get very much for it but a new friend of mine says he might be able to get me some work. I'm waiting to hear about that.

I've wanted to talk to you about things. I almost called the other day but I was afraid one of the children might answer. Things are difficult. I can't sleep any more without dreaming of him. I wonder how it's possible that you knew nothing for so long when you were just across the hall.

Sometimes I wonder what life would be like if things had gone differently. I wonder who I would be now. I wonder if Sebastian and Elise would have even made it into this sick, sad world. It's a pity for them that they did.

C.

Memories of the city came flooding back. Her mother had returned there! She had been just a few hours' drive away and had not thought to visit her children, even for the day. Disappointment seeped through Elise's veins but was lost in the sadness that wept from Catherine's words. Even though the letter was more than three years old and events had long since passed, Elise worried for her. She had to sell her car. She had little money. She was tormented by nightmares. Rage boiled Elise's insides. Perhaps she should wait for Uncle Edward to come, she thought. Then, she could seek vengeance for the things he had done.

The world turned upside down and Elise held onto the bed with all her strength as she remembered her mother's words: "I can't sleep any more without dreaming of him. I wonder how it's possible that you knew nothing for so long when you were just across the hall."

Nana had known after all. And yet she had allowed him into her home and into her grandchildren's lives—lives he had infected with his filth, his dirt. The letter slipped from Elise's fingers and sailed down to the floor. The cracks in her heart widened, growing down to its foundations. Pieces fell away into darkness and then the whole thing was collapsing, finally gone.

Nana May had lied to Elise. She had endangered her grandchildren by allowing her son to come near them.

'Why, Nana? Why?'

No longer able to hold back her tears, Elise picked up the next letter. There was no date, no signature. This was no mere letter. This was anguish. This was fury. This was an open, festering wound that refused to heal.

You bitch! You liar! You let your bastard son ruin me before you called him off. I hope you fucking burn!

'It's not true!' Elise cried out.

How could Nana May have known and yet still acknowledge her son? It was too disgusting to contemplate. Throwing the letter down, she moved onto the next. And caught dwindling hope in her hand.

Tuesday, 1st August

Mum,

I expect this letter will be greeted with much shock and surprise, as it's been more than two years since I wrote.

I can only imagine the grief and worry I've caused and I'm sorry. I'm sure by now the kids have well and truly forgotten who I am, and who could blame them? They must look so different, so grown up. I bet they're as tall as buildings! I don't know what they think of me, or if they even think of me at all. But lately, they are all I can think about.

I think about the lives they've led and the terrible times they've been through. I think about what a terrible mother I've been.

I hope that one day they might forgive me for the life I gave them. I know I can't forgive myself. But they must be happier with you. You've shown them more love than I ever could.

Two years is a long time. Too long to write down in a single letter. I will tell you that I have been to the brink and back many times. I will tell you that I have seen things I never wanted to see and things that I needed to.

I will tell you that my head is a lot clearer these days, and that each day is new and exciting. Bad times do still visit me and my dreams are far from peaceful, but I'm getting help now.

I think that if I were meant to die because of all that's passed, I would not be sitting here today, writing this letter to you. I think then, I am meant to live, and to see you and my beautiful children again.

Your Catherine.

P.S. The photograph is of me at the promenade, taken last month. I wanted to show you that I'm doing much better. To show you who I could be.

Elise picked up the photograph. It was true. Her mother looked happier than she ever remembered seeing her. And she wanted to see her children again! She still loved them. She had called them beautiful.

'Sebastian!' Elise cried as she pulled out the next letter. 'Come here now!'

Sunday, 17th December

Dear Mum,

I hope you're well. Christmas is almost here and I wanted to send money so you can buy extra presents for the children. You don't have to tell them they're from me. I can imagine the house is all decorated and you have a nice tree in the living room. I was reading that you have heavy snowfall this year. I bet the children are excited, although I expect Elise is old enough to have worked out the truth about Santa by now.

I don't think I'll be celebrating much as I've found a job in the city and will be working over the festive season. It's nothing special but the money is okay. Soon I'll be able to afford my own place again and that makes me very happy. I'm tired of sleeping on friends' floors. I'm getting there, Mum. I'm starting to feel clean. Merry Christmas.

Catherine.

'Sebastian! Get here now!'

Elise giggled and rocked on the bed as her eyes pored over her mother's words. Whatever transpired in those missing two years had had an extraordinary effect. Her mother was getting better. She had a job and money and soon, she would have a place to live. She was happy and most importantly, she was still thinking about her children.

Elise thought about last Christmas and tried to remember the gifts she'd received from Nana May. There had been a new dress, new shoes and a doll to add to the mounting collection that sat on her bedroom shelf. She had come to an age where dolls were no longer of interest, but Nana May had either chosen to ignore her granddaughter's growing maturity or had passed it by unnoticed. Elise wondered if this was the gift that her mother's money had been used to buy.

Looking up at the shelf, she found the doll that had been given to her that Christmas. It looked like all the other dolls sitting there— slim, blonde and frighteningly happy. It was not the kind of gift she hoped Nana May would have chosen on such a special (and secret) occasion. Then she smiled, remembering the book of fairy tales.

Nana had spent her whole adult life telling stories to her children and to her grandchildren. She had encouraged her daughter to do the same, and Catherine had done so on her happier days. Elise remembered evenings when she had lain in bed, stunned and elated to find her mother perched by her side, reading from the book of tales given to her by Nana May. That book had been left behind with the rest of Elise's life the day she had come to her grandmother's house. The book she had been given last Christmas was a reminder of those rare moments, a secret message that told her never to forget.

There was one unread letter remaining.

Wednesday, 14th March

Dear Mum,

I never meant to leave it so long before writing. Christmas left me with a broken heart and I lost myself for a while. Do you think I'll ever feel normal again? I think about it all the time. My heart tells me to keep fighting but my head is tired. I think about all the terrible things I've done. I think about all the hatred and anger I have vented upon the world. I wonder if I was born bad and if that is why my life has turned out so. I wonder if I deserve all that has happened to me.

Lately, I've been missing you and the children too much. It's been almost four years since I left. How I long to see you all again but I am full of shame. How will I ever face Sebastian and Elise? I gave them lives of misery. I took their smiles away. I disposed of my children like pieces of rubbish. Me. Their mother. I did that.

Will there ever come a day when I can throw caution to the wind and turn up at your door, with hope of salvaging some sort of relationship with you all? It would be nice to hope I could find it in me to do that.

I love you all,

Catherine.

There was little need for Elise to search for more hidden letters. Her mother's words dripped with finality. Catherine was saying goodbye.

How does one person carry so much sadness? Elise wondered. In both arms of course. Perhaps her mother was not saying goodbye forever—she had, after all, signed off by saying she hoped to return one day. She had used the word "hope".

There was another possibility swimming through the other thoughts in Elise's head. It stayed low, cutting through the shadows. She's dead, it said. She killed herself. Gathering the letters together, Elise laid them out beside her feet. She picked up the photograph, looked at it one last time and placed it on top of the letters.

There were too many thoughts in her head, all fighting for her attention, all demanding to be heard. Thoughts too adult in their nature for the contemplation of a child. Yet they persisted, wearing her down until pain ripped through to her temples. Elise was twelve years old, almost thirteen, and already she felt as if she had lived her life twice over.

As she stumbled out of her bedroom and headed towards the stairs, a hundred homogeneous voices deafened her ears. The throb in her head intensified, spreading from her head to her neck.

'Nana,' she moaned, grasping the stair rail. 'I don't feel good.'

She pushed her feet forward and the stairs seemed to change angles. Painful spasms tore through her chest and she cried out. The voices barraged her consciousness, until she no longer heard words but a steady, deafening roar.

'Nana!' she cried. 'Please, help me!'

Above the roar, a single voice could be heard. At first, she thought it was her grandmother answering her plea. Then, as the din began to fade, she realised it was Sebastian. He was talking to someone, perhaps to Nana May.

Elise pushed herself down a step, willing the cacophony of thoughts into a whisper. Sebastian's words became clearer, and a new surge of pain drove deep into the centre of Elise's brain. Sebastian was not talking to Nana May. Nana May was dead. Sebastian was talking on the telephone. He was talking to Uncle Edward.

'Yes, Uncle Edward,' he said, his voice small and guilt-riddled. 'No, Uncle Edward. You just need to come.'

On the stairs, Elise's entire body went limp.

'Oh, Sebastian,' she mumbled as the world fell into darkness. 'You really are an idiot.'

Chapter 27

Her mother's voice was calling to her, floating through the air like a faraway song caught on a breeze. 'Wake up, Elise. Wake up now.'

In the back seat, Elise opened one eye. 'Are we here?'

'Almost. Just a little further to go.'

Catherine sat in the driver's seat, her hands gripping the wheel as the engine purred. They were at the mouth of the lane, the car unmoving. Elise pulled herself up and stared at her mother's reflection in the rear-view mirror.

'Where's Sebastian?'

'Who?'

'Sebastian. My brother. He should be here.'

Catherine shrugged. 'Oh, him. You shouldn't worry about him.'

'What do you mean?'

'He went away,' her mother replied. 'He doesn't need you anymore.'

The girl pulled her knees up to her chest. She looked out of the passenger window to see that the woods were on fire. Flames licked at the tall trees. Putrid black smoke curled around their trunks. A fox darted from the undergrowth, its copper coat ablaze.

'That's taken me by surprise,' Nana May said, clicking her tongue. Her voice startled Elise. She hadn't noticed her grandmother sitting beside her.

'The fire?' Catherine asked.

May shook her head. 'Even a fool knew that was on its way. I'm talking about Sebastian. He was always such a needy boy, but now look at him. What are you going to do, Elise?'

'I don't know.'

'I think you do.'

'She doesn't,' Catherine sighed. 'She's missing something.'

Nana May cackled. 'Isn't that the truth!'

Wind blew up through the woodland, lifting the fire from the ground and up to the treetops. Birds screamed as flames engulfed them. They fell from branches like burning rocks. Roots tore up from the earth. A large oak toppled and smashed across the lane.

'Oh dear!' Nana exclaimed. 'Can't go that way now. You'll have to walk.'

Elise turned full circle in the back seat, observing the surrounding inferno.

'I can't do that!' she squealed. 'It's too dangerous!'

'A little danger's good for the soul!'

Elise looked up to see Uncle Edward sitting in the passenger seat, next to her mother. Nana May was gone. Rage erupted inside the girl.

'Get out of here!' she screamed at him. 'Stay away from my mother!'

Uncle Edward laughed and ran a hand through his black, lacquered hair.

'I can't stay away,' he said. 'She won't let me.'

His hand moved down to his lap and across to Catherine. Then his fingers were running up over her knee, disappearing beneath the hem of her skirt and travelling along her inner thigh.

'That's not the truth,' Catherine giggled.

'No,' said Uncle Edward, bringing his hand higher still. 'It's not.'

Flames had reached the edges of the lane and were now burning their way in between the potholes. Tendrils of smoke searched for a way into the car. Another tree fell, then another. Elise tore her gaze away from the front of the car and covered her face with her arm.

'Stop it!' she wailed. 'Leave her alone!'

Something was touching her. She uncovered her face to see that Uncle Edward was no longer sitting in the front of the car but sitting right beside her, his hand on her knee.

'Don't be scared,' he said, exposing spiny teeth. 'It only hurts the first time.'

Elise screamed. The passenger door swung open and hands took her by the shoulders, dragging her from the car. Elise landed on the ground, the air punched out of her lungs. Flames lapped at her feet. Heat seared her skin. The cries of burning trees were all around.

'Get up!' Sebastian shouted. 'You have to get up!'

Elise sat up with a shriek. She was no longer sitting on the hard stone of the lane but on the soft carpet of her bedroom floor. Sebastian knelt over her with lines of worry creasing his brow.

'Am I awake now?' she asked him.

Sebastian nodded. He sat back on his heels. 'Are you all right? I thought you were . . . I couldn't wake you up.'

Elise pulled her knees up to her chest and wrapped her arms around them. The light in the room had changed to a dusty watermelon pink and from where she sat, she could see the sun setting at the corner of her window.

'What time is it?'

Sebastian looked at the alarm clock sitting next to Elise's bed.

'Nearly nine.'

Outside, the clouds were melting into rivers of blue and red, and the light in the room changed again. The sun flickered as it began its descent behind the tree line. The first stars of the evening winked at the watching children.

'I did something,' Sebastian said.

Elise nodded. 'I know. He's probably left already.'

'Are you angry with me?'

'I was,' Elise said. 'But not anymore.'

Sebastian let out an enormous sigh. 'Good.'

He looked at the piles of clothes sitting on the bed and the big suitcase that sat next to them. He couldn't understand how running away was going to help them. It would only serve to complicate their already troubled lives. He looked down and saw the photograph of his mother smiling at him from the floor.

'Where did you get this?' he asked, his breath snatched away.

'It was inside my case along with those letters. Nana must have put them there.'

Sebastian spied the letters, picked them up and shuffled them in his hands. 'I don't understand. Who are the letters from?'

'Mum.'

'Don't be daft.'

Elise stood and padded over to the window. The sun's blazing crown was all that remained on the horizon. Clouds were reforming, rolling in across the sky like great curtains. They thickened and grew dark with rain.

'She's been writing letters since she left. Nana kept it a secret from us.'

'Nana wouldn't—'

'Read them if you don't believe me. There are some things you're not going to like.'

Elise took the letters from Sebastian, placed them in chronological order and handed them back. Sebastian stared at the envelopes in his hands. He took out the first letter and began to read, stopping to reread difficult words and whole sentences when their meanings escaped him. When he was finished he looked up at Elise, who was standing at the window watching the last light of the day. He wanted to ask questions about the parts that confused him, but his sister was lost to him, submerged in her own thoughts. He opened the next letter and in the failing light, tried to understand his mother's words as best as he could.

'She's gone back to the city?'

'Keep reading,' Elise muttered. 'That letter was written a long time ago.'

'Who is she dreaming about?'

'Keep reading.'

The third letter didn't take long to read. At the window, Elise watched mounting horror crawl over her brother's face.

'Do you see now?' she asked. 'Do you see what you've done?'

The letter shook in Sebastian's hands. He read it again, over and over, the words hammering nails into his mind.

'I don't—' he said, his voice wavering. 'I don't know what it means.'

Elise pressed her forehead against the windowpane and stared down at the garden. Blades of grass parried one another. Flower petals fluttered in the new wind. Shadows grew long and wide, until they merged into one to become the darkness of night.

'It means I told you the truth,' she said. 'It means we have to leave soon because Uncle Edward is coming for us.'

The letter slipped from Sebastian's hand.

384

'She didn't write for another two years,' she told him. 'But when she did, she was much happier. She got a job in the city last Christmas and was saving up to get a place to live. She wanted to see us but she got sad again.'

'Why?'

'Because of Uncle Edward. Because of what he did to her. She says she was a bad mother and it's true, she was. We're her children and she left us behind. I've been so angry with her all this time but I don't think I can be any more. I knew why she was so sad and crazy, Sebastian, but I never knew <u>how</u> sad she was.

Nana was right. Our mother didn't want to hurt us anymore. How could she get better when she was worrying about you and me? She had to leave us. She had to.'

Sebastian sat on the floor for a long time. The world no longer made sense to him. His mother was gone, his grandmother had died just days ago, and he and his sister had been left alone. Now, even though he could not contemplate how or why, he had learned the one person whom he had thought could lift him and Elise from this pit of horrors was the person who had put them there. He slumped against the side of the bed.

The world made no sense because the world was a lie.

Elise sat down beside him and ran fingers through his hair. He rested his head against her shoulder.

'Uncle Edward is bad,' he said.

'And Nana May knew all about it,' she replied. 'And I don't understand it all either, but I think we can't know the whole story because if we did, then that would make Nana May a bad person too.'

'Nana May would never hurt us.'

'Never ever. But we can't stay to find out what really happened because Uncle Edward is coming here now.'

Sebastian gripped Elise's arm. 'I didn't tell him about Nana May. I was going to but I got scared. I just told him he had to come because it was important, and he said he didn't know what I was talking about and he asked me what was wrong and I wouldn't tell him, and he said he was worried now and I put the phone down. Then, I think he called back because the phone kept ringing but I didn't answer it. I went and watched TV and looked out of the window for the shadow man but I couldn't see him. Then, I called Uncle Edward again and there was no answer. I thought he must be coming and then I came upstairs and found you.'

Sebastian took a breath. 'Elise?'

'Yes?'

'Is Uncle Edward really a bad person?'

Elise nodded. 'Yes, he is.'

They were sitting in darkness now, holding hands. High above the house, a battalion of clouds swarmed the sky, blotting out the moon and stars. They swelled to bursting point, splitting at their seams. The first drops of rain spattered against the window.

'We need to go,' said Elise. She jumped to her feet and switched on the bedroom light. Both children shielded their eyes and waited a few moments for their sight to adjust. Elise began to fill the suitcase with the clothes she had gathered. Sebastian remained where he was, blinking away black spots from his vision.

'Where are we going to go?' he asked.

'The city. I thought that might be a good place to start.'

'We don't like the city.'

'I know, but Mum might be there. She said in her letter that she wanted to see us but she was too ashamed. If we find her, we can show her that we don't care about that anymore. Maybe she won't feel so sad. Maybe she'll be ready to take us back.'

'You think so?'

Elise nodded as she put the last of the clothes inside the suitcase. 'It's not as if we have anybody else to go to. She'll have to take us back.'

'But how will we find her?'

'We could go to the last place we lived,' she said. 'She might be back there again. Or we could go and see Aileen. I bet she knows where Mum is. They were best friends.'

Clouds tore open in the dark sky and a huge torrent of rain plummeted towards the earth. It hit the house hard, battering the roof and windows. It smashed into the yard and shot gravel bullets through the air. The cats raced for cover, screeching as they ran. Sebastian stood up and moved over to the window. He thought about Red, and worry fell down with the rain. His kitten was out there somewhere, lost in the woods.

'We can't leave the cats,' he told Elise, raising his voice above the din of the rainfall. 'There'll be no one to feed them.'

'We can open all the cans we have and leave them in the garden,' she replied. 'After they've eaten them they'll have to catch their own food. Cats are supposed to be hunters, you know.'

'But what about Red?'

'He'll come back. The other cats will look after him.'

'But I don't want to leave him. He's mine.'

'We don't have time to find him. I'm sorry Sebastian, but we have to go.'

The boy watched the rain cascading down into the garden. Leaves and plants were being torn apart by the force of its descent.

'How are we going to get to the city?' he asked Elise. 'We don't have any money or a car, and we can't drive even if we did have one.'

'There's money in the house. Nana puts it in a jar every week, after she comes back from the post office. She hides the jar at the back of the top cupboard, next to the stove. There's always a big bunch of notes inside it. We can use that money to take the bus into town, and then we can buy tickets for the train and get to the city that way. But if it's nine o'clock already we're going to miss the last bus in. We'll have to walk.'

Sebastian turned away from the window. 'But that will take ages and it's raining. Can't we ask someone for a lift?'

'No. We don't want anyone from the village to see us. We can take a shortcut through the woods. We'll come out a few miles from the town and we can walk through the fields from there.'

'But we're going to get soaked!'

Elise nodded. 'I'll find our raincoats.'

'But what about the shadow man? He's probably outside right now. I don't want to go outside if he's there! He'll get me!'

Sebastian began to sob again. Elise was surprised that he still had tears left to expel.

'I don't think he'll be hanging out in that rain,' she said, trying her best to sound reassuring. 'Besides, whoever it is would be stupid to come back again.'

'Why?'

'Because we know not to go anywhere without each other now. It'll be two against one. He can't get both of us at the same time, can he?'

Sebastian didn't look convinced.

'We'll be careful,' Elise said. 'We'll keep our eyes open. I'll bring torches so we'll be able to see if anyone is sneaking up on us, okay?'

'I don't know. I guess.'

Elise nodded. 'I have to go and get some things.'

* * *

She left him with instructions to pack toothbrushes, toothpaste and towels, then made her way downstairs.

The hallway was steeped in darkness and she fumbled along the wall for the light switch. She thought about the shadow man. If he were watching the house just as Sebastian thought, putting all the lights on would give him a better view. Her fingers withdrew from the switch. Rain hammered against the front door. Elise thought about the journey ahead. Panic attacked her and she struggled to fight it away. She had planned as far as getting to the train station. After that, she and Sebastian would be relying on hope and good fortune—things that had evaded them for most of their young lives.

Pushing the kitchen door halfway open, the girl peered into the darkness. From here, she could see rain hitting the windows and the glass panes of the back door. It was difficult to make out the garden beyond.

Closing the door behind her, she moved across the floor until she could see through the windows. Relieved to see that the rain was the garden's only unwelcome guest, Elise moved towards the cupboards. Using a stool to stand on, she found Nana May's money jar. It was large and heavy and half-filled with coins. A roll of notes was stuffed on top. Elise heaved the jar onto the table.

A large, hulking shadow filled the glass of the back door. Two white eyes burned into her. Elise shrieked, slammed into the table and tipped the jar. It balanced on its bottom edge before standing upright again.

Elise returned her gaze to the door.

The eyes were gone.

She stood for a moment, listening to the rain and the thud of her heartbeat, hoping that the apparition she'd just seen was born from panicked imagination.

Unscrewing the cap of the jar, she fished out the roll of notes. She had no idea how much was there, but judging by the thickness of the roll, she assumed it was a lot—at least enough to get them to the city, to feed them and to pay for a place to stay if they needed it. The weight of the coins would slow them down, so Elise screwed the cap back onto the jar and returned it to the cupboard.

Being in the kitchen reminded her that they hadn't eaten in hours. She was not hungry at all but she would need strength for the journey ahead.

Gathering together bread, cheese and butter, she made rough rounds of sandwiches. As she worked, she glanced out into the garden. The rain had eased off a little but showed no sign of relenting any time soon. With the moon smothered by clouds it was hard to see beyond a few metres of the garden. The trees of the woodland were cloaked in blackness and Elise hoped that they were the only things hidden by the night.

The shadow man.

She could not let herself think about him because to do so made her tremble so forcefully that the knife in her hand clattered against the kitchen table. To think of him brought up all kinds of frightening questions. Who was he? What did he want? Why did he take the outhouse key? How many times had he been inside the house?

She wondered if he had crept about while she and Sebastian slept. She wondered if he had come into their rooms and watched the rise and fall of their chests.

The knife slipped from her fingers and hit the table. She snatched it up and finished making the sandwiches, switching her thoughts to her mother and the reconciliation they were going to have. The possibility of not finding Catherine did not occur to her for a single second. How could they not find her? Their mother was now the only hope Sebastian and Elise had left. With the sandwiches made and stacked on a plate, with a fat roll of banknotes tucked away inside her pocket, Elise stole through the darkness of the house to return to the light upstairs.

Sebastian remained where she had left him, standing at the window and staring out into the night with unblinking eyes.

'I've made sandwiches,' she said to the back of his head. 'Cheese ones. Eat some of them and then put on warm clothes. Did you get the things from the bathroom?'

Sebastian shook his head.

'I'll get them. Start eating.'

She ducked out of the room. Sebastian turned away from the window and stared at the plate of sandwiches sitting on the bed.

His stomach growled at the sight. Sitting down, he picked up a sandwich and began to eat. His head felt strange, as if it were filled with a billion bubbles all bursting at once. He devoured the sandwich with three large bites and picked up another. He looked up at Elise's shelf of dolls. A row of pretty faces smiled at him.

Elise returned carrying toothbrushes, toothpaste and towels. She dumped them into the suitcase, flipped its lid closed and snapped the clasps together. Setting the case onto the floor, she took its place on the bed and picked up a sandwich. They sat there for a while, eating in silence, Sebastian staring at dolls and Elise willing the rain to stop. When the plate was empty, they glanced at each other and then they both looked away.

'Ready?' asked Elise.

'Uh-huh,' said Sebastian.

'Let's go.'

Chapter 28

They put on dark clothes and hiking boots that Nana May had bought them for long country walks. Elise turned off the upstairs lights. Now the entire house was as black as the night outside. As they descended the stairs, Elise could hear Sebastian's frightened breaths coming fast and heavy beside her. She carried the suitcase in her left hand, and although it was light, it was awkward to manoeuvre, banging against the wall and bumping along the steps. She frowned, thinking about the burden of carrying a suitcase through the pitch-black woodland.

As they reached the bottom of the stairs, Sebastian grabbed Elise's free hand.

'I'm scared,' he whispered.

Elise squeezed his hand. 'I'll get the torches.'

There was a small door cut into the side of the stairs. Elise dropped the suitcase and moved towards it, pulling Sebastian behind her like a carriage to her train. She liked this door. It reminded her of Alice finding the door to Wonderland. She opened it and felt around. A few seconds later, the cupboard filled with light. Elise passed a torch to Sebastian.

'Hold this.'

Sebastian directed the light back into the cupboard. Searching for a second torch, Elise spied a hook where rope had once hung. Images of Nana May tied to the rocking chair flashed in her mind.

'I can't find another one. We'll have to share.'

Sebastian shone the beam in her face. 'I want to hold it.'

'Okay but switch it off until we're out of the yard,' she replied, pushing the torch away. 'Just in case.'

'In case of what?'

Elise pressed the torch switch, and the children were plunged into darkness once more. Sebastian knew the answer to his own question: In case of the shadow man. He found Elise's hand and held onto it. She pulled him towards a door that lay between the living room and the kitchen. Inside, a multitude of coats and jackets hung from hooks, with several more layers thrown on top. It looked as if all the coats in the world had been squeezed into one small space, and that pulling out the wrong one would result in an unstoppable textile avalanche.

'Torch,' Elise commanded, and the cupboard filled with light. She waded in, removing layer after layer, letting the garments fall to the floor until she held two matching blue raincoats in her arms.

'Switch it off.'

Sebastian switched off the torch, then struggled with his raincoat.

'What do we do now?'

Elise took in a deep breath. 'We leave.'

Pulling Sebastian behind, she picked up the suitcase and marched to the front door.

Sebastian waited as Elise pulled back the two iron bolts. Nothing made sense and everything was terrifying, but he was convinced that as long as he held onto his sister's hand and had the torch to guide him, he would be safe.

The sensation of bubbles bursting inside his head returned. It was a strange feeling—a collision of calm and fear, of clarity and confusion. It made him dizzy and he wanted to sit down.

Stepping out from behind Elise, he saw the front yard yawning like a great mouth. The rain fell, fizzing as it hit the gravel. Great trees bowed in and out of shadows as the wind whipped through their branches. The lane that led to the road seemed to lie a mile away, invisible in the distance.

Sebastian looked over his shoulder, into the darkness of the house. He wondered if he would ever return here. He wondered what Uncle Edward would say when he found the place abandoned and the children gone.

He stopped thinking.

The place in his head for thoughts about Uncle Edward was torn and battered, no longer recognisable. It was the twisted wreck of a car. It was the ghost of a bombed building. Any happy memory that had once lived there had been snatched by unseen hands and dragged down, way beneath the foundations.

'Put your hood up, Sebastian,' Elise whispered. Then, they were stepping out into the yard.

Once they had reached the lane, they were to cut through the woodland until they were close to the road. When the trees gave way to fields, they would take their chances crouched down behind hedgerows and stone walls, following the route of the road until they came to the town.

They had covered half of the yard already and were coming up to the old shell of the pick-up truck. Raindrops played a lonely melody on its rooftop as they passed by.

Elise quickened her pace. The suitcase was already weighing her down and she wondered how long it would be before it became impossible to carry.

Sebastian struggled to keep up. As he was dragged along, he looked behind, whimpering at the distance growing between himself and his home.

They had almost reached the trees. The darkness of the woodland reached out to greet them. Sebastian's index finger hovered above the torch switch.

'I don't want to go in there!' he howled, digging his boots into the ground.

'Quiet!' Elise hissed. She broke into a run, lifting him off his feet. Darkness snatched the children up in both hands and dragged them into the woodland.

Terror consumed Sebastian. He spun around, trying to wrench free from Elise's grasp. He screamed and wailed, pulling towards the house like a panicked dog on a leash. Darkness stopped him at every turn, disorienting him. He fell to his knees and vomited on the ground.

'Sebastian, please!' Elise begged. 'I can't do this without you! I need you to stay calm.'

The night was all encompassing and it swallowed the world whole, forbidding her to see her brother's face. High above, the rain hit the canopies, sounding like gentle applause. The sound calmed her. She squeezed Sebastian's hand and, amid his tears, he squeezed back.

'Have you still got the torch?' she asked.

A blinding flash answered her question.

Elise took Sebastian's arm and directed the beam towards the ground. A soft, golden glow balled upwards, allowing enough light for the children to pick each other out in the darkness.

A circle of thick tree trunks surrounded them, and in the eerie light they looked like the legs of giant, fantastical beasts.

Elise stared at Sebastian. In the torchlight, he was a weeping ghost, transparent against the pitch-black night.

'You have to stop crying,' she told him. 'We don't want anyone to hear us or we'll get caught.'

'But I'm scared!'

'I know. I'm scared too, but if we get through the woods as fast as we can, then we won't be frightened any more. We'll be on our way to find our mother. Think about it, Sebastian. Think what it will be like when we find her. She'll be so surprised!'

Sebastian looked up. He wiped his nose and eyes with the back of his hand, shooting torch beams through the trees.

'We'll be okay,' Elise nodded. 'Just keep hold of my hand and shine the torch down and in front of us. Don't shine it through the trees. Someone will see it if you do.'

'We forgot to feed the cats,' Sebastian squealed.

'The cats will be okay too. There are lots of mice and birds around for them to eat. They just have to practise their hunting skills, that's all.'

'But Red!'

'I told you. He'll come back and the others will take good care of him. Now, come on. We have to go.'

Elise swapped her carrying hand with her holding hand and the suitcase became more manageable.

As they advanced through the trees, Sebastian did his best to shine the torch beam at the correct angle and distance. His eyes were everywhere, searching the darkness for signs of the shadow man or any other threat that might creep up on him. A shrill cry of an unseen bird made his hand tremble with fear. The beam of the torch shot upwards, revealing a skeleton of bony branches.

'Keep the light down!' Elise hissed, her voice shaking with fright.

Sebastian concentrated and brought the torch down in time to see a thick bog blocking their path. Elise pulled him around it. Sounds invaded his ears—the pitter-patter of raindrops splashing against leaves and the surfaces of marsh pools; the squelch of wet mud as their boots sank into the ground; the desolate moan of the wind as it roamed through the trees.

There were other sounds—rustles from the under-growth, twigs snapping, strange animal cries—that filled Sebastian with such fear he thought he might vomit again. He blocked the sounds out, picturing the wonder and surprise that would light up his mother's face when she and her children were reunited.

Detouring around the bog had pushed them away from the lane and deeper into the woods. The ground was softer here and parts of it were flooded. The stench of dead water saturated the air. Elise crinkled up her nose and breathed through her mouth.

She was struggling with the suitcase. Her arm ached and Sebastian's poor direction of the torch beam meant that the case was continually bashing against unseen tree trunks and bushes. Elise thought about ditching it all together. There was enough money in the bundle of notes she'd taken from Nana May's jar to buy new clothes. But how much time would it take to find their mother? As long as that question remained unanswered, buying new clothes would be a waste of limited funds.

Wet from the thigh down and cold to her core, Elise ploughed on, the suitcase slamming into her side.

Above the woodland, the rain came to an end. Clouds parted and the moon appeared, spilling monochrome light onto the land. Stars glinted.

Elise looked up through a parting in the branches and saw an infinite black sky.

'Let's stop for a minute. My arm aches,' she said.

Sebastian dipped the torch so that the light bounced off the ground between the siblings' feet. He felt as if he had been dropped into a bath of ice-cold water.

'I can't feel my fingers,' he complained.

Elise looked down at their linked hands.

'I don't think we could let go now, even if we wanted to. We're stuck together forever!'

They both giggled and the sound of their laughter was a blanket of warmth and comfort.

'We can't be far from the road now,' Elise said. 'It will be easier then.'

She tugged on Sebastian's hand and they were on the move once more. The journey seemed a little easier now it had stopped raining. The wind had also dispersed, allowing some feeling to return to the children's extremities. Although they were still wet and cold, their spirits rose.

'Did you hear that?' Elise asked, stopping in her tracks.

Sebastian cocked his head. 'Hear what?'

'A car!' she replied. 'I heard a car go by.'

Pulling her brother along, Elise hurried in the direction of where she thought the sound had come from, then stopped still.

'Quick, give me the torch!'

'No!' Sebastian clutched the torch to his chest and sent a beam of light shooting skywards.

'Fine,' growled Elise, annoyed by how self-important he could be, even in the most imperative of situations. 'Point it over this way, straight ahead.'

Sebastian did as he was told. A few metres ahead, the trees thinned out and just beyond them, hidden by shadows, was the top of a stone wall.

'There!' Elise cried, jumping up and down with excitement. 'You see? The road's on the other side. All we have to do now is follow that wall along and we'll be in town before you know it!'

Sebastian shared his sister's relief. The trek through the woodland had terrified him, and although just a small circle of light was still all that stood between him and the dark, having the road alongside attached him to the world of people, making him feel secure.

'Mum's going to be so happy when she sees us,' he said, smiling.

Elise grinned. 'She won't believe her eyes!'

An explosion of noise erupted behind Sebastian.

He spun around, the torch cutting through the darkness.

Large, muscular hands reached out of the shadows, swooping down to lift the boy from his feet. The torch beam shot upwards, plunging the siblings in darkness.

Elise was knocked backwards. She screamed as she fell against the trunk of a tree, striking her head.

The suitcase burst open on the ground, expelling their clothes and their mother's letters.

Sebastian's hand was wrenched from his sister's grasp.

Elise sat up to see him disappearing into the night, the torch waving in his hand. He grew smaller as he was carried through the trees. The torch beam danced further and further away until it was a mere pinprick. Sebastian's screams became an echo.

Then there was silence. Then there was darkness.

Chapter 29

Elise jumped to her feet and screamed Sebastian's name. Silence answered her. She charged forward, narrow shafts of moonlight illuminated spots here and there, but not enough to light a clear path.

She ran, stumbling through prickly undergrowth that tore at her trousers and scratched her skin. Her mind raced alongside, careering through a hundred horrifying images of the shadow man. He had taken Sebastian!

Elise lowered her head and, tucking her arms close to her sides, increased her speed. She had to get him back. She had to! Her shoulder glanced off a tree, sending her spinning in a half-circle to fall sideways into a thick pool of mud. Pain ripped through her body.

'No!' Her voice bellowed up to the sky. Her feet slipped from beneath her as she tried to stand. 'No! No!'

Pulling up onto her hands and knees, Elise dragged herself out of the mud. Her shoulder throbbed. Her head hurt. Tiny white dots peppered her vision. She ran on. Thick clots of mud weighed her down. She pulled off her raincoat as she moved, throwing it into the darkness.

The spiny points of a holly bush whistled past her eye and scored her neck. She raised a hand to protect her face and skin was ripped from her knuckles as she collided with a low-hanging branch. She lurched forward, snapping the branch clean off. Her foot caught in exposed roots and she slammed into the thick trunk of an oak tree. Tears came.

'Please!' she shrieked. 'Give me back my brother!'

Sliding to her knees, Elise clung to the tree trunk, hugging its wet mossy bark as she let out great braying sobs.

Something glinted at the corner of her eye.

The torch lay at her feet, its lens reflecting moonlight.

Elise stopped crying.

She snatched up the torch and flicked the switch. Light burst out and she brandished it like a weapon. Any weakness she felt was vanquished.

She ran, ducking and weaving through the woodland, swinging the torch beam from side to side.

The watery bog she and Sebastian had narrowly avoided was up ahead. She circled it, breathing hard. She shone the torch to her left and, through the trees, she could see the lane that joined the house to the road.

With a startling cry, Elise hurled herself out of the woodland and landed in between the potholes.

She didn't need to rest or catch her breath; adrenaline was crackling through her body like electricity. She bolted down the lane and the yard swung up in front of her. Elise stopped still. Light filtered out from Nana May's bedroom window. For a second, she wondered if Uncle Edward had come, but his car was not sitting in the yard. The shadow man had taken Sebastian home.

Switching off the torch, Elise sank down to a crouch and moved towards the side of the house. Nana's window was like an eye, its gaze roaming over the yard. Slipping under its radar, Elise reached her destination and slid up against the wall.

Cats appeared, whining as they rubbed themselves against her ankles. She kicked them away and they stalked off into shadows, swinging their tails.

It was quiet then, and the girl panicked, petrified that the shadow man was inflicting all kinds of unthinkable cruelties upon her brother.

Uncle Edward was going to be here soon, and whatever tortures the shadow man didn't impress upon the children, he most certainly would. If she could get inside the house, she could call the police and then neither the shadow man nor Uncle Edward would be able to hurt them.

Calling the police would mean being found out. It would mean being put into care, but if that kept Sebastian away from these monsters, then so be it.

Finding her mother no longer seemed so important. She had risked Sebastian's well-being too many times. How strange, she thought, when her sole purpose had been to protect it.

The outhouse was just ahead of her. For a solitary moment, she had forgotten all about the building and what it contained. Elise covered her mouth and nose, protecting her senses from the stink that gathered there. The smell was not as pungent as it had been that morning and she was glad for it. There were no words in her vocabulary to describe the remorse she felt for putting Nana May inside that building. But her remorse needed no words—it had pain instead. Elise hurried past, then drew in a horrified gasp.

The door to the outhouse was wide open.

Elise raised the torch. Her thumb pushed down on the switch.

The inside of the outhouse lit up as if it were day. A small pile of coal rode up one corner. One of the cats lay dozing on top and it opened a slanted eye, grumbling at the intrusion. On the floor, scuff marks and scrapes made patterns in the coal dust. Among these were boot prints far bigger than any child's. Nana May and her chair were gone.

The torch slipped from the girl's hand and bounced off the gravel, shattering the bulb inside. Elise ran into the garden and ducked down amongst the rose bushes. The kitchen light was on. The back door was ajar. He had taken her body! Why had he done that? For one sickening moment, she convinced herself that Nana May would be propped up at the kitchen table, waiting for her return. She stared up at the kitchen door, just as a tall shadow moved behind it, making the light in the garden flicker.

A low whine came from behind her head. One of the cats sat on its haunches, its eyes glowing in the darkness.

'Go away!' she whispered. The cat remained where it was, griping and complaining. What was it with these damned cats? Thoughts derailed and collided inside the girl's head.

Her subconscious was trying to tell her something. Something about the cats and the shadow man. There was a link between them, but what was it? What <u>was</u> it? Then she knew.

'I lied to him!' she gasped. 'I told him one of our cats had gone missing and the next day one of them did!'

Elise was horrified. "Something's gone and died in there", those were the words he had used, like he already knew.

It was him. It had to be. But why?

Her legs quaking beneath her, Elise jumped to her feet and charged towards the kitchen door.

'Mr Elliot!' she shrieked. 'I don't know why you're doing this but you leave my brother alone!'

The man standing in her kitchen was not Tom Elliot. Nor was it Mr Tonkin, or Mr

Brooke, or any other man that had made her list of potential suspects.

The man in her kitchen was a stranger.

He stood over six feet tall and was dressed in long, black, stinking rags that hung from his wiry frame like the shredded sails of a ghost ship. His lice-infested hair hung down to his shoulders in black matted clumps. A thick gorse bush of a beard covered most of his features and two razor-sharp cheekbones rose like mountains from it.

His eyes rolled in their sockets as he bore his rotting teeth like a rabid dog.

Elise opened her mouth to scream. She turned and fled through the kitchen door, out into the garden.

The shadow man came up behind her. His huge, dirty hands wrapped around her ribcage and he lifted her from the ground.

Elise screamed and kicked. She snatched handfuls of his lank hair and pulled with all her strength.

The shadow man laughed as he threw her over his shoulder and carried her back towards the house.

Chapter 30

Kicking the door shut, the shadow man slipped a hand inside his mass of rags and pulled out a key. He locked the door then dumped Elise on the floor, who scrambled backwards and slammed into the table.

'Thought you could outrun me, did you?' The shadow man's voice was deep and undulating and as ancient as the trees. His laughter boomed through the house.

Elise twisted herself around, putting the table between them. Her gaze shot to the open hallway door and back to the shadow man. Amused, he watched her.

'Where's my brother?' she demanded.

The shadow man smiled, observing the frightened girl before him. Her back was arched and her knees bent, ready to pounce in any direction that would lead to escape. Her eyes, wet with tears, jolted about in their sockets; two white orbs gleaming from a face slicked with mud.

'Where is he?' she asked, her voice quivering.

The shadow man nodded his head towards the ceiling. Elise bolted from the harbour of the table and dashed out into the darkened hallway. The shadow man did not follow. She hit the lights as she raced past, clearing the stairs in seconds.

'Sebastian!'

He answered in a voice shrill with hysteria. 'Elise! I'm here, in Nana's room. I can't get out!'

Elise saw the door handle move up and down. She pushed against the door, throwing her weight at it, but it would not open. Muffled cries came from the other side and she punched the door in frustration.

'It's locked!' she called.

'I'm scared, Elise! Let me out!'

There was a loud thud as Sebastian's body smashed against wood. The handle moved up and down. He threw himself at the door, again and again, screeching in terror.

'Stop it!' Elise shouted. 'You'll hurt yourself!'

A terrible thought struck her. 'Is it just you in there?'

'Yes, now get me out!'

'All right! But you need to calm down for me.'

She looked along the landing and wondered why the shadow man had not come for her. Dropping to her knees, she peered through the keyhole. She saw Sebastian walk away from the door and sit on the edge of Nana May's bed. His clothes were soiled and sodden. There was a deep cut above his right eye, where bruising was already discolouring his skin.

'Hang on, Sebastian,' Elise urged. 'I'll find a way to open the door.'

He looked up from the bed, and his eyes were empty and glazed, as if they had seen all they were ever going to see.

Getting to her feet, Elise darted into the bathroom and pulled the light cord. The first thing she saw was her own reflection, staring out from the cabinet mirror. She was a feral beast born of the woodland, moulded from the same cast as the shadow man. She opened the cabinet, ridding herself of the offending reflection, and peered inside. She growled, not knowing what she was looking for. The only way she was going to open the door was with the key, and the shadow man was in possession of that. But then an idea came back to her like a long-lost friend.

'I have to go downstairs now,' she whispered, returning to the door. 'I'm going to call the police. They'll come and arrest that man. They'll let you out.'

Through the keyhole, she saw Sebastian rise from the bed and come towards her. He knelt to meet her gaze.

'Don't leave me in here,' he begged.

'I can't get you out. That man must have the key.'

'Who is he, Elise? Why is he here?'

Elise looked over her shoulder. 'I don't know. But if I don't call the police he's going to hurt us both.'

'Where is he?'

'He's in the kitchen. Did he hurt you, Sebastian?'

'If you call the police they'll find out what we did. We'll be in so much trouble.'

'We're already in trouble, stupid. I won't be long.'

She turned to leave.

'Elise?'

'Yes?'

'I pissed myself.'

'Well, you needed a bath anyway.'

She headed towards the stairs, a ball of fear knotting in her stomach and reaching up to her chest and into her throat, choking the air from her lungs. Taking off her boots, Elise descended the steps one at a time, her feet silent against the carpet. When she reached the bottom, she ducked her head around and checked the kitchen door. She could see little at this angle, but she could hear the shadow man crashing about and raving to himself.

Elise stole across the hallway. The telephone sat on the bookshelf, next to the kitchen door. Her heart raced. She wondered how she could make the call without being seen. Then, she noticed the cord of the telephone hanging in the air. It had been cut in half.

'No!'

She had no more ideas, no more cunning plans. She was an empty vessel, no longer useful or required. Her fate was clear to her. Sebastian's too.

'There's no good in just standing there,' boomed the shadow man in his hollow voice. 'Bring yourself into the kitchen.'

Elise was frozen with fear. She tried to step back towards the staircase but her legs were like stone.

'Bring yourself into the kitchen!' the shadow man repeated, and there was such menace in his voice that she dared not disobey him. She shuffled her feet forward until she reached the doorway.

The shadow man had his back to her and was bent over, shovelling coal into the oven. She watched him drop the shovel onto the top of the oven and close the furnace door. He turned to face her.

'Don't want the fire going out now, do we?' he said, his smile revealing brown stumps and bloody gums. Elise felt sick in her stomach, yet she dared not remove her gaze from him for a second. The shadow man moved away from the fire. He didn't walk, she noted, but lurched, swinging his body forward with his long, sinewy arms, while dragging the rest of him behind.

'Why don't you come and sit down?'

It had not been a question. Elise shook her head. Tears slipped down her cheeks.

'Come and sit down,' he commanded, his eyes growing as black as the coal now crackling in the furnace.

Elise shuffled forward like a marionette manipulated by torturous hands. She reached the table and stood still. The shadow man loomed over her. He stank of the earth and the rain, of rotten leaves and decay, of misery and despair. To Elise, he was Death, standing in her kitchen, eager to squeeze the life from her hapless soul.

'Wh-Who are you?' she stammered.

'You don't know me?' he replied, and there was surprise in his voice.

Elise looked up at his frightening face. There was a familiarity there, something about his eyes.

'You should know me,' the shadow man said.

A memory struggled to free itself from Elise's mind.

'I don't.' Even as the words fell from her mouth, she knew they were a lie.

The shadow man pulled back a chair and sat down, then rested his hands on the table. His fingernails were encrusted with half-moons of dirt. His knuckles were battered and bruised.

As Elise stared at them, the memory pulled and twisted.

Then it tore away.

'I do know you!' she cried. 'I remember you sitting at this table! Nana gave you a meal and sent you on your way. You tried to steal her coal. She felt sorry for you because you were homeless.'

It was his eyes she remembered. He had been sitting at the table eating hot stew when Elise had entered the kitchen, thirsty for a glass of milk. He'd put down his spoon and had not stared at her, but into her, and his eyes had burned black like cinders.

'Go on to your bed,' Nana May had said, seeing the fear crawling over her granddaughter's features. 'There's nothing for you to worry about here.'

Elise had run all the way to her bedroom and hidden beneath the blankets. Too afraid to sleep, she had lain awake until morning had come.

'That was a long time ago,' Elise said to the shadow man. Invisible hands pushed her towards the table and into the chair opposite. 'Why have you come back?'

The shadow man looked at her. It was the same look he had given her that night in the kitchen, and it paralysed her even now.

'Can't come back from somewhere if you never went there in the first place,' the shadow man grinned.

Elise looked back at him, a chill running the length of her spine. 'What do you mean?'

'I've always been here. Watching you and your brother. Watching your Nana May. I've watched you help grandma baking her cakes. I've watched Sebastian playing with his cars in the yard. I've come into the house while you've all been asleep. Once, I even lay down next to you, on the floor beside your bed. Such a pretty girl when you're sleeping. All those worries floating away with your dreams.'

The shadow man leaned forward and seemed to double in size. Darkness glowered from the pits of his eyes.

'But can't do that anymore. Not now Grandma's dead. Not since you hid her away and forgot her like a dead star.'

'What have you done with her?' Elise couldn't listen to the words oozing from his lips.

The shadow man sucked on his rancid gums. 'What a nasty pair you are, treating Grandma like that. Took you in she did, when your own mum didn't want you. Gave you food and a roof and love to last you a lifetime. What a fine way to repay her!'

Elise sobbed. 'Tell me!'

The shadow man shook his head. 'Not for you to know.'

'How do you know about my mum?'

The shadow man smiled. There was not enough distance between her and this monster in her kitchen, and the closeness made her nauseous and faint.

'Please, let Sebastian go,' she moaned. The room spun around her. She looked up and saw the shadow man had split into three separate entities.

'No,' they said as one. 'Can't have you running away after what you've done. Wouldn't be fair.'

'I won't run. I'll stay. Just let him go.'

'Can't do that. We're all one happy family now. I'm going to take good care of both of you.'

Elise tried to stand up. Gravity pushed her back down. White spots flashed like fireworks in front of her eyes and then the world turned yellow.

'Please,' she muttered. 'I don't feel well.'

The shadow man sat back and shook his head. 'Nor did Grandma, and she died. I saw it. I saw the life go out of her. One minute she was baking cakes and the next she was gone.'

The words edged Elise back towards consciousness.

'You saw?'

The shadow man looked up and his eyes glinted with tears. They spilled over his face, painting pink streaks in the dirt.

'I hid in the trees and I watched her die. It was the saddest thing and it was the most beautiful thing. I wanted to go to her, to tell her how sorry I was, but she needed no apologies. She was smiling, content to be returning to heaven. Then, she was gone. You came along and when you saw her, you fell on the ground. Made your head bleed, it did. And I thought, this is an angel so full of love that her heart will surely break into pieces. But I was wrong. You're not full of love. You're full of darkness. Like me.'

Elise found the strength to stand.

'Give me the key to Nana's room.'

The shadow man let out waves of deep laughter that resounded through the kitchen and made overhanging cooking utensils shudder on their hooks. Elise shivered. There was something about the way his mouth curled as he laughed that was familiar.

His amusement vanished and was replaced by fire. He jumped up, tipping his chair, letting it clatter on the flagstones. Lurching around the table, he snatched the girl's face up in his hand and bent down until his eyes were level with hers. Elise choked on his stench. She stared into blackness.

'Perhaps I should lock you in with your brother. Let you starve to death. Would you like that? It would take days for you to die. You'd probably go mad, tear the flesh off each other's bones with your bare hands and swallow it down raw like animals. And when you were dead, I'd lock you up in the coal shed, just like you did to Grandma.'

Elise whimpered, shaking her head as she tried to wrench free. The shadow man tightened his grip, making her wince with pain. He brought up his other hand and ran long fingers through her hair. He leaned in and kissed her on both cheeks.

'Such a pretty girl,' he cooed. 'Such a pretty, pretty girl.'

'Please,' she begged through clenched teeth.

The shadow man released his grip on her jaw. Then his arms were swooping down and wrapping around her ribcage. He pulled Elise towards him, burying her face into his chest.

'And sweet too. Like sugar and spice.'

He released her from his hold. Elise stumbled backwards, retching and gasping for air.

'What are you going to do to us?' she cried.

The shadow man picked up his chair and sat back down at the table.

'I'm going to take good care of you.'

Elise backed away. 'I don't know what you mean.'

The shadow man smiled and she caught the curl of his mouth again.

'No one to look after you now that Grandma has gone,' he said. 'So I shall look after you. And I'll do a good job, you'll see.'

'You can't do that,' Elise replied, edging towards the hallway. 'My uncle is on his way here, right now. He's not going to let you do that.'

'Edward? He won't be here for another week.'

'Sebastian called him. He'll be here soon.'

Elise was in the doorway now. The shadow man's knowledge of her family frightened her. How long had he been watching them from the woodland? How many times had he been inside their house? How many times had he come into her room to brush his fingers against her cheek while she slumbered?

Elise squeezed the keys in her hand. She had delved deep into the shadow man's clothing when he had pulled her in for an embrace. The stink of his rags had brought her close to vomiting but she had held her breath and fumbled through holes and pockets, until she held a key in each hand. She did not know if either key belonged to the bedroom door, yet she had to hope because the shadow man had no intention of taking care of her and Sebastian in the same way as Nana May.

'You've gone to such lengths to remain here alone,' he said, and there was a hint of uncertainty in his eyes. 'You've spent so much of your energies convincing Sebastian that Edward would wash his hands of you once he knew about Grandma.'

'He didn't believe me. He phoned him this afternoon. Uncle Edward will be here any minute.'

'I am not afraid of Edward!' the shadow man cried. 'Let him come! Such a ridiculous man, riding in his expensive car, thinking one weekend in a month is thankfulness enough for the life he was given!'

Fury thundered across the shadow man's features. The kitchen light flickered above his head. All the shadows in the room seemed to stretch and grow towards him.

'A ridiculous man! Always hanging from her skirt like a frightened pup. Always snivelling and sickly. Never letting her out of his sight for fear of being left alone. And she adored it! She bathed in his attention as if it were nectar!'

The force of his rage rolled across the room in great waves. Elise held onto the door frame, quaking with terror. The shadow man came towards her.

'A fine pair they were, he and your mother! Everywhere together, inseparable like Hansel and Gretel. But she was such a pretty girl! Such a pretty, pretty girl blessed by the angels. He was not worthy of her love, yet she showered it upon him!'

The world became unbalanced. Elise looked up at the shadow man. The curve of his mouth was so familiar. And the shape of his eyes. And it was not because she had met him before.

'Who are you?' she asked. 'Who are you really?'

For a moment, the shadow man looked small and afraid, like a child lost in the woods. Without anger or bitterness, his face softened. Elise knew why he was so familiar.

'You look just like Uncle Edward!' she cried.

The shadow man turned away, covering his face with his hand, and backed into a corner of the kitchen. Elise stared in awe, in disbelief.

'That's impossible!'

The shadow man lowered his hand.

'Is it?'

The world tried to right itself and tipped Elise into confusion. 'But how? I don't . . . This doesn't make sense!'

'It does,' said the shadow man. 'If you know everything there is to know.'

'Who are you?' she asked him. 'What are you?'

'I am nothing. I am a shell. Once, I was a boy with a name. Then darkness came and stole all the good in me. I was cast out, forced upon the land like vermin. I ate the flesh of feral creatures. I drank the rain and the morning dew. I watched.'

The shadow man crouched down in his corner and looked up at the light.

'I watched them all. They worried for her after I was gone. She was like a flower whose petals had been torn in the wind. They said she was damaged, that she would not recover, but they were wrong. She still shone. The angel Catherine shone and her light was more magnificent than ever!'

'My mother!'

'Then one day sickness came. Father grew ill and my pretty girl was all but forgotten. The farm fell to ruin. All the animals were sold. I hid in the cow shed and slept on old straw. I stole eggs from the hens of neighbouring farms. At night, I could hear father's cries echoing across the yard as the sickness ate away his insides. Once, I dared to go home. Just once. My angel had become captive to melancholy, her room a sad cell. I did not see her, but I felt her light seeping through the walls. It was warm and magnificent, blissful against my skin. When Mother saw I

446

had come home she flew at me like a frightened bird. She took her fists to me and I fled. Father went to heaven that same evening. I watched through the window as Mother rocked in her chair, waiting for him to expel his last breath. When he had, an angel came down and sat at our mother's feet, and we all wept rivers of mourning.'

Elise's legs trembled beneath her. She moved over to the table and sat back down.

'I know this,' she said, dumbfounded by the shadow man's story. 'You're talking about my grandpa.'

The shadow man did not hear her. He continued to stare at the light, ranting in his strange way.

'They buried my father. Then, they put their things into boxes and a big blue van came to take them away from me. They left. Mother, Edward and my lovely girl. They drove away and I chased after them. I ran fast but I fell behind. I saw my mother's face as she was driven away, and it was stained with sorrow. I cried out to her but she did not hear my voice.

'After they left me, I returned to the house. There were locks on the doors and people in the yard. Strangers moving into my home! I left that place. I wandered for days, lost and alone. I fell into despair. Night came and darkness made me its companion for many, many years. I became nothing, a ghost, haunting each town and village that I passed through. Eventually, I grew tired of the world. I wandered through the moorland until I fell among the trees. Darkness lifted and I found myself here. I heard Mother's voice and I thought it was a dream. Then I saw her, standing in her garden, talking to the birds. It was a vision of such beauty that I fell to my knees and wept.

'Memories of my old life came back to me and my heart yearned for my angel. I watched for her, waiting day and night, but she had gone away. Mother was alone now. I saw her go about her day, filling it with meaningless chores, and I knew I could not leave her.

'The trees became my home. One day, the angel Catherine returned, and with her she brought children of light. She, herself, had lost her shimmer but the little ones shone bright enough for them all! She left them here, a gift to remedy Mother's loneliness. Then, the angel went away and she did not return.

'The children grew melancholy at first, longing for her arms. But Mother was Grandma now, and she had enough love for them both. I watched for a long time, basking in their glorious light as they talked and played. How I longed to hold them close! To feel their radiance upon my skin. I became bold, entering the garden at night, peeking through the windows. Mother caught me one evening, mistaking me for a coal thief. She cried out when she saw her son. It was late. She took me into the kitchen and gave me hot food. She watched me in silence as I ate. You came into the room then, the daughter of an angel, and I was blinded by your brilliant light and humbled by my reverence. You stayed only for a moment and when you were gone, a look came over Mother's face. "You cannot stay," she said. And I was cast out on the land once again.'

The shadow man looked across at Elise and smiled. 'But here I stayed anyway.'

Elise grew as pale as moonlight.

'Mum wasn't talking about Uncle Edward,' she said. 'She was talking about you.'

The shadow man said nothing.

'He didn't hurt her. It was you. You did those things to her. You turned her into what she is. You made her leave us behind.'

The shadow man rocked in the corner. 'Left you behind, she did. Presents for Grandma that lit up her face. Poor, dear Grandma. Gone to heaven on a silver cloud.'

'But I thought it was him! Everything I've done was because I thought it was him. Oh, Nana, I've been so wrong!' She glared at the shadow man, fury scorching her features. 'But I didn't know about you. They hated you so much for what you did to my mother they left you behind. They threw away all the photos. They never mentioned your name. They pretended you didn't exist.'

Elise stood, erupting with years of suppressed rage. Amused by her anger, the shadow man emitted a child-like snigger.

'I hate you!' she bellowed. 'You ruined our mother's life and you ruined ours!'

She loomed over him and spat in his face. The shadow man stopped laughing. He wiped the saliva from his cheek and rubbed the palm of his hand against his lips. Then he lunged at her. Elise hurled herself back towards the hall. Leaping to his feet, the shadow man emitted a terrifying, high-pitched scream.

'What you did to Grandma!' he thundered.

Elise pounded past the living room and headed for the stairs. Catching the end of the banister, she swung herself around and onto the bottom step.

The shadow man reached over and snatched at her hair, tearing clumps from her scalp.

Elise screamed in pain. She pressed forward, channelling her strength into her arms and legs. She reached the top of the stairs and slammed into the wall. Pushing off it, she propelled herself towards Nana May's bedroom. She took the key she held in her left hand and rammed it into the lock.

'Stand back, Sebastian!' she screamed.

The key refused to turn.

Behind her, the shadow man had reached the top of the stairs. His eyes rolled in their sockets. Spit and foam flew from his mouth and caught in his beard. He saw Elise and stampeded towards her.

With a cry, she wrenched the key free from the lock and tossed it away. Inserting the second key, she twisted it and there was a sharp click.

The door was unlocked.

The shadow man was upon her, lunging forward with outstretched arms.

Screaming, Elise dropped to the floor.

The shadow man stumbled over her crouched form. His face slammed into the wall with a sickening thud. He fell, spinning a full circle before hitting the carpet, where he howled like an injured dog.

Elise sprang up and wrenched open the door.

Sebastian stood in the centre of the room, Nana's bedside lamp held high above his head. He screamed as Elise raced inside then kicked the door closed.

One twist of the key and the door was locked again.

Outside, the shadow man wailed and shrieked.

'No angels here! All the light's gone out! Darkness now! Only darkness!'

Sebastian threw the lamp on the bed. Elise fell to her knees and began rocking back and forth.

'Elise!' he cried.

It was as if she couldn't hear him. Wrapping his arms around her body, Sebastian held her tight. They rocked together as the shadow man defiled the air with curses and thrashed his body against the door.

Then it was silent.

Sebastian looked over his sister's shoulder. They waited for the door to be smashed apart, to be torn from its hinges.

Elise made a noise against Sebastian's chest. She began to laugh, filling the room with high-pitched cackles. Tears leaked from her eyes and she began to cry.

Sebastian held her as they waited for the sun to come up, his eyes never leaving the door for even a second.

Chapter 31

Uncle Edward pulled into the yard at exactly ten to five in the morning. He was exhausted after a nightmarish journey in which his brand new, metallic silver convertible had broken down on the motorway, just forty minutes after leaving home.

It had taken almost two hours for the mechanics to show up and another two for them to make their repairs. While Edward had waited, he'd called the house several times from his mobile phone, his worry gathering like the rain clouds above him with each unanswered call.

Now, as he sat in the driver's seat, the car engine ticking and hissing beneath the bonnet, an uncomfortable sensation tickled his insides. He quickly checked his appearance in the rear-view mirror. Then he climbed out of the car.

The sun had begun its morning ascent but was not yet high enough to warm the land. He looked up at the fiery sky and smiled in wonder. Sunrise never looked so beautiful anywhere else.

Stepping away from the car, Edward moved his small frame towards the house. He was thirty years old and not one inch over five feet tall. His father had once joked that if given the opportunity, the cows would have eaten him for breakfast. Edward had always struggled to find the humour in his father's jokes.

He reached the front door of the house and pulled down on the handle. Cold spots numbed the back of his neck. The door was locked. He stepped back, staring up at the house. He had never known the door to be locked—not while growing up here and not when returning for his monthly visits. He thought back to Sebastian's phone call. He had sounded so panicked. So afraid.

Edward made his way around the side of the house, noticing the open door of the outhouse and the unpleasant essence that lingered at its entrance. He wondered if he should have called for the police or for an ambulance, and he chastised himself for being an irresponsible uncle and a neglectful son.

As he made his way through the garden and stepped through the open kitchen doorway, Feline eyes spied on him from the undergrowth.

'Mum?' He waited for a response. 'Mum, it's Edward. Everything all right?'

Streaks of dried mud lagged the floor. Broken dishes lay heaped in a corner. A torn sack of coal lay beside the oven, its contents spilled on the flagstones like an unfinished game of draughts. Edward stepped into the centre of the room and the silence closed in on him.

'Sebastian? Elise? Are you here?'

Stepping into the hallway, he pushed open the living room door. Thick red curtains stopped the morning light from penetrating the shadows that lurked there. Ornamental animals regarded him from the mantelpiece. He closed the door, half-expecting them to come to life now that he had left the room. He reached the foot of the stairs and looked up. There were more shadows lingering at the top, remnants of an endlessly dark night.

'Kids? Mum?'

The shadows seemed to move by themselves, spreading dark tendrils along the walls. Edward climbed the stairs. He reached the landing and moved towards Elise's bedroom. The curtains were open and soft light filtered in, illuminating a hurriedly made bed, which had not been slept in. Returning to the hallway, he saw more mud streaked along the carpet. Panic set in. Edward burst into Sebastian's room. Drawers were pulled out of chests. Bed sheets draped the floor.

He reached his mother's bedroom. The door was locked. Kneeling, he peered through the keyhole and saw the key had been inserted on the other side.

'Mum? It's Edward. Are you all right? What's going on?'

He hammered his knuckles against the door.

'Mum! Kids? Unlock the door! It's me, Edward. I'm worried!'

He took three steps back, ready to throw his weight at the door. A voice stopped him in his tracks.

'Uncle Edward? Is it really you?'

'Yes, it's me!' he nodded. 'It's me, Sebastian. Let me in! What the hell is going on here?'

The key was pulled from the lock and a wide, frightened eye filled the hole. It blinked as it stared at the man in the hallway. Then, the key was replaced and the door was unlocked. Edward pushed it open and stared open-mouthed at the children standing in the doorway. Both were caked in dirt and mud. Dried leaves and bits of twigs adorned their hair. A multitude of cuts and bruises tattooed their skin.

Uncle Edward tried to speak. He put a hand on each of their shoulders.

'What happened to you?'

The children looked at one another. They reached for each other's hands and linked fingers. They looked back at Uncle Edward.

'Where's Nana May?' he asked. 'Where's my mother?'

Chapter 32

The Past

Nana May sat in her chair next to the back door, gently rocking back and forth. Knitting needles clicked in her hands as she wove together the beginnings of a bright green sweater.

Lounging on a large blue blanket on the lawn, Sebastian and Elise ate sticky toffee cupcakes baked by their grandmother that afternoon. Above the treetops, the sky was ablaze with a thousand colours.

'The fading light of day is a wonderful thing,' Nana said, then looked down at her grandchildren and smiled. 'Once, there was a woman graced with such beauty that men fell on their knees in her presence and wept. But that's men for you—soft as jelly. Such was the power of her extraordinary loveliness that, wherever she went, a trail of broken hearts was left in her wake. Some people believed she was born from the moon and the stars. Others believed faerie magic was responsible for her bewitching looks. One boy thought she was an angel.

'His name was Henry and he was not the brightest of sparks. On the day he was born, the doctor took one look at him and announced to the world, "By the blankness of his face, I would guess his father was the village idiot!" Henry's mother nodded and sighed. "You guess right. And now I am blessed with a fool for a son."'

'That's not very nice.' Elise wiped crumbs for the corner of her mouth. 'You can't call your children idiots. They're still learning.'

Sebastian grinned. 'Yes, you can. People call you an idiot all the time!'

He filled the air with laughter. Elise pinched the skin of his upper arm and twisted it in her fingers. Nana May stopped rocking and the children fell silent.

'Henry didn't do well at school,' their grandmother continued, her feet waving in the air as she set the chair rocking once more. 'He'd never learned to properly read or write and when it came to arithmetic, well, all the numbers got tangled up until his head was full of spaghetti! The other children laughed at poor Henry, thinking him the most foolish boy to ever walk the Earth.

'Henry's mother had a job at the mill. She worked long hours to earn money for food and clothes, but she and Henry were still very poor. While all the other children ran out to play after school, Henry had other responsibilities such as cleaning the house and preparing the evening meal.

'He had never been the greatest of cooks and his mother had to write everything down to make sure he could get it right. But because Henry and reading were like chalk and cheese, the dinner table was always an interesting place to eat. "Oh Henry!'"his mother would say, as she ate cold pink soup with slices of potato and raw cabbage floating on top. "It is a miracle I am not poisoned yet!"

'One morning, she gave Henry a large shiny coin and said to him, 'This is all the money we have until the mill pays us in a week. It may be that I am taken by madness to entrust you with this coin, but as I have to work late into the night, I am left with little choice. Our larder is empty and I cannot leave you to starve. So you must go to the market after school and bring home the things I have written on this list. You cannot lose this coin Henry, or the rats will be dining upon both of us come the end of the week.'

'Henry regarded the coin with great fear and responsibility. He held it in his hand as he walked to school and kept it in his pocket while he sat in class, tapping it with his fingers every few seconds to make sure it was still there. When school had finished and the other children had done laughing at him for the day, Henry walked to the market, holding the coin in a vice-like grip.

'It was a long road to walk to the market but Henry had heard of a shortcut through the forest that would lead him into town and back before darkness fell. Leaving the road, he hurried through the trees. He didn't much like being in the forest. People told frightening stories about the awful spirits that haunted there, so he kept watchful eyes while he made his way through.

'As he walked, he heard what sounded like singing, and he stopped to listen as the song soared high above the treetops and swooped right down to the ground. It was the most beautiful voice he had ever heard! So bewitching was it that Henry fell to his knees and wept with joy. But this was no ordinary voice and before he knew it, Henry had fallen into a deep sleep.

'It was dark when he awoke. So dark that he could not even see his hands in front of his face. The forest surrounded him with frightening noises. Beady yellow eyes blinked at him. He ran in all directions, trying to find his way out.

'The coin his mother had entrusted to him was lost. Heartbroken and afraid for his life, Henry sat down and began to sob so loudly that all the hungry beasts of the forest fled in fear.

'Above the sounds of his sobbing, came the song that had lulled him into enchanted sleep. Henry looked up to see a ball of light floating through the trees. It came closer and closer still, until he could see that, at the centre of the light, was the most beautiful woman he had ever laid eyes on! "An angel!" he cried out. "An angel has come to save me from the wolves!" The woman stepped forward. She smiled and the forest lit up as if it were day. "Are you lost?" she asked him. Henry replied that he was. The woman took him by the hand and the light that surrounded her enveloped him too. "I will show you the way home," she said.

'As they walked, Henry asked the angel lots and lots of questions. What was it like to be an angel? What did angels eat? What did it feel like to sit on top of a cloud? How did a person get to become an angel? The woman listened to his questions and smiled. "I am no angel," she told him. "Once I was a woman deemed so beautiful that men would fall at my feet and weep in my presence. Wherever I went, a trail of broken hearts was found in my wake. At first, I was revered. Then I was hated, for women feared I would steal their husbands, and men feared I would steal their souls. None of these things I tried to do. I had always looked upon my beauty as a curious and wretched thing, as a wall of impenetrable thorns.

"But I was branded a witch, a jezebel. So hated had I become that I feared for my life in the world of people. I came to the forest and found solace among the animals. Beauty has a different aspect here, you see. Flesh is merely food but beauty is the heart and the soul. It is the colours of the leaves as the seasons change. It is the night sky and the moon."

'They had reached the edge of the forest and before them lay the road that would take Henry back home. "Don't you get lonely?" he asked, looking back into the darkness of the trees. The woman leaned down and planted a kiss on his cheek. "You are the first person I have seen in many an age," she said, "and although you are but a simple boy, your kindliness reminds me of happier days. What a wonder it is to be a child! So innocent and carefree! I am never alone. Look for me in the fading light of day and you will see. You shall be the sun and I shall be the stars, and we will dance through the evening until morning comes."

'The woman returned to the forest, leaving Henry with a head full of wonder. It was late when he returned home. His mother rushed forward, sweeping him up in her arms. "My darling boy!" she wept. "I thought you were lost to the wolves! Where have you been?" Henry replied, "I fell in the forest and could not find my way. Forgive me mother but the coin that you entrusted to me is lost, and now the rats will surely chew on our bones." His mother looked at him strangely. "You really are your father's son!"

'She pulled open the larder door and Henry gaped in wonder. The larder was filled with food. "If you lost the coin, how did you pay for all that you brought home from the market?" his mother asked. Henry's hand went to his pocket and pulled out the coin given to him that very morning. He gasped, and he smiled, and he said, "With the help of an angel."'

When Nana May was finished telling her story, she chuckled to herself and set her knitting to one side.

'Look! There they are now. Henry and the angel, waltzing across the sky.'

The children stared up to see the sinking sun and stars that sparkled around it. Clouds framed them in a perfect circle. Sebastian and Elise smiled at such a strange and enchanting sight.

'It's daytime and night-time at the same time!' laughed Sebastian.

'It's like magic!'

Nana May looked down at her grandchildren. 'Watch the sky at this time and a thousand eyes will be looking at the same thing. No matter where she is, she'll be looking and thinking. Her heart will swell till it almost bursts.'

Elise caught her grandmother's eye and Nana May nodded and smiled.

'Getting cold now,' she said. 'Best be getting in.'

Chapter 33

As Sebastian did all the talking, one single, shameful thought played over and over in Elise's mind: I was wrong. I was wrong. I was wrong. And it was strange, because even though she had been wrong about Uncle Edward, she still felt uneasy around him. She didn't understand why then, but years later, when she thought back to that morning, as the three of them stood in Nana May's bedroom, she realised it had been a confusing mixture of guilt and habit plaguing her.

As Sebastian told Uncle Edward of the ugly events that had passed during the last five days, Elise bowed her head and remained silent. Uncle Edward turned pale when he was told of his mother's death, and it was as if someone flicked a switch inside his mind because he stopped listening.

Tearful and distraught, Sebastian was forced to repeat the entire story over and over again.

When all the talking was done, it was clear that Uncle Edward needed to sit down. Taking an arm each, Sebastian and Elise guided him to the bed.

He sat on the edge of the bed for a long time, starting sentences and not finishing any of them. Sebastian and Elise stared at him, then at each other. Finally, Uncle Edward looked up at Elise, and his eyes were red and watery.

'You should have called me the very minute it happened,' he said.

He started crying.

Elise bit down on her lip. Her eyes found the floor. Sebastian slipped his hand into her hers and squeezed.

'We thought you were bad,' he told Uncle Edward. 'Nobody ever told us Mum had another brother.'

Uncle Edward pulled the children towards him.

'There's too much,' he wept. 'I can't take it all in.'

Sebastian threw his arms around Edward's neck and although it felt unnatural to do so, Elise rested her head against his shoulder. Uncle Edward, as it turned out, was a good man who had just lost his mother. He deserved some comfort for that.

Some hours later, the full truth of what had transpired hit Uncle Edward with horrifying clarity.

By noon, a search party had been assembled, comprising two police officers, Uncle Edward, Tom Elliot, and a handful of concerned villagers.

Sebastian and Elise remained at the house. A police officer named Irene made them take hot baths and put on clean clothes. Tom Elliot's wife, Beth, cooked sausages and baked beans, and filled mugs with hot coffee while Irene asked the children lots of questions and wrote things down on her notepad. In return, Sebastian asked lots of questions about the officer's police radio and hunting down bad guys. Elise sat solemnly at the table, thinking about her mother and dear Nana May, and how odd it felt to have finally uncovered the truth.

It didn't take the search party long to find what they were looking for. The shadow man had put together a crude shelter on the other side of the river, where Sebastian and

Elise had always feared to go. It was a roughly fashioned construct, made from fallen branches, scraps of tarpaulin, and large pieces of skinned tree bark, just ten metres from the riverbank.

Nana May was lying inside it, covered by soiled sheets.

They found the shadow man soon after, hanging from a nearby tree, choked to death by the rope that Elise had used to tie Nana May to her chair.

'I'll walk you back to the house,' Tom Elliot told Uncle Edward, taking him by the arm.

Uncle Edward stared up at his brother. A hundred memories hung between them; shards from a life lived so long ago it was all but forgotten. He turned away, wishing not to remember.

'Where is her chair?' he asked.

The search party looked but it was never found.

It was late afternoon when the men returned. Tom led Uncle Edward to a seat at the kitchen table and helped him sit down.

'We found her,' he said. 'She can be at rest now.'

An unsettling hush fell upon the room. Tom took a small hip flask from his trouser pocket and handed it to his wife.

'Give the boy some coffee,' he said, glancing at Uncle Edward. 'Load it up with this.'

Beth unscrewed the cap and sniffed the contents. Aware that this was not the time to scold her husband for ignoring his doctor's plea for teetotalism, she set about making the coffee.

Sebastian and Elise huddled at the far end of the table, their chairs pulled together. They looked at all the adults milling about the kitchen. They looked at Uncle Edward and his blank face. They looked at Tom Elliot, who returned their stares with an expression that said, "I knew you were up to something." The world felt very large. Tom's face softened.

'Why don't you kids watch some television while the grown-ups do what they have to do?' he suggested. 'Then, if it's all right with your uncle there, if that's what he needs, Beth will take you to stay with us for the night.'

The children nodded and climbed out of their seats. They gave Uncle Edward one final, sorrowful glance and walked hand in hand out into the hallway.

'What will happen to us?' Sebastian asked Elise, when they were sitting in the living room. A soap opera played out on the television. Elise turned the volume down low.

'I don't know.'

'Will we go to jail? The police have got handcuffs. I saw some on Irene's belt!'

Elise stared at the television. 'I don't know.'

'Is Uncle Edward going to be all right? He looks funny.'

'I don't know.'

Sebastian was quiet then. He turned to the muted soap opera, guessing the story line as he watched.

'What's going to happen to Nana May?' he asked, after a long while.

Elise looked at him. She looked away.

'She'll be buried. There'll be a funeral.'

Sebastian returned his gaze to the television.

'Oh,' he said.

Chapter 34

The funeral took place on Saturday afternoon. The sun was merciful, wrapping itself in clouds and sparing the mourners in their black clothes.

The children were driven through winding country lanes, following a long back hearse that carried their grandmother to the churchyard. It was not the village church they were heading for, but one close to where Nana May and her family had once lived, in a time long since forgotten.

Uncle Edward sat between the children in the back seat of the car, holding their hands in his. Sebastian wore a smart black suit with a white shirt and shiny black shoes.

His hair had been scraped into a flawless side parting and fixed there with cream. Elise wore a black polyester dress that came down to her shins. It made her skin itch the whole time she wore it.

No one spoke until they arrived at the churchyard. Then, as they stepped out of the car and onto the gravel of the church path, Sebastian said, 'I want to go home.'

Tom and Beth Elliot came over to stand with the children for a while. Beth gave each of them a white rose. The children looked down at the flowers, confused.

'To put with her,' she explained.

They watched as Uncle Edward and men whom they did not recognise, carried Nana May's coffin inside. Tom and Beth guided the children forward and the rest of the villagers followed behind.

Sebastian and Elise were taken to sit at the front, next to Uncle Edward. Tom and Beth sat to their right. Elise looked over her shoulder. The whole village was there and she caught the villagers' eyes as she looked across each row.

Some stared at her. Others turned to their neighbours to whisper. Elise felt her face burn. To her relief, she found Lamorna sitting somewhere in the middle and to the left. There was no accusatory glare here. There were no scandalous whispers. In Lamorna Brooke's smile there was warmth and compassion and, if Elise was not mistaken, there was also respect.

Sebastian's gaze was frozen on his grandmother's coffin. He tried to imagine her inside it. He pictured her sleeping. Horrified, he pictured her imprisoned and screaming.

The vicar, an old man who was as pale as the robes he wore, spoke kind words about

Nana May. Neither of the children could listen.

Organ music filled their ears and the mourners all stood and sang hymns. For once, Lamorna Brooke sang at an acceptable volume and in the right key.

Uncle Edward cried into his hands and the children stared at one another, overwhelmed and afraid.

Nana was carried outside to the graveyard. The procession drifted past headstones and sprays of both fresh and decaying flowers, until they came to a large hole dug deep into the ground.

The vicar began to speak again but the children did not hear. They stared into the black pit and their legs trembled beneath them. Then Nana May was ever so carefully lowered into the ground.

Uncle Edward fell to his knees and he made a sound that reminded Sebastian of the seals he had once seen at the zoo. Tom

Elliot put a hand on his shoulder and helped him back up.

Beth brought the children forward and one after the other, they dropped their flowers onto the lid of the coffin.

'It's dark down there,' Elise whispered.

'Your Nana will be just fine,' Beth said, leading her

away. 'Look, they're putting her next to your grandpa.'

The children read their grandfather's name on the adjacent headstone.

'Besides,' Beth continued, 'where your grandma really is, it never gets dark. Never ever. It's always full of light.'

'How will she get to sleep then?' Sebastian asked.

Beth smiled as she led them back towards the church gates. 'You know your Nana. She'll find a way.'

Leaving the church, Tom rode with Uncle Edward in the long black car, back towards Nana May's house. Beth took the children and drove them to her home, where they had been staying the last week.

Uncle Edward had been away, busy rearranging his workload and planning his mother's funeral. Sebastian and Elise changed into more comfortable clothes and packed their belongings. When they were ready, Beth drove them out of the village and towards the house in the woods.

Nobody talked much along the way. Beth switched on the radio and a man talking about market prices and mass production filled the silence. She shook her head and muttered words of disapproval. Sebastian and Elise gazed out of the windows, watching fields and hedgerows shrink behind them.

'Do you think they're all right?' Sebastian asked, pointing at the cats that were waiting on the doorstep to greet them.

'Hell, they ought to be!' Beth laughed. 'Those lazy good-for-nothings have had Mr Elliot running around like a blue-arsed fly! He's been down here every morning at the crack of dawn, feeding those urchins before he goes off to work. Outdoor cats, my backside! They couldn't catch a mouse if it served itself up on a plate!'

Sebastian heaved his shoulders, wondering if Red would ever return. Elise tugged his arm.

'Come on. Let's go and see if Uncle Edward's all right.'

They climbed out of the car and walked towards the house. They had not been back here since the police had come.

Memories of that day flooded Elise's mind. From them, a question formed and found its way to her lips.

'Beth? What happened to the shadow man?'

Both Beth and Tom knew what had happened. All three remaining members of the Montgomery family felt that these were people whom they could trust.

The rest of the villagers knew only snippets, but they had already woven together a story so inaccurate in its telling that even Mrs Thorn, a woman who thrived on the downfall and demise of others, found it impossible to believe.

Uncle Edward had paid for the shadow man to be cremated. Leaving the crematorium, he had taken his brother's ashes and emptied them into the gutter. He had chosen not to tell the children of the shadow man's death.

'I think,' Beth lied, 'that he was caught by the police. Anyway, you don't need to worry about him anymore. He'll never be coming back here again.'

'How do you know?' Elise asked.

'Because I'm a grownup,' Beth replied. 'Grownups know everything.'

'What was his real name? He must have had one.'

'I'm sure he did once, but that's for another day, when your Uncle Edward is ready to tell you.'

An enormous thud shook the windows of the house. Sebastian froze in his tracks.

'What was that?'

The sound came again and the children held on to Beth's arms. The sound shattered the quiet for a third time.

Elise pointed to the side of the house. 'It's coming from over there.'

She ran towards the sound and Sebastian chased after her, careering around the corner of the house and along its side.

Both siblings slid to a halt. Mr Elliot stood up ahead. He had removed his jacket, shirt and tie, and was wiping his hands on his vest. A heavy sledgehammer stood on its head beside him.

'Thomas Joseph Elliot, what in God's name do you think you're doing?' Beth cried, as she rounded the corner of the house.

Mr Elliot glanced over his shoulder. He was panting like a dog on a hot day.

'Helping,' he said.

'Helping? You're an old man with marshmallow bones! You go and rest yourself this instant!'

The sound of metal striking stone hurt the children's ears. They ran forward to see Uncle Edward pull a sledgehammer behind his head, and with a cry full of rage and sorrow, swing it with surprising strength towards the outhouse.

The left wall exploded in a cloud of dust. Shrapnel shot through the air and hit the ground.

Uncle Edward swung the hammer, again and again. He was still dressed in his mourning suit, his tie impeccably knotted.

Elise slid to the ground, resting her back against the side of the house. Sebastian sat down beside her. Beth moved towards them but Tom held her back.

'They'll be fine, my lovely. Let's leave them be.'

They left soon after, patting the children on their heads as they went.

Mesmerised, Sebastian and Elise watched Uncle Edward tear down the outhouse. Walls crumbled. Slates smashed to pieces as the roof caved in. After a while, there was only dust choking the air, and rubble that could have once been anything.

When he was finished, Uncle Edward sat down beside them. He was panting and sweating, but his jacket remained buttoned and his tie still hung from his neck.

The children waited for him to catch his breath. When he had, he said, 'We'll clear that up in the morning. Then we'll plant something nice there. An apple tree perhaps. Or a rose bush.'

'An apple tree would be good,' Elise nodded. 'We'd have our own fruit.'

Sebastian moved around so that Uncle Edward was sandwiched between them.

'What's going to happen now?' he asked.

Uncle Edward hung his head and stared at the ground. He wiped his eyes with the sleeve of his jacket.

'I'm not entirely certain.'

They sat for a while, the three of them staring into the trees. Then Elise turned to Uncle Edward, and with tears spilling down her cheeks, she said, 'I'm sorry.'

Uncle Edward caught a tear on his finger and he watched it roll down to his palm, leaving a thin streak of sorrow in its trail.

'Me too,' he said, and he wrapped an arm around her shoulder and pulled her close to his side. Sebastian shifted his small frame until he too was held in his uncle's protecting arms.

'Shall we come and live with you?' he asked.

Uncle Edward shrugged his shoulders. 'I guess. If that's what you want. I mean, of course.'

Sebastian saw a strange look wash over his uncle's features.

'I don't know if I'd be any good at looking after the two of you,' Edward confessed. 'I've never had children. I don't know the first thing about raising them.'

'It's all right,' Sebastian replied. 'We'll be on our best behaviour. We can all take care of each other.'

Uncle Edward nodded. 'We'll have to find somewhere new to live. Somewhere bigger than the place I have now.'

'Can we have our own rooms?'

'I think that would be wise.'

'With our own television sets?'

'We'll have to see about that.'

'And can we get bikes?'

'Steady on, Sebastian!'

'And we'll have to make room for the cats.'

'But there are so many!'

'We have to stay.'

Uncle Edward looked down at his niece.

'We have to stay,' Elise repeated. 'It's the only place where Mum knows to find us.'

'Your mum may never come back,' Uncle Edward replied. 'You must know that by now.'

'I know.'

'And we have as much chance of finding her as we do of getting Nana back. Believe me, I've tried.'

Elise nodded. 'But if there's a chance then we should stay. Nana would want that. You know she would.'

Uncle Edward smiled, and it was such a sad smile the children moved a little closer to his sides.

'She wouldn't just want it,' he said, shaking his head. 'She'd expect it.'

And so, they stayed. Elise, Sebastian, and Uncle Edward. And weeks later, on the first official day of autumn, when the leaves on the trees turned as crimson as sunset and shivered on their branches, Red pawed his way through the foliage and back into Sebastian's arms.

'Look!' he cried. 'The cat came back! The cat came back!'

Above the yard, the sun was molten in the sky. All the stars had come out. And in the fading light of day, Sebastian and Elise wondered if Red's return meant something bigger than the Earth and the air put together.

Then Uncle Edward was calling them to the dinner table and they were racing back towards their home.

Also by Malcolm Richards

CIRCLE OF BONES (PI BLAKE HOLLOW BOOK 1)

For over eighteen years, private eye Blake Hollow has been tormented by the disappearance of her best friend. Now back in her hometown, Blake learns the daughter of another old school friend has vanished.

Blake is determined to find Lucy Truscott alive. But when her search takes a tragic turn, local police detectives soon find themselves hunting a cold-blooded killer.

Convinced Lucy isn't the first victim, Blake launches her own murder investigation. But is she wasting precious time by trying to connect her long-missing friend to Lucy's murder? Or has Blake uncovered a secret serial killer whose grisly intentions are about to reach terrifying new heights?

OUT NOW IN LARGE PRINT.

Also by Malcolm Richards

THE COVE (DEVIL'S COVE TRILOGY BOOK 1)

The smallest towns have the darkest secrets…

When Carrie's son, Cal, vanished from the Cornish town of Devil's Cove, she thought she'd lost him for good. Seven years later, a teenager has been found washed up on the beach.

It's Carrie's son. And he's alive.

No longer the sweet boy she remembers, Cal is deeply troubled, wildly unpredictable, and a growing danger to everyone around him.

Now, Carrie must unravel the mystery of what happened to her son before it's too late. Because a serial killer is stalking the streets of Devil's Cove. And another young child is missing…

OUT NOW IN LARGE PRINT.

Also by Malcolm Richards

NEXT TO DISAPPEAR (EMILY SWANSON BOOK 1)

When troubled nurse Alina vanishes one night, it's assumed she ran away from her violent husband. Until disgraced ex-teacher Emily Swanson moves into the couple's former home.

Emily's life is in ruins and she's meant to be making a fresh start. But when she learns about the missing nurse, she sees a chance for redemption. Because finding Alina could help right the wrongs of Emily's past. All she needs to do is follow the clues.

But what Emily doesn't know is that Alina had a horrifying secret. One about the care foundation where she worked. And the closer Emily gets to uncovering the truth, the closer she gets to terrible danger.

OUT NOW IN LARGE PRINT.